MURDER ON
SKIS

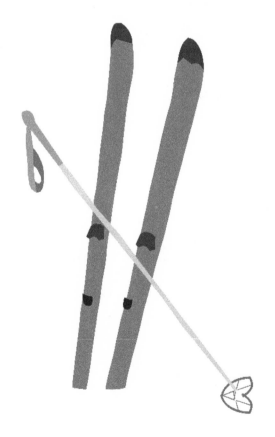

MURDER ON SKIS

PHIL BAYLY

SHIRES ✺ PRESS

4869 Main Street
Manchester Center, VT 05255
www.northshire.com

MURDER ON SKIS

©2019 BY PHIL BAYLY

WWW.MURDERONSKIS.COM

ISBN: 978-1-60571-609-1

Cover Design: Debbi Wraga
Author Photo: Carolyn Bayly

Building Community, One Book at a Time
*A family-owned, independent bookstore in
Manchester Ctr., VT since 1976 and Saratoga Springs, NY since 2013.
We are committed to excellence in bookselling.
The Northshire Bookstore's mission is to serve as a resource for
information, ideas, and entertainment while honoring the needs
of customers, staff, and community.*

Printed in the United States of America

To Carolyn, for her love and intelligent feedback. And to mom and dad, who woke us before dawn, drove north for hours, pushed us out into the bitter cold and said, "Have fun!"

No man chooses evil because it is evil. He only mistakes it for happiness.

—Mary Shelley, author of *Frankenstein; or, The Modern Prometheus*

1

A frozen body may never decompose. A mountain climber's body was discovered on Everest in 1999. He died, likely in a fall, in 1924.

When he was found, his skin was still white and there was still meat on his broken bones.

On the other hand, if an unfortunate victim survives a near-death encounter with freezing temperatures, fingers, toes, nose and ears could turn dark purple when they thaw. Any or all of them may have to be removed.

"There is something to be said for eternal beauty," Bob Platz told the woman lying on his stainless steel table.

She'd only been delivered to the medical examiner that morning. The ski patrol said that she resembled a snow princess in a deep sleep. Only a beautiful face and a torn jacket protruded from her blanket of snow. She was found at sunrise.

Dawn exploded onto the south face of Grizzly Mountain that morning. It was a brilliant flash of light, but no sound followed. Sun poured into the shadows of chutes called "Hoppel's Horror" and a ski run called "Marsha's Moguls." Grizzly Mountain was waking up.

Every morning, the mountain came alive like this. But for millions of years, no one saw it. The cold and snow during winter was too much for the First Natives, the Crow Indians.

The first white mountain men, even the wildlife they hunted, stayed closer to the valley. These heights were too cold, too barren.

After World War II, a young man looking for an exciting new life found this remote spot.

Walter Prospect had enlisted in the United States Army even though he lived most of his life in Canada. The Army saw that he was born in Alberta, so they asked him, "Can you ski?"

MURDER ON SKIS

"Yep," he told them. In truth, the answer was "Nope." But his name was added to the rolls of a new fighting outfit, the Tenth Mountain Division. They were going to be taught to fight the Germans on skis. Hitler already had a division of skiing soldiers.

Young Prospect had never put on a pair of skis in his life. He did know how to ice skate. He'd played pond hockey.

And he had been told by his family that it was twenty degrees below zero when he was born inside his grandparent's farmhouse. So, Prospect was a better fit for the new ski troops than the guys from Brooklyn and Miami.

By the end of the war, the young soldier had never gone to battle while on skis. The plan to engage the enemy in the Alps was abandoned by the U.S. military. Instead, Prospect's unit had distinguished itself fighting on Italian soil. It was conventional warfare.

But Prospect had learned to ski. He was taught by Austrians who fled Hitler's vision of a Thousand-Year Reich. When the war broke out, many Austrian immigrants were already ski instructors in the United States. Suspected of being spies, the U.S. Army told them to enlist or spend the war inside a prison camp.

The Tenth Mountain Division also had instructors from Dartmouth College, the best collection of ski racers in the country. A few had competed in the

3

Olympics. Many of them grew up privileged. But the Austrians and the Ivy Leaguers proved to be courageous in combat.

And then the war was over. Walter Prospect didn't want to return to farming. And the thought of living in a big city to do combat on the corporate ladder didn't appeal to him either.

He wasn't alone. Like others who trained and fought alongside him, Walter Prospect was hooked on skiing.

After WWII, small ski slopes began to appear on hillsides in Minnesota, Massachusetts, Michigan and nearly every state that turned white during the winter. Many proprietors of these new ski hills were veterans from the Tenth Mountain Division.

When Walter Prospect found his hillside, it was summertime. The terrain was covered by grass and wildflowers.

He cleared a slope on the lower elevations of Grizzly Mountain. He erected a rope tow. It was powered by an old Buick perched on gray concrete blocks.

That winter, skiers came. More skiers followed. In winters to follow, the rope tow was replaced by a chairlift, and then multiple chairlifts. The ski resort climbed up the mountain and added its first gondola.

The comfort of a lodge and a warm fireplace offered protection from the same deadly elements that had kept rugged Crow and mountain men away.

Now, human eyes could witness sunrise on Grizzly Mountain at eleven thousand feet. It was a twenty-first century playground.

On this morning, gas-powered grooming machines were finishing their rounds. They were not unlike the half-tracks utilized by the Army when Prospect was a young soldier.

The groomers crawled over the ski resort's runs all night. They smoothed the snow for the coming day's customers. "Corduroy," they called it.

The machines looked like glowing insects from below. Groomers worked in the dark, guided only by their headlamps.

Because it was so dark, it was easy not to notice the blue fabric torn from the snow as one machine rolled over its surface. The driver of the powerful groomer couldn't even feel the tug of the cloth catching on the steel tracks.

They rarely groomed this run, called "Marsha's Moguls." The driver could not know that in the darkness behind the machine, there was now a human body exposed, the face of a woman frozen in a blanket of snow.

2

Marsha Prospect walked toward the gondola shed with grace. Somehow, she avoided that stumbling footfall forced on others who wore ski boots. Mrs. Prospect seemed to glide across the crunchy snow. Others lurched or limped, or both.

Grizzly Mountain Ski Resort employees admired Marsha Prospect. They would have even if they didn't work for her. She now owned the sprawling ski resort that was started by that old soldier, decades ago.

The ski resort's treacherous expert run, "Marsha's Moguls," was named after her. It was one of the few nice things Marsha's ex-husband did for her during the last years of their marriage.

The name of the mogul field with the huge bumps was a double entendre. Marsha Prospect's moguls were more than ample.

The divorce was messy. She'd married the billionaire Paul Prospect when she was an unassuming Montana girl from the small town of Livingston. One of the things that she did assume was that her husband would be kind and faithful to her. He was neither of those.

He was born in Montana, too, the son of Walter Prospect. But Paul gravitated toward New York City, where the money was. For Marsha, the marriage added up to thirteen years of bad luck and neglect.

Her husband's cheating began discreetly when he was away on business trips. By the last few years of their marriage, he carried out affairs under her nose at Grizzly Mountain.

The mountain employees were all aware of Paul Prospect's escapades. He especially lusted after the athletic young women who worked at his ski resort.

At the beginning of a new ski season, his trip to Montana aboard a corporate jet from New York City seemed to have less to do with inspecting his investment and more to do with inspecting the new crop of "girls" who came to work for him. Employees called Mr. Prospect's lustful explorations "grooming the slopes."

Marsha Prospect's workers felt sorry for the woman. There was a sense of celebration when word arrived that she was filing for divorce.

Grizzly Mountain was all she really wanted in the divorce settlement. She could have gotten a lot more.

Paul Prospect didn't like relinquishing a good investment, but he knew he would produce greater profits with that money invested elsewhere. His sentimental attachment to the ski resort barely occurred to him. His father was dead and buried. Paul Prospect was a bastard, but he had the Midas touch.

Marsha Prospect was forty years old but looked twenty-nine. There were very few lines in her face. Her brunette hair hung to her shoulders. She had a long, thin body and a good figure. She looked a little fragile.

Her brown eyes always looked like they were smiling. She was pretty, but when one got to know her, she became more beautiful.

Following her divorce, she proved she could be a success on her own. She was smart and had a way with people.

In the second winter of running the ski resort without her ex-husband, it was showing signs of being even more successful than Paul Prospect's projections.

MURDER ON SKIS

Grizzly Mountain was the biggest employer around. Most employees were from the nearby town. Some were from overseas on temporary work visas. There were also the ski bums. They came from across the country.

There was a bit of "ski bum" in Marsha Prospect, despite being worth millions of dollars. She even kept the price of a lift ticket a few dollars lower than she knew she could get. She really adored skiing and skiers.

Every morning, she made the first run off the gondola. The rest of the day might be filled with meetings or running the mountain. But Mrs. Prospect always showed up for her run off the gondola first thing in the morning.

She often invited resort guests to join her in the car. Sometimes, that involved visiting movie stars, politicians and other famous faces.

She was careful to attend to the needs of celebrities who chose to vacation at Grizzly Mountain. Word-of-mouth among the rich and famous could go a long way, especially in the age of social media.

No one fitting that description was visiting on this day, though. That was OK, too. She was looking forward to skiing instead of socializing. She deliberately left her cell phone at the office.

Lately, her duties included taking phone calls about the body of a woman found in the snow. The victim still

9

hadn't been identified. It appeared that she froze to death. The ski resort's CEO was waiting for a lawsuit. But so far, no one had claimed the body.

"Pile on," Marsha Prospect told the imaginary plaintiff's attorneys in her head. A lawsuit was already sitting on her desk from another death that winter, a backcountry skier who died in the strangest way.

The chief executive climbed into Grizzly Mountain's new twelve-million-dollar gondola. It was on all the brochures for the resort this year. It was hyped as the newest, state-of-the-art gondola in the world. U.S. Forest Service regulations wouldn't let them build a faster gondola, so Mrs. Prospect built one that would cause skiers to be in less of a hurry.

The gondola cars were sealed tight so there wasn't a draft. The windows didn't fog to prevent skiers and snowboarders from enjoying the spectacular views of a Montana winter. The seats were cushioned instead of hard plastic or metal.

There was piped-in music. You could select a genre of music or plug in your own digital device. The sound system was also used to inform riders where the best snow was that day and which lifts had the shortest lines.

The new features helped contribute to the sense of community among skiers and boarders. It put them in a good mood and on the same wavelength. Marsha

Prospect's new gondola was attracting attention from across the country.

Of course, the gondola was also becoming a legendary rendezvous for lovers. More than once, staff working in the gondola house at the peak had to gently inform an amorous or partially clad couple that their ten-minute trip had come to an end.

Marsha Prospect was wearing an expensive one-piece ski suit with a Western theme, embroidered cowboy boots and spurs and six-guns. She climbed into the gondola alone.

Before the doors automatically closed, one of the gondola operators stuck his head in.

"Excuse me, Mrs. Prospect, would you mind accompanying a box of medical supplies to the top? The ski patrol wants to re-supply the first aid sled."

"That's not a problem. Let me help," she responded.

"Nope, not a problem." And he slid the unsealed cardboard box onto an empty seat.

The employee's name was Trip Lake. He was a twenty-four-year-old ski bum working at Grizzly Mountain for his second year. As he reached to strap down the box, she couldn't help studying the young man's familiar round shoulders and muscular arms. His strong back pressed against his red cotton turtleneck sweater. He preferred cotton to the normal sweat-wicking fibers modern skiers had adopted. He said cotton was comfortable.

He knew she was admiring his physique but didn't let on. She was grateful for that. He spoke to her without looking up, but you could hear the familiarity in his voice.

"If the lift stops, reach into the box and swallow the little red pills. You'll float to the top without the gondola," he joked.

"You're a bad boy," she told him.

He gave her a glance that said, "All the girls like bad boys, don't they?"

He backed out of the gondola and it pulled ahead. The doors automatically closed with a hiss. The world's newest gondola began to climb toward the summit and into the sunlight. Its lone rider considered the music selection.

With the craft safely out of earshot, Trip Lake's co-workers began to tease him. "Man, you are going to get yourself in trouble talking to your boss like that," one joked.

"Naw, she's hip," Trip responded with a smile. Another fellow employee suggested that Trip would never have joked like that with *Mister* Prospect.

Before Trip could respond, another co-worker reminded them *Mister* Prospect wouldn't have let Trip into the gondola in the first place. And *Mister* Prospect would already have a waitress from the base lodge half-undressed. They all laughed and agreed.

Trip Lake looked like a movie actor who was on the cover of nearly every magazine at the supermarket checkout counter, right now. Trip was handsome, polite, and you couldn't wipe the smile off his face. Every young woman on the mountain wanted a piece of him.

He lived with more than a dozen other ski bums in a collection of campers and vans in the corner of a distant Grizzly Mountain Resort parking lot. They called it "Fort Affordable."

For some reason, Grizzly Mountain's management allowed the skier commune to stay there. Marsha Prospect said, "They aren't hurting anyone, and they lend a little ambiance."

Trip was a little different from the other residents at Fort Affordable. He always looked like he had enjoyed a good night's slumber, the kind you get sleeping in a condo rather than a sleeping bag in the back of a van.

He was rarely at the commune when his fellow ski bums woke up in the morning. They figured he was living off his good looks. They wished they could, too.

It was hard to imagine Trip Lake, or an assortment of young men and women at Grizzly Mountain, being anything other than ski bums. Their shaggy hair and tanned faces wouldn't look right looming over a necktie and business suit.

The gondola at Grizzly Mountain rises over four thousand feet to the summit. After clearing the gondola shed, it rides over multi-million-dollar homes. Much of the trip then passes over jagged rock and sheer drops. The car is carried far above timberline and sometimes travels unnoticed from below.

So, the skiers and snowboarders on an intermediate run called "Silverback" didn't notice when Marsha Prospect began pounding on the windows of her gondola. She clawed at the doors. She couldn't breathe.

She was alone in the car, so no one saw her. In her desperation, she split her manicured fingernails. She shed blood on the windows of the gondola as she tried to spread open the doors.

Something she couldn't see was killing her. "Killing me?" she thought. That made her fight harder. But she grew weaker. Tears blurred her vision. She slipped to the floor of the gondola car.

She couldn't breathe. Her fists barely made a sound now.

She couldn't move.

She worried about missing her ten o'clock appointment that day ... and she had plans for dinner with friends.

She wondered when she last went to church. She thought about dressing up for Sunday school when she was a child. She wondered if it was all good enough to go to Heaven.

On a catwalk called "Collie Dog," a snowboarder turned hard on his edge and came to a stop. He dropped to the seat of his pants to wait for his friends.

If he had looked up, he would have only seen an empty gondola car. Marsha Prospect lay below the windows, breathless, dying. Tears ran down her face, her heart broken because it was all coming to an end.

3

"Racer ready!" the starter shouted. JC Snow watched the ski racer ahead of him slap his skis on the floor and push out of the start house.

That meant JC was next. He finished his pre-race rituals. He pulled the thumb loops down on his skintight racing suit. He wrestled his ski boot buckles to the tightest setting possible. He pulled his gloves on. They were padded on the knuckles to lessen the sting when his hands slapped the racing gates.

JC pulled his goggles down from his helmet and over his face. He looked over the racecourse in front of him, down a run called "Montezuma's Revenge."

"Why is it called 'Montezuma's Revenge?'" JC had asked the racer behind him.

"Why not?" he responded.

But another racer wisely offered, "Because if you take that headwall the way you're supposed to, you'll probably shit yourself."

"That's why I race," JC told his companions. "To search great minds about the mysteries of the universe." They shared a nervous laugh. Ski racing was fun, but it was "scary fun."

"Racer ready!" That was JC's call to the starting gate. He slid forward so his shins were only inches from the timing bar. He reached over the wand and drove his ski poles into firm snow.

The air on JC's face was cold and crisp. "Three, two, one ..." the starter bellowed. JC catapulted himself downhill.

JC believed ski racing was a metaphor for human existence. The start of a race was like birth, full of promise and hope. Anything was possible. Crossing the finish line was like death. Everything was over. It was time to assess a man's existence. In between, there were triumphs and disasters.

The beauty of racing was that life's metaphor was condensed into seventy seconds. And he would be reborn in the start house of the next race, promised another chance.

On rare occasion in races, there really was death. Some racing crashes at high speed ended with a racer's literal killing. More commonly, racers broke legs and arms. Torn ACLs were not a matter of "if" but "when."

JC crossed the finish line in a tuck. He'd nailed the headwall. As he threw his skis sideways, skidding to a stop, he was already searching for the clock. He was atop the leaderboard after the first of two runs.

There was a smile on the racer's face. His chest heaved to suck in the cold air. His hands shook with exhaustion as he tried to pull up the zipper of a jacket over his speed suit.

"It takes two runs to win," JC modestly responded to the racers who congratulated him.

"Yeah, and it takes only one run to screw it up and hand the race to me," cracked his friend and primary competition, Al Pine.

Pine had been JC's friend since they were thrown together in the same dormitory room in college. They would both be trying out for Colorado State University's ski team.

"You steal your sister's ski sweaters?" Pine had cracked as he watched JC unpack his suitcase in their dorm room. It was just minutes after they'd first met. JC could have taken the wisecrack as an insult. He didn't. He thought it was funny.

Pine had grown up in West Yellowstone, at the famous national park's border. He had a lot of cowboy in him then, including a belt with his name embossed on the back.

JC saw the belt and retaliated, "It's handy when you forget your name. Does that happen often?" They were already cementing a friendship that would last for life.

Al's real name was Bob. But JC had given him the nickname "Al."

"Must you?" Bob Pine had asked.

"I could call you Porky," JC had offered.

"Porky Pine?" Bob frowned, "No, Al will be fine."

Now, the two friends found themselves at the head of the pack, one-two, after the first run of an adult giant slalom at Grizzly Mountain.

"You look every bit as good as you did when you were twenty," Pine said. He was only half-joking.

JC put an arm around his old friend and said, "Anyone at this age who says he can do the same things he did when he was twenty, wasn't very good when he was twenty."

JC was handsome, with a thick head of brown hair and a mustache. His face always had a tan and a bit of wind burn. It was his green eyes that first got your attention.

They were full of emotion. Often, it was amusement, but when things weren't to his liking, those eyes could expose the gravity of the matter.

He was born and raised in upstate New York, Saratoga County. He literally couldn't remember when he didn't know how to ski. On weekends, his parents would pile the children into a station wagon. They would drive until JC and his siblings thought their bladders would burst.

Some of the ski hills, when he was growing up, were small. It took about eighteen seconds to the bottom, if you turned a lot.

JC didn't begin to ski because he wanted to. His older brothers and sisters wanted to, and he was too small to leave home alone.

He remembered how cold the winter was in the Adirondacks. When he was little, the freezing temperatures would reduce him to tears.

His mother would bribe him into coming out of the lodge. She'd promise to reward him with a patch from the ski area they visited that day.

Eventually, his ski parka was covered in patches from little hills in the Adirondacks, the Catskills, the Berkshires and the Green Mountains.

Eventually, he would never feel quite at home unless he was in ski country.

In time, those little ski hills grew into ski mountains, just like Grizzly Mountain. The "Ski Boom" had arrived.

JC was named by his parents after the hero of the 1968 Winter Olympics. The Frenchman named Jean-Claude Killy won all three gold medals in skiing's alpine races.

Jean Claude Snow was a spectacular ski racer in high school. He was above average in college. But when he realized he wasn't good enough to be an international champion, he turned his attention to getting an education.

He discovered poetry and politics. He began to read as though he were racing against the clock.

A college internship at a Rocky Mountain radio station turned into a job as a "cub reporter." He won awards for his journalism. In time, he was hired by a Denver television station.

That's what brought him to Montana, this time. He was on assignment to report on the death of Marsha Prospect. The mysterious tragedy struck a chord with television viewers in Colorado's Ski Country. Grizzly Mountain had been negotiating to purchase a Colorado ski resort.

It was a perfect assignment for JC. He was back with his college buddy. He'd even come north a day early to squeeze in a Sunday race. He was in his element. What could go wrong?

4

"So, what the hell happened, Al?"

JC was asking what Pine knew about Marsha Prospect's death. The two old friends were eating lunch between runs in Grizzly Mountain's adult giant slalom. The second and final run was about an hour away.

"Al" was a U.S. Forest Service ranger. Grizzly Mountain was on Forest Service land, so Al Pine had a role in the investigation of the death of the ski resort owner.

Al shrugged and told JC what he knew. She was dead but they didn't know why.

"Heart attack? You should have seen that gondola cabin." Al was almost whispering so he wouldn't be overheard by other racers eating nearby. "She tried to claw her way out of that car. Why?"

"Who was in the car with her?"

"No one. There was nothing but her and a box for the Ski Patrol," Al told him. "We're waiting for tox." The toxicology report might show if she'd ingested something. A full report would take a long time, but a preliminary exam might provide a clue.

"She wasn't a needle popper or a druggie," Al offered. "You ever see her?" JC shook his head no.

"She was beautiful. She looked healthier than I do." Both men smirked at that comparison.

"There was another one found a while back." Al told JC about the body uncovered by the groomer. "We don't know much about her. But it's getting a little creepy around here."

"Are they related?" JC asked of the two deaths.

"No," Al shook his head as he took a bite of his sandwich. "No reason to think so, anyway. It looks like an accident."

Outside the ski lodge's windows, large snowflakes had begun to fall. They looked like goose down. A Rocky

Mountain blizzard was going to spice up the end of their race.

It was not the kind of spice ski racers liked. Fresh powder brought universal joy to a ski resort, unless a race was underway.

At the top of the race course, the snow continued to fall on the gathering of racers. The light was going flat. Ruts in the soft snow were getting deep and dangerous. There were crashes.

One ski racer moaned in anguish, waiting for the ski patrol, after catching a tip and falling. He'd be heading for surgery.

Another racer launched off a rut and into the safety netting. He was hanging off the ground as if caught in a spider's web, until he had help getting down.

"Racer ready!" The official starter, wearing a headset and thick down parka, stood next to the starting gate.

"Go fast. Get this thing over with, so I can go sit by the fireplace in the bar," he said. JC smiled and reached his poles out over the timing wand.

"Three, two one ..." the starter shouted. JC pushed out of the gate with a loud grunt. He struck the first four gates with his upper arms as he raced by. He felt fast. He rolled forward on his toes as he entered the steep headwall.

But he was blind to the deep ruts that had formed, until he was in them. His skis were vibrating violently.

That's probably why he didn't see the gate he cut too close. He caught his ski tip and was launched forward, head first. He'd taken off without filing a flight plan.

The snow felt like concrete when he came down. First his leg, then his ribs and then his head made a crunching sound. His ears rang and his vision blurred.

His race was lost, now it was a matter of survival. He was sliding down the hill. The snow felt like glass against his face. His leg felt like it was going to explode.

JC ground to a halt against another racing gate. It worked as a cowcatcher. JC felt like hamburger.

He didn't move a muscle. He was still searching for one that didn't hurt. His face was covered in little bleeding cuts from being dragged across the snow. But when he rose, his left leg protested but supported him.

He checked his other leg, then his arms and his hands. Then he waved off the gatekeepers. They had been watching to see if another ski patrol sled was going to be needed. JC was fine. He had only lost the race.

5

Two Black Dog beers dropped onto the table from JC's hand. He was with Al Pine at a ski village bar called Shara's Sheep Ranch. It was packed with the après ski crowd.

They wore thick sweaters, turtlenecks, Polypro or tee shirts stiffening with dried sweat. Their hair was matted after pulling off their helmets or knit caps.

Their faces were tanned. Their eyes glowed as they recounted the adventures of the day, shouting to be heard over the roar of the music and the crowd around them.

Some of the story tellers embellished their exploits of the day. Their listeners responded with good-natured jeers. And then it began again, with someone else's tall tale.

A lot of shops in the ski village and the nearby town of Sierra had signs hanging in their windows. They said "Be back soon" or "Gone skiing!"

On powder days like this one had become, the whole valley's attention turned toward the slopes. Hoots and hollers from delighted "powder hounds" echoed off the mountainside. A few shouted, "Whoo, 406!" Montana's area code.

Marsha Prospect's body lay nearby at the morgue.

JC and Pine toasted Al's victory that day. The crowd pressed them against a tall two-man table that had their wet ski clothing piled on top of it.

Al Pine was six-foot four-inches tall. He was broad, too. He was a good-looking man, beneath a big beard and long brown hair braided into a ponytail.

He had a ranch on Route 191, with a herd of a hundred elk. He didn't own them or feed them. They just liked to call his land home.

"You had a helluva first run, but you left me a small window of opportunity," Al said with a coy smile.

"Open the window and watch the flies come in," JC said back with a grin.

The proprietor of Shara's Sheep Ranch was an old friend of the two men, more than an old friend to JC. He hadn't seen her in years.

Another skier pushed his way to their table. Al knew him and introduced JC to Sierra County Sheriff's Deputy Alex Cochran.

"Hey, don't I recognize you?" The deputy looked at JC and asked Al, "He's a TV reporter, isn't he?"

JC knew that many cops, maybe most, didn't like reporters. At best, reporters were trying to get law officers to say something interesting. And most law officers knew that the sure way to avoid trouble was to say nothing.

"Yeah," said Al, "but he tells the truth."

"Wow, I'd heard about reporters like that," Cochran said, "but I thought it was just a myth, like Bigfoot."

"No, the myth is that all reporters are good-looking," Al said smiling as he gestured toward JC.

"Oh, this is good. Now I'm having lunch with two guys who think they're comedians," JC rebutted.

Deputy Cochran was off duty. He'd just enjoyed the day skiing. Al and JC made room for him at their small table. The mountain of wet clothing grew a little taller.

"So, show me some TLC, since you stole my race," JC said as he looked at Al.

Pine told Deputy Cochran, "JC nearly snapped his leg in half when that storm came during the race." JC had a bag of ice on his knee.

"So, you knew Marsha Prospect?" JC asked Al. JC was going to be "on the clock" tomorrow. He had a lot to learn before his initial report on television regarding Prospect's death.

Deputy Cochran gave Al a wary look, but the Forest Ranger shook him off, "He's alright, I told you." Al's face grew serious as he began to recount the last twenty-four hours since the ski resort owner had been found dead.

"Yeah, I did know her," Al stated. "Nice lady. The body had been lowered back down to the base by the time I'd gotten there. Gondola operators from the top of the peak said there was nothing out of the ordinary in the car, other than her body. They thought it was natural causes, despite Mrs. Prospect's relatively young age."

"We spoke with her physician," added Cochran. He was still looking at Al. It was an adjustment for the deputy to confide in a journalist. "She didn't have any health problems. No family history of heart problems. She saw her doctor at her annual physical about a month ago."

"Not much blood, right?" Al asked the deputy to confirm.

"A little, not much."

Al turned toward JC. "This is probably going to be a heart attack, despite her trying to dig her way through the gondola's door. God knows, living with Paul Prospect for a *week* would give me a heart attack."

"Not a nice guy, huh?" JC asked.

Al shook his head. "I know your TV station would prefer a mob hit or murder-suicide, but it's probably not that."

The three men were interrupted by a middle-aged woman who approached the table.

"Mr. Snow, I don't mean to interrupt, but I just wanted to say how much we enjoy your reporting. I didn't expect to see you here!"

JC smiled at his fan and nodded his head to the powder piling up outside. "We live for days like this, don't we?"

"We sure do! My kids are still out there, somewhere," she replied, smiling as she also grimaced a mom's grimace. "Well, I won't keep you. I just wanted to say hi."

JC thanked her again.

"Shit, no one gets all huggy with me cuz I'm a forest ranger," Al mocked insult.

"Maybe if you were a better forest ranger," JC jabbed. Even Deputy Cochran laughed. He was getting to like JC, even if he was a journalist.

JC's TV viewers knew he was a skier, so being in a ski bar wasn't out of context. Colorado skiers came to Montana, too. And Denver television did get some viewership in Montana, especially with online streaming.

"Don't flatter yourself," Al said with a smile. "Up here, you're on TV opposite 'Rodeo Today.' Your ratings finish behind that and any fly-fishing show."

"Well, I'll come back when someone murders a fish."

Al broke a pause in the bantering. "You wanna take a look?" He was inviting JC to the gondola shed.

"Absolutely. I love field trips."

6

The gondola shed was the same timber and boulder architecture as the rest of the ski resort. But inside, it was spartan. It was unheated and cavernous. The space had to fit the massive gears, cables and motors carrying the cars to the windy peak.

With the machinery shut down to accommodate the investigation, voices and metallic collisions made faint echoes. JC and Al walked across the waterlogged carpets. They were there so the skiers' boots didn't slip.

"This is a dirty garage that houses some very expensive cars," JC shared. Al agreed, "Yes, it is."

They peered inside the gondola where Prospect's corpse was found. Blood was smeared on the window of the door and along some edges.

JC had covered hundreds of police investigations as a reporter. He learned to look for the same clues the police were looking for. In fact, his conduct led many at the scene of the investigation to believe he was a cop.

"She got in alone and she was still alone when the gondola door opened at the top, as if there was any choice," Deputy Cochran told them.

There was no midway station on the way to the peak. For most of the ride up, the car was a hundred feet in the air. And no one was going to jump from the nearby rocks or treetops.

JC repeated what he had been told, just to be sure he understood, "The only thing in the car besides Mrs. Prospect was the cardboard box carrying medical supplies for the Ski Patrol?"

"Oh, and a small tape recorder she must have been carrying. She was probably going to do some work on the ride up," Cochran informed the reporter.

"Are you done dusting?" JC asked the deputy.

"We don't dust for fingerprints if it's a heart attack," he responded.

JC asked, "I can pick up the tape recorder?" Deputy Cochran nodded his approval.

JC pushed "play" on the pocket-sized recorder. But rather than dictation from the ski area's CEO, there was disco music recorded. "Why would she spend all that money for a gondola with a great sound system, and then listen to music on a tape recorder with fifty-cent speakers?" JC asked.

The deputy shrugged and offered, "Maybe she doesn't like the gondola's playlist." His facial expression made it clear that he was joking. "Honestly, we figured she was probably going to record over the music."

"Maybe," JC said as he turned things over in his mind. "Any idea when she died on the ride up?"

"Impossible to tell," the deputy responded. The cardboard box with the medical supplies was still perched on the seat of the gondola across from where Marsha Prospect had been seated. The box was open.

JC asked who opened the box. The deputy told him they found it that way. "We looked through it and it all checks out. Maybe she was looking for medicine when she began to feel ill," theorized the deputy.

"Maybe." JC pushed "play" on the tape recorder again and listened to another disco hit from the '70s. He pushed "rewind." Another disco song played.

JC coughed and gave the tape recorder to the deputy. He coughed, too.

"It's disco music, I've always been allergic to it," joked JC.

"I was all about country music," offered Al, proudly.

Ranger Pine pulled JC aside by the elbow with an earnest look. They walked to a corner of the hut. Al spoke in a quiet tone only the two of them would hear. "Look JC, in all seriousness, you've seen more of this in your line of work than I have. I deal in forest fires, hungry bears and missing hikers. If there's something out of sorts here, I wouldn't mind a heads-up."

JC knew it was true. As a reporter, he had covered more suspicious deaths than Al or the Sierra County Sheriff's Department put together. Recreational accidents were their strong suit, from climbing accidents to drownings. Lots of drownings.

People rarely came on vacation to the Rockies to kill, not since Ted Bundy murdered a woman vacationing in Aspen, Colorado. Her body was found in a snowbank.

JC knew that deaths at ski areas usually fell into a very narrow category. There were avalanches, heart attacks or a skier who lost control and hit trees. More ski accidents claimed the lives of good skiers than beginners, and more men than women. The good skiers who died usually did so on an intermediate trail going like a bat out of hell.

A helmet will save a skier's head when he hits a tree, but he'll probably break his neck. Speed kills and trees forgive little.

Al told JC that this was the third weird death at Grizzly Mountain that winter. There was the woman whose body was found by the groomer. She was presumed to be a snowboarder who died in a fall and was covered by snow that night. Or perhaps she was knocked unconscious beneath some deep powder and froze to death. They still didn't know who she was. "Sounds crazy, but the snow really piled up that night, and she was on the edge of a trail that isn't groomed daily."

"And then there was the extreme skier," Al told him and shook his head. "Talk about bad luck."

The forest ranger explained that the backcountry skier was hit by an explosive fired from one of the cannons used to knock loose avalanches each morning. The ski area wasn't open for the day yet. Investigators announced to the public that he shouldn't have been there.

"We think he talked one of the lifties into letting him ride while the gondola was still warming up," Al said. "Then, we think he climbed up the rest of the way. The victim was traversing across the high chutes called 'Hoppel's Horror' when he was hit square in the back."

No lift operator had confessed to being the one who allowed him onto the gondola. Al told JC the two ski patrol members firing the cannon that morning were devastated by the accident. "There's a honey of a lawsuit being filed for that one," Al stated.

"The ski patrol guys were both suspended, of course, and they've been vilified in the press," Al told him. "It's too bad. They're good guys. They're taking it hard."

As Al and JC walked across the gondola shed, one of the deputies assigned to keep the scene secure spoke up: "You look familiar." Al rolled his eyes.

JC extended his hand and introduced himself, "JC Snow."

The uniformed inquirer just returned a blank stare. "Nah, that's not it." He searched JC's face for a memory. "Do you play softball in the Big Bear League in Bozeman?" JC shook his head no with a smile.

"You must look like someone else," the deputy said as he turned his attention to other matters.

JC just smiled as Al called out to the deputy, "Marty, what time is 'Rodeo Today' on?"

The deputy quickly responded, "Five o'clock. I taped it in case I'm still here. Man, I love that show." Al smiled back at JC.

But JC was lost in thought, still trying to explain how Marsha Prospect met her fate.

"Al," he said in a whisper, "Ask Alex who saw the victim alive last."

Al asked and the deputy responded, "The last guy to talk to her was one of the gondola workers, a guy named Trip Lake. We've already questioned him. He happens to be in there." The deputy pointed to an office with glass windows looking out on the gondolas.

Trip Lake looked like he hadn't gotten much sleep since Marsha Prospect's body was found. His blond hair was brushed straight back from his face. He was unusually pale. His eyes were red and he was biting his lip.

JC wanted to know what Lake had to say about the cardboard box. "He says a ski patrol guy gave it to him," Deputy Cochran told JC and Al. "These guys are busy with their own job when they're just getting the mountain running in the morning, especially when you know your boss takes the first ride up every day. We can't find anyone else who even saw this ski patrol guy."

"So, how do you know there was a ski patrol guy?" JC asked.

The deputy paused and said, "We don't, if you want to put it that way. But Trip Lake definitely said a guy wearing a ski patrol jacket handed him the box."

"And who knew that Mrs. Prospect rode the first gondola every morning?"

"Who didn't?" The deputy explained that Prospect's routine was so well known it even appeared in newspaper and magazine articles.

Al said he'd talk to Trip Lake later, if it proved to be necessary. The deputy told them that Lake lived in the ski bum's compound in the far parking lot, just below the snowboard park.

"They get a good view of the half-pipe from there," the deputy said.

"I suspect they get a pretty good view of the bong pipe," Al told him. They shared a small laugh.

As JC and Al left the gondola house, the sun was setting, and the snow was still accumulating. JC was limping a little. His leg was pretty sore after his fall in the race.

Many skiers had decided to take rooms at the resort, rather than drive home through the storm. Steam could be seen rising from the outdoor hot tubs and swimming pools. The sound of laughter could be heard.

JC and Al parted company. JC gathered up his gear from a rented locker in the lodge and dragged his throbbing leg toward his four-wheel-drive SUV. He was carrying a bag with two pair of skis over his shoulder. His ski poles were in his hand and his boots and helmet were in a backpack.

JC could smell the smoke coming from fireplaces in the houses and condos spread across the valley. He was getting hungry. He was tired. And the race left his ego bruised.

His face stung from those little cuts he suffered in his fall. Maybe that's why they call it a face-plant. He could use some ibuprofen, he thought.

But he stopped and turned around when he heard his name called. It was Al. He had pulled up in his green U.S. Forest Service truck. The big man with a beard climbed out of the cab and pushed through the snow as he announced he had news.

"It looks like a heart attack. The autopsy was just done in Sierra. Sorry, newsman," Al said with a broad smile. "Get your scoop on someone else's turf. There hasn't been a murder in Sierra County in thirty years."

7

The roads near Grizzly Mountain are lined by "jack fences." The barriers are brilliantly designed to meet a rancher's needs. They're built with three or more horizontal rails that hang on two poles. They're tied into an A-frame at each end. The fences are wide at the bottom and narrow at the top. They are portable and can be reconfigured to need. There are thousands of jack fences in Montana.

The state of Montana is three times the size of the state of New York but has fewer residents than the island of Manhattan. Only three percent of the land in Sierra County is privately owned. The rest is state and national forest.

As JC drove down Route 191, he passed ranches identified by the brands hanging from the gate over the dirt road leading into each property. The ranches each had names like "The Lazy 8 Bar-K" or "The Tumbling Circle C" or "The Rocking T-bar."

The land had always known conflict. The Spanish Peaks were named after Spanish trappers from Mexico who were ambushed and killed by Crow warriors in 1836.

The canyon that Route 191 wanders up was frequented by gamblers, gold miners and gunslingers.

Grizzly Mountain rises above the surrounding peaks like a spike. It is about nine million years old. That makes it a youngster in geologic terms.

The peak sort of looks like the Eiger in the Swiss Alps. Skiers frolic at the foot of the Eiger while mountaineers climb above. Sometimes the mountain climbers die. JC was skiing in Wengen, Switzerland, while a climber who had fallen to his death some months before could still be seen dangling in the wind at the end of his rope. It took a long time for rescuers to get the man's body off the difficult, concave face.

The lodge of the Grizzly Mountain Ski Resort has a towering sculpture of a grizzly bear in the lobby.

Arriving guests are startled by the size and realism of the bronze work. They might have been even more concerned if they knew how close they were to the real beasts, sleeping their winter away.

Grizzly Mountain is a destination resort. It draws skiers from California to Florida. Minnesota is a lucrative market. Montana has a sibling relationship with Minnesota going back a century. That's when immigrants from Sweden and Finland began moving west to work in the timber industry.

It is a posh resort for those who desire it that way. The slopes are peppered with large homes and spacious condominiums. The most expensive land prices could approach a half-million dollars for an acre. The homes built on top of them could cost millions more. Locals who grew up near Grizzly Mountain complained that they couldn't afford to live there anymore. Many had moved down the valley.

Grizzly Mountain Lodge looked like a castle in the Alps. It was ten stories tall but was still dwarfed by the peaks surrounding it. The lodge had rustic stone floors and log walls. Huge timbers held up the ceiling in the lobby.

As JC wandered through shops in the lodge, he saw everything from cowboy boots to lumps of gold jewelry fashioned into the shapes of bear and buffalo. There were cotton sweatshirts that looked a foot thick when folded on the shelves. Lettering across the chest said "Grizzly Mountain Ski Club" or "Grizzly Mountain Bit Me."

The ski area offered four thousand vertical feet of skiing. Experts could tempt fate in the chutes. The bowls ranged from double diamond to intermediate.

Extreme skiers were allowed to venture over the backside, but they had to wear a beeper. That would allow rescuers to find them, or at least their bodies.

The discovery of Marsha Prospect's body was getting all the attention. But JC wondered who the other woman was, the one found dead under the snow?

He wondered why she hadn't been identified. If she was a local resident, or even if she wasn't, why hadn't someone reported her missing by now?

JC made a mental note to look into it further. But this might be his last night before returning to Denver. Tomorrow, he'd report that Prospect's death appeared to be a heart attack and then he'd be summoned home. If that were the case, he had something to do first.

8

JC pulled his 4x4 into the parking lot of the bar called "Shara's Sheep Ranch."

The restaurant and bar's large windows looked out on the ski runs, dark now except for the lights provided by the groomers. The mahogany bar itself dated back to the days of a saloon in the Wild West. The bar's owner, Shara Adams, purchased it on the condition the bar remained in Montana. If she ever sold the restaurant, only a buyer from Montana could obtain the bar.

The idea of naming a saloon "The Sheep Ranch" recalled a battle going on in this area 150 years ago. Back then, if a cattle rancher shot a sheep rancher to death, it might be called justifiable homicide. This was cattle country.

Cattle ranchers would tell you that sheep cut the grass too short for cattle to graze on. Sheep required fences and cattle needed to roam. There was once a range war here. Nobody won, but a lot more sheepherders died.

Over the bar at Shara's Sheep Ranch hung a huge comical picture of cowboys on their knees with their hands up. They're being held at gunpoint and have embarrassed looks on their faces. So do the sheep a few feet away. Below the picture were the words, "Where men are men and the sheep are scared."

Many of those who frequented the Sheep Ranch believed the most decorative fixture was the bar's owner, Shara. She had long red hair, though some insisted she was a borderline brunette. She was athletic-looking with strong legs and a narrow waist. She was only thirty years old but strong-willed. She ruled the bar with a two-fisted toughness that was required of a woman running a business by herself.

She didn't mind if men there made fools of themselves trying to win her attention. They were paying customers and she was part of the floor show.

But it was only a show. Look but don't touch. And don't try to rip her off.

Her parents named her Shara after a war goddess in Sumerian mythology. "They grew up in the '60s," she'd explain to the bewildered.

The first time JC ever saw Shara was at a ski team workout at CSU. They were both eighteen years old.

She'd missed the introductory team meeting and showed up at the field where they were playing soccer. They played a lot of soccer that fall, to work on their fitness until they could find snow to train on.

She was a Northern California girl. She grew up skiing in the Sierra-Nevada mountains.

Watching her run the field that day, never yielding in pursuit of the ball, JC thought she was the sexiest woman he had ever laid eyes on.

Now, he was seeing her for the first time in eight years. Nothing had changed. He noticed that his heart was racing.

He seated himself alone at a table and watched her work behind the bar. She saw him and continued to grab a glass and fill it with beer for a customer. But she smiled, and he knew it was his smile.

She worked her way over to his table, interrupted a few times by customers, but always drawing nearer. JC thought to himself that he could just sit and watch her move for a lifetime.

"I heard you were in town," she said as she pulled out a chair and sat next to him.

"Ooh, look at your face," she said as she gently ran her fingers over the scratches, "What did you do?"

He told her about the race.

"Do you think you're still twelve?"

"No," he responded with a little boy's smile. "I've got a driver's license. I'm the envy of twelve-year-olds."

She folded her arms, leaned on the table, and looked at him. Al Pine had told JC that Shara had moved up to Grizzly Mountain. It was a few years ago when the bar became available.

She'd gone to law school and made good money in the banking industry in New York City. It was a lot of work and no sleep. She'd even squeezed in a failed marriage.

When the saloon at Grizzly Mountain became available, she realized she had just enough savings, and not a cent more, to leave the law bar and just buy a bar. Take a second chance at life.

A banker's mind saw that the business could be more than what it was when she bought it. There was a dark corner where guests could partake in video poker and keno. She opened up the space and added some lights and ambiance. The new gambling parlor was separated from the restaurant by an old fence with rusty barbed wire hanging overhead. It was there for all to see, but only those over eighteen, to play.

The video gambling area was corralled by cowboy attire, old rifles and six-guns on the wall, and there was an antique stuffed horse in a corner. Welcome to the Wild West.

The supplier of the gambling equipment split the take with Shara and the ski resort. Marsha Prospect had arranged it. But they all watched profits rise since Shara had taken over the bar.

Shara had been a friend of Marsha Prospect. Their friendship was founded on their roles as single women succeeding in a man's world. And a lot of these men were rednecks.

Shara and JC sat at a small table with a little light on it and two beers from a craft brewery down the road. A black Labrador Retriever was on the label. An authentic, ninety-pound black lab wearing a red bandana emerged from behind the bar and laid down on the floor next to Shara.

"This is the man in my life, Jumper," she told JC as she scratched behind the dog's ears.

"It's funny you should show up tonight, of all nights," she said to JC, sad and sweet. "I wanted to know that all of my other friends were alright. You're someone I thought about."

"Marsha Prospect?" he asked.

She nodded, "She was so nice," she said, her voice trailing off. She suddenly sounded tired. Her mind wandered. "I'm sorry about your race. How's your leg?"

"It throbs, but it's OK. I think you've lived through a few falls, too."

"Yeah, but we were kids then. I know I'm not a kid anymore," she said and smiled at him.

They sat and talked and caught up with each other's lives for a little while. The black Lab lay on the floor, glancing up at the two of them occasionally. The bar was beginning to empty out now.

She said that the shock of Marsha Prospect's death had worn her down. She was tired and wanted comfort. She had no energy left to be distant with someone she used to be so intimate with. "Do you remember," she asked JC, "the first night we spent together?"

"Oh yeah," he said. He was laughing at how well he remembered. That made him a bit embarrassed and his grin gave everything away. She giggled. Then she showed him that look he used to think was reserved only for him.

They made love for the first time eleven years ago. It was at the end of a party at a house she shared with other girls who they went to college with.

It was late and the house was empty. Even her roommates had gone elsewhere. Shara was nineteen years old and adored this well-behaved and unassuming boy. She felt it was time to take matters into her own hands.

She looked into his eyes and without uttering a word, led him upstairs by the hands. She closed the door to her bedroom behind them, softly kissed his lips and undressed.

"We were young and scared to death," she remembered. "You were so gentle."

JC smiled and protested, "You couldn't keep your hands off me. You were like a coiled rattlesnake. I was defenseless." But he was laughing as he said it. She gave him a gentle slap on his arms as she laughed, too.

He was still smiling as he pictured her soft shoulders and vulnerable neck. The pace of his heart began to race, like a wave coming into shore. He remembered her small waist and her snow-white breasts. He remembered the touch of her fingers and the taste of her skin.

Now, eleven years later, they caught each other exchanging a look and shy smiles. It seemed hard to imagine, at this moment, why she left him abruptly after graduation. Of course, that was his view of things.

Shara had told him she wanted a man instead of a boy. Things had changed during their last year of college. She was determined to pursue adulthood. He thought he already had everything, with a beautiful woman living in a beautiful land.

No matter how adorable that boy was, she believed that it was time to get serious. And he just didn't want to. She wasn't certain what JC loved more, her or his skis.

"You broke my heart," JC finally told her in the nearly empty bar. She already knew that, though.

"Your heart broke every time your skis got scratched," she replied with a sad look.

JC just smiled. He knew that she was right.

9

JC woke up in his dark room at the "Bearly Inn" as narrow rays of sunlight began to penetrate where the curtains didn't quite meet. Tiny particles of dust danced in the bright thin beams of light. He was alone.

Grizzly Mountain was waking up beneath a new blanket of deep powder. The sky was blue. Author AB Guthrie labeled it the "Big Sky" and Montana was forever after known by it. Their license plates told visitors and each other that they were from "Big Sky Country."

The roads were buried under the blinding bright new layer of snow. JC's leg ached a little from his fall in the race the day before. He called work in Denver and the assignment desk told him they'd hired a local crew in Sierra to shoot his live shot that night. Since he was coming back after reporting that Marsha Prospect's death was a heart attack, the television station hadn't seen the need to send its own truck and crew up for one day's work.

He put some ice on his knee and thought about Shara Adams. He wondered what it would have been like to sleep with her last night. He decided that it would have been a disaster. Getting his heart broken once by Shara Adams was enough.

After telling the desk clerk that he'd be checking out of his room the next morning, JC drove up to the base of the ski area. He passed Sierra County Highway Department plows and their deafening grumble, as they scraped the snow down to the pavement.

He wanted to stop by Marsha Prospect's office and pick up an official biography. He'd go live during the evening news and again in the late night show. Then he'd get some sleep and rise early for the long drive home through Idaho and Wyoming.

He'd stop for lunch in Jackson and drive through Rock Springs and Laramie. He'd pick up 287 to Fort Collins and then I-25 to Denver. It wasn't the shortest route, but it was his preferred route. In the summer when snow didn't close many roads, he'd add the Wind River Indian Reservation to his path.

He pulled up outside the Grizzly Mountain administrative offices and hopped out of his 4x4. He saw Shara Adams picking her way across the snow-covered street. She was walking in his direction. Her hair was blowing gently in the wind. She had her eyes on him and a big smile on her face. His heart began beating faster.

"Get a grip," he whispered to himself.

"Maybe Mother Nature wants you to stay around awhile," she said in a loud voice to be heard over the noise of the trucks.

"It's a beautiful day," he responded. He watched a big black Labrador with a red bandana riding past in the back of a pickup truck.

"Isn't that your dog?"

She looked over her shoulder and said, "Oh shit!" She turned in the direction of the pickup truck and said, "Jumper, get over here!"

Obediently, the dog hung his paws over the back of the moving truck and slid down to the pavement. He trotted over to Shara and sat down beside her with his tail wagging.

"He does this all the time," Shara said in a huff. Jumper seemed to have a happy look on his face. "He thinks the whole world is his carnival ride. He loves to ride in pickup trucks and I don't even think he checks to see who's driving!"

Shara told JC stories about phone calls she'd received from nearby towns, someone telling her they pulled their truck into their driveway after a visit to the ski resort, and there was a happy black Lab sitting in the truck bed. Shara had her phone number stitched into Jumper's collar.

"It's an obsession with him. No wonder they call them retrievers. I've been retrieving him all over Sierra County." And JC began to notice how many pickup trucks slowed down as they drove by, rolling down the window, and happily greeting the woman and her dog.

Life at Grizzly Mountain could definitely be a "dog's life." Aside from the free rides in pickup trucks, Jumper had hobbies like chasing tennis balls in the snow, and sometimes getting to chase skiers down mogul runs. He was one of the mountain's most popular residents.

JC informed Shara that he was just stopping into Marsha Prospect's office to get a bio.

"Trip Lake must feel terrible," Shara said quietly as her eyes looked at nothing in particular.

"Trip Lake? Wait, I know that name." He thought a moment. "The gondola operator?"

"Yes. They were a thing. I don't see any harm in saying it now that she's gone. It was hush-hush."

Shara told JC that Prospect and Lake had been having an affair for about a year. Marsha had told Shara that Trip spent nearly every night at Marsha's condominium. She said Marsha adored the sex, but Shara thought it might just be something she had to get out of her system after the divorce.

"I suppose it had to feel good to finally have someone who cared for her and treated her like she deserved," said Shara, "after living with that rat Paul Prospect for thirteen years."

Shara did not like Mrs. Prospect's ex-husband. "You know, I met him when I was living in New York. He hit on me while he was still married to Marsha. What a creepy coincidence."

But Shara also felt a little sorry for Trip. She always felt it was inevitable that Marsha would tire of her "boy toy" and return to the comforts of her own socioeconomic strata.

"And that's what happened," she said.

JC asked, "She broke up with him?"

"Only a month ago," Shara replied. "He was crushed. He really loved her, and somehow thought it was going to work. If she had only waited another month." Her voice reduced to a whisper, and then no sound at all.

"So, that's why that ski bum commune was allowed to stay in the parking lot," JC supposed out loud.

"Probably. Of course, the whole relationship was kept a secret, for lots of reasons. Anyway, it got kinda ugly at the end."

"Breaking up is never unanimous, even when they say it is," he offered.

"Trip was mad that she wanted out," Shara explained. "She didn't want to hurt him, so it dragged on longer than it should have. And then he'd get mean. He'd make her cry and then come back and beg her not to leave him. It got scary sometimes."

"Was he ever physical when he'd want to hurt her?"

"I don't think so, not that she ever told me. He's such a laid-back kinda guy, but sometimes Marsha would just make him crazy. She started going out with other guys and Trip went berserk. I guess he was just hurt."

"Love doesn't always tell the truth," JC said.

After talking a while, JC told her he'd be returning to Denver early in the morning after his live shots that night. He promised he'd stay in touch and kissed her on the cheek. His lips lingered just a little longer to brush her soft skin. And smell her fragrance. He had to look away.

10

The business office at Grizzly Mountain was occupied by a staff looking like they hadn't gotten any sleep. It appeared that they didn't quite know what business to conduct. Their boss had just died.

JC was directed to a middle-aged woman. She was wearing a ski sweater with bears and big snowflakes on it. She was going through a file cabinet. She looked up with a "grin and bear it" expression, and said, "How may I help you?"

"Oh," she said, suddenly sounding startled. She recognized JC from television. "I watch you all the time. My children live in Denver."

He asked for a biography of Marsha Prospect.

"Oh dear," the woman said as she closed the file cabinet. "I'm Lila Seneff, Mrs. Prospect's personal secretary. Let's see, let's go into her office and see what we can find."

JC followed her through a door. It led into a big, wood-paneled room with a large window looking out on the ski runs. The office was a handsome blend of mahogany bookshelves and furniture reflecting the Old West. The glass top on the coffee table disclosed a pedestal made from two huge moose antlers.

There was a pair of matching chairs blending elk antlers and soft leather. She gestured him to one of the chairs. Her eyes swept the room as if it might disclose where that bio might be hiding.

"It's a little much," said Mrs. Seneff of the posh office, "but Mrs. Prospect's husband ... uh, former husband, did all this. She never would have fussed over herself like this."

But Marsha Prospect did know how to make the right impression on anyone who needed impressing. There were pictures on the walls of Mrs. Prospect with a dozen movie stars during their visit here. There wasn't a single picture of Mr. Prospect.

There was a racing bib signed by the winner of a World Cup race held at Grizzly Mountain a few years ago. There was an assortment of oil paintings and watercolors replicating the ski resort.

Mrs. Seneff was going through the drawers of the big desk. She was a friendly woman. "Here we go! Will this do?"

She handed JC two pieces of paper pulled from a file. It was a slick and carefully worded capsule of the woman who now would not need it. The résumé was the work of a public relations firm, JC suspected, probably from New York City rather than local. Another lingering influence of Paul Prospect.

"This is perfect," JC said with a smile.

As they were preparing to leave the room, JC pointed at a computer tablet and asked, "Is that hers?"

"Oh yes, she never left the office without it. If she intended to do any work, it went with her." Mrs. Seneff paused and looked at the tablet as though it triggered pleasant memories.

"So, was it with her on the gondola?"

"Oh, she never worked on the gondola. That was her 'me time,'" Mrs. Seneff smiled. "She said that the rest of the day could be wasted on work."

"But they found her tape recorder on the gondola."

"She doesn't own a tape recorder," Mrs. Seneff responded. "She wrote notes on that tablet and she didn't take her tablet on the gondola." The secretary said this with a tone that carved out her turf.

"She didn't own a hand-sized tape recorder?" JC feigned absentmindedness, but he liked repeating the point when he wanted to make sure he hadn't misunderstood. It gave the person being interviewed a chance to change their story, or forever live with it.

Mrs. Seneff required no time to reconsider her position: "She did not."

JC apologized. "You've been very helpful. I'm sorry for your loss."

Mrs. Seneff had a warm nature. It appeared to JC that she may have enjoyed being grilled by the famous TV reporter. It would give her something to tell her family over dinner that night.

JC walked back into the cold winter air of the busy resort village. "Then whose tape recorder was it?" he asked himself.

He pulled out his cell phone and called the satellite truck he'd be working with that night. He was told that their photographer was running late because of snow on the roads near his remote home.

"That's alright," JC said over the phone. "We have some time to work with. If we can meet at the lodge in a few hours, we'll have enough time to do some shooting and get it edited. I think I'll have my copy written by the time you get here."

As he held the phone to his ear, JC stood with his car door open and watched a faraway pennant wave above Fort Affordable. JC thought about Trip Lake. He also recognized an uneasy feeling in his stomach. Why was he chasing loose ends in a heart attack? Because he'd never seen a heart attack with so many loose ends.

11

"What the hell, why not?" JC muttered to himself as he was driving past the ski-bum compound, Fort Affordable. He pulled his forest green SUV into the parking lot.

He climbed out of the car and encountered a bundled-up man who introduced himself as "Ski Fish." He said he got that name because when he skied tight parallel turns, his friends said he wiggled like a fish.

"I think that's a compliment," said JC.

"That's how I took it," Ski Fish responded with a proud smile. He had the face of an adolescent, with a sparse goatee and mustache. Aviator goggles were resting on his forehead.

The ski mountain had just opened for business. The gondola had reopened and most of the compound's inhabitants were already heading up to make fresh tracks in the new powder.

But Ski Fish said Trip Lake was still inside the compound. "He's pretty shook up. Take it easy on him." Then Ski Fish squeezed by with a pair of fat skis on his shoulder and marched up a beaten path in the snow to the gondola.

Fort Affordable was comprised of about a dozen vehicles parked in a circle, bumper to bumper. JC thought it looked like a wagon train under attack in an old TV Western. Typically, the Wagon Master would have just yelled, "Circle the Wagons!"

Colorful flags flew overhead, blowing in the wind. They brandished the logos of ski and snowboard manufacturers. The flags were probably freebies from a snow show or an industry rep. The residents of Fort Affordable weren't picky. If you brought a flag bearing a snow industry logo, they'd run it up the flagpole and see if anyone would salute.

JC pictured Woodstock in Antarctica. Blankets and towels hung inside the windows of the cars so no one could see in. Marsha Prospect had provided portable toilets. Someone had even dropped off a portable generator to provide a little heat and light. At night, there was a string of illuminated Christmas bulbs hanging around the perimeter.

That surreal glow during darkness helped earn the compound a bohemian kind of respect. Ski bums were not hobos. They generally held jobs and did not have criminal records. They just were consumed by their art, namely skiing and snowboarding.

There were stories in Colorado of skiers living inside caves and old gold mines. In resort towns, ski bums weren't that hard to spot. Their tans and windburn were deep, except for the white skin around their eyes protected by goggles. And there were those who thought duct tape was a fashion accessory.

Some shared a two-bedroom apartment with four or five friends. Even that was expensive in a ski town, and there wasn't much comfort. "We suffer for our art, man," one of them had said.

Most of them would eventually relent to the lure of love, material wants or just growing up. When that time came, they'd pack up, ship out, and for the rest of their lives look back on their time as a ski bum as something magical.

Right now, doctors, lawyers and CEOs looked out from the windows of their expensive rooms at the lodge and saw Fort Affordable. They were filled with envy. They'd switch places, if only they could.

JC found Trip Lake hovering over a portable stove on a picnic table in the middle of the circle of vehicles. He had a cup of coffee in his hand and a blanket over his shoulders. His eyes were red and his blond hair wasn't combed.

The weary young man in front of JC was one of the best skiers on Grizzly Mountain. That's what the reporter had been told. Trip made money on the side, being photographed wearing a manufacturer's ski jacket. On other days, he was paid to show off a brand of skis and poles.

He'd soar off a rock ledge or race down a steep chute. Skiers like the perception that they are doing something dangerous. Trip would provide the pictures.

JC introduced himself. "Shara Adams told me how close you were to Marsha Prospect."

Trip glanced up at the visitor. He looked grateful that someone knew his secret.

"I had enough with being a second-class citizen," Lake told JC with bitterness. "I was the boss's dirty little secret."

Trip took a gulp of coffee and stared in the direction of the half-pipe, snowboarders just getting in their first runs.

"They say she died of a heart attack," Trip said as he laughed a little. He looked up at JC. "I'd forgotten she had one."

"A heart?" JC completed the despondent man's riddle.

Trip almost appeared to be in a trance. JC had watched a lot of people grieve, and none did it exactly the same as another.

"She was such a beautiful blend of woman and child," the gondola operator said, seeming to be speaking to anyone or no one. There were pauses between his spoken thoughts.

"She was fifteen going on forty. I'd see her on the job and she was all business. But when we were alone, she'd turn into a teenager. She was a little kid."

JC asked Trip who the ski patrol member was who gave him the cardboard box.

"I don't know," he responded as he stared at the fire on the stove.

"Really? You've worked here two years. I thought you'd know everybody."

"Well, I guess I don't."

"Had you ever seen him before?"

"No."

Trip Lake's demeanor had changed when JC began to ask him questions. He grew aloof. The TV reporter wasn't even certain why he was asking the questions, other than because that's what he always did.

The two men stared silently at the flame on the stove. JC was told to expect an official declaration from the medical examiner: "Death due to heart attack."

Then who was the ski patrol guy, and where did the tape recorder come from? Also, there was a lovesick secret boyfriend and a caustic ex-husband. Marsha Prospect had secrets, and JC probably wasn't aware of all of them.

At that very moment, back inside the gondola house, an operator was struggling to close the door on a car loaded with skiers. The door seemed to be stuck.

The employee with dirty hair and a dirty company-issued pair of overalls got frustrated. "Fuck!" he said and shut down the lift.

"It's stuck," he barked as another lift operator came to investigate why the gondola was shut down. The realization came to the dismay of a growing line of skiers and snowboarders.

The second lift op pulled with all his might but couldn't move the door either. Then he glanced at the number on the car and spoke so just the two of them could hear: "Oh great, the fucking thing is haunted."

They didn't inform the four skiers waiting inside the gondola, but the freshly scrubbed car was the same one that Marsha Prospect had died in only two days before.

The two employees asked the skiers to remove themselves from the gondola and wait at the head of the line with the others.

The lift ops dropped to their knees to get a better look at the door. One of them ran his finger along the oily track the door had to follow. He grunted, "Huh." He pulled out a thin and partially crushed metal tube. He drew it closer to his eyes for inspection.

The other employee rose to his feet, shut the door without difficulty, and restarted the gondola.

There was an enthusiastic cheer from those waiting for their ride up the mountain, as the mechanism roared back to life.

A supervisor had arrived at the shed and approached the two lifties. It was too loud for anyone to hear their conversation, but one employee held up the small bent metallic tube for his boss to see.

12

A Country-Western musician was singing a song on the radio about how much he loved bears. JC was driving to Al's ranger station down Route 191.

JC's SUV pulled into the plowed dirt and gravel parking lot for the Sierra District Ranger Station. There was a county sheriff's patrol car parked there, too.

As JC walked into the one-level brown building, it was empty except for Al Pine and Deputy Alex Cochran. They were behind the counter and gave each other a nervous glance. Cochran looked at Al and nodded.

Al was holding a clear plastic Ziploc sandwich bag. Inside the bag was a metal tube, not much longer than three inches. It looked like it had been crushed.

JC summed up the bag's significance: "You don't put evidence of a heart attack in a plastic bag." He knew that plastic bags were reserved for evidence of a crime, to protect fingerprints and fibers.

"What do you make of this?" Al handed the bag to JC.

He turned it over in his hands and shrugged, "Haven't a clue."

Al said, "Open up the bag and take a little breath." Then Al put a cautious hand on JC's arm, "I said a little breath."

JC opened the bag and did as instructed. He coughed. For just a moment, he found it hard to get a breath. His eyes watered a bit as he looked at the two other men.

"You must hate me. What the hell is that?" He choked the words out as he handed the bag back.

"I do hate you, but that's not the point," Al smiled at Cochran, as he resealed the bag.

"This came out of the gondola Marsha Prospect died in," Al said with a serious look on his face.

"They weren't looking for it, so they didn't see it when deputies looked through the gondola." Al was telling JC this as the forest ranger was looking at Deputy Cochran with disapproval. Cochran returned an embarrassed look. It was his people who screwed up, JC thought.

Al continued, "An employee found it a few hours ago when it jammed up a door in the gondola car. Where it came from, we're not sure. The medical examiner says he found some residue in the cartridge that might match something he found on Mrs. Prospect's face and in her lungs."

"What exactly is it?" JC asked.

"The M.E. was in the Army. He thinks he knows what it might be. He's in the morgue now taking a closer look, then he'll send it to a lab in Bozeman."

"So, what's he think it might be?"

"He was a young doctor in the Cold War," said Al. "They were trained, just in case, to deal with stuff Soviet spies were using. He tells us that there was a concentrated gas that paralyzes a victim's breathing apparatus, just long enough to kill them. It's not easy to detect unless you're looking for it."

The forest ranger had an astonished look on his face as he looked at JC. "Congratulations, newsman, you may be on hand for the first murder in Sierra County since Ronald Reagan was president."

13

A voice from Denver came over the headset. JC was driving back to the ski village to meet the freelance satellite truck. Now, they'd be reporting that Marsha Prospect's death was suspected to involve foul play.

JC was told by his assignment desk to expect the TV station's own truck and crew tomorrow. Their stay was open-ended. He could expect to be there as long as the investigation proved interesting.

The assignment editor asked JC, "Who killed her?"

"That is the ten thousand-dollar question, right now," he responded. If the metal tube turned out to be old army stuff, police would look at paramilitary groups scattered across Montana and neighboring states.

But there were also jilted lovers to look at, a boyfriend and an ex-husband.

JC returned to the Bearly Inn. It was a good name, he thought. He was barely ever there. Tomorrow his crew from Denver would join him.

The motel was a three-story log structure. It looked like a big hunting lodge. There were life-size wooden bears carved into posts and beams. Some literally hung from the rafters. There were also some hanging from second-story porches, as though they were climbing up.

JC needed to meet the freelance crew he'd be working with for the evening.

But first, he had time to make another stop. His 4x4 pulled in behind a small red building with a white cross painted on it. Inside, he introduced himself to Elise Du Soleil.

She was the director of the Grizzly Mountain Ski Patrol. She told the reporter that she was in charge of sixty seasonal employees and volunteers. From time to time, they were the difference between life and death during ski season.

Du Soleil was a forty-year-old black woman. She had black hair to her shoulders. She had dark eyes and wore little makeup. She was big-boned and athletic-looking. She told JC that her last name meant "of the sun" in French.

"You're surprised I'm black," Du Soleil asserted at the start of the visit. "I'm told there aren't many of us around here. But my mom's black and my dad's black. My brothers and sisters are black. I see black people here every day."

JC smiled. He already liked her. He had known leaders in the Army and police force. He thought Du Soleil fit the mold. Inside her ski patrol hut, she demonstrated that she was in command. At the moment, she appeared to be double-checking paperwork that had been done by those who served under her.

JC asked, "Who delivered the box of medical supplies to the gondola that Marsha Prospect was on?"

"I'm not sure what you're talking about," was the reply he got.

"The box was intended to resupply your sleds at the top of the mountain. A lift op says one of your people handed him the box and he put it in the gondola."

"I wasn't there," Du Soleil told him. "Did the lift op know who it was?"

"No," JC informed her, "Do you find that strange?"

"Do I find what strange?"

"That he wouldn't recognize the ski patrol guy," JC answered. "I thought everybody knew everybody."

Elise Du Soleil said, "It's not that strange. We have a lot of ski patrol members, and their shifts change. And there always seem to be three or four new ones in training. It's a tough job. No one needs to know their name. They need to know the jacket."

"The red jacket with the white cross on it," JC affirmed.

"Yes," responded the director. "Most of our customers aren't in the mood to chat. They've been hurt, they want help. When they see the red jacket with a white cross on it, they know they're going to be OK."

"Don't get me wrong," Du Soleil continued, "a lot of us get to know each other. We meet during the shift or at the bar at the end of the day. But, I can't tell you who every lift operator is."

"I have to ask this," JC said. "Has anyone on your staff had a problem with Marsha Prospect? A significant problem?"

Du Soleil stopped rummaging through her inventory of gauze and plastic gloves. "You mean, a problem so big that they'd want to kill her? Come on." She made a face like JC was fishing in the wrong pond.

"Do you have anyone new? Anyone you can't really vouch for?"

"You mean, have I hired anyone who just got out of the state pen, or is facing murder charges?" Du Soleil returned to counting her inventory.

JC broke off their eye contact and looked at the floor. He asked, "You know, whatever killed Marsha Prospect may have been inside that box of ski patrol supplies."

The director stopped what she was doing. She looked at him. "Are you serious?" His look assured her that he was.

He asked, "Did it have to be one of your people who gave that box to the gondola op?"

"You just told me it was," Du Soleil replied.

"You made me think ... about the jacket," JC said. "The gondola operator said he didn't know the guy who handed him the box. He just knew he was wearing that red jacket with a white cross."

JC was thinking through the whole exchange of the box with Trip Lake again. Maybe there was no ski patrol guy. That would mean Trip Lake filled that box. The ex-boyfriend might be the murderer.

"Who's the gondola operator, anyway," asked Du Soleil.

"Trip Lake."

"Oh," Du Soleil said, "the cute one." JC smiled, allowing her a perky moment. The heart wants what it wants.

"OK, let me ask you something else," said JC. "Who gets to wear those jackets?"

"Only members of the ski patrol, no exceptions," she replied with some pride.

"What about if I want to go skiing and I have a friend on the ski patrol. So, I say that I'll wear the jacket and help him with his duties and I'll get to ski for free?"

Her eyes became piercing and her voice forceful. "If I catch it, they'll need to call two sleds. One for you, and one for the guy who gave you the jacket. There is no funny business with these jackets."

JC was gaining an understanding about how this woman controlled a staff of mostly men with "Type-A" personalities.

He asked Du Soleil if the ski patrol's locker room is locked at night.

"It's not necessary," she said. "There's always someone coming and going. What if a groomer gets hurt in the middle of the night? The medical supplies are locked up, the medicine. That's what a thief would be after, not someone's jacket."

"Oh!" Du Soleil exclaimed and looked at JC. His point had registered. "Could someone have walked in and stolen a jacket?" she asked rhetorically. "This is Grizzly Mountain. Most people don't even lock their ski lockers. If you left a dollar on the floor, it would still be there tomorrow."

"Let me ask you about something else," JC said. "The woman found buried in the snow, the snowboarder ..."

Du Soleil gave him a look like he was picking at a scab.

"Did your patrollers overlook her?" the reporter inquired. "They swept the mountain when it closed the afternoon before, right?"

The ski patrol director's look told him that she was asking herself the same thing. Someone would pay if they screwed up. "It was snowing like crazy that night," she said. "You could have buried a barbeque."

JC thanked the woman and told her that he had to be going. His live shot for that evening's newscast was approaching.

"But one more question." He already knew the answer.

"If I decided to drop by at five in the morning to borrow a ski jacket, there wouldn't be anyone or anything to stop me, would there?"

"Nothing happens overnight," she insisted. "Guests are exhausted from a day of skiing. If they aren't, we finish them off in the bars and on the dance floor. If you have any energy left to prowl around at five in the morning, you'll be the first."

"Maybe, the second," JC responded.

JC's live report for television broke the news that Marsha Prospect's death was being investigated as a homicide. Deputy Cochran confirmed that it was being called "suspicious" and being investigated. He wouldn't go into details.

A couple of employees spoke affectionately of their late boss in interviews. A snowboarder was asked if the death made him question his own safety on the mountain. He replied, "That's one of the reasons we do it, dude. It's better if there's risk."

JC wrapped up his report by telling the anchor and their audience that a memorial had been scheduled for the following day. Prospect's body wouldn't be there. Police were holding on to the corpse until the cause of death could be confirmed.

Al pulled up in his Forest Service truck while JC and the crew were still breaking down their equipment, following the live shot.

"So, did you tell them how dumb we are, up here in the sticks?" Al asked with a grin.

"They've been here, they know," JC laughed at his own joke. "Besides, little buddy, I'm not going to tell my audience who killed Marsha Prospect ..." His smile grew. "... Until after I tell you."

14

Cannons could be heard on the morning of Marsha Prospect's memorial. Some who attended the service thought it was a salute to the late ski resort owner. But the explosions were part of the mountain's routine, to knock loose avalanches before the slopes opened.

The memorial was held in the little town of Sierra. She would be buried in an old cemetery on a hill overlooking town. It was called "Boot Hill" a century before. The oldest graves had their share of gamblers, prospectors and prostitutes from the 1850s.

MURDER ON SKIS

A respectful distance was kept by four different television news crews sent to capture arrivals and departures at the memorial. The footage would show mourners outside the chapel. At the request of family, the cameras weren't allowed inside the service.

This was now an intriguing news story to a lot of news outlets. There were newspapers from out of town, including one from New York City. Learning that this was the third death on the same mountain this winter, a headline on a tabloid newspaper screamed, "Grizzly Mountain eats its own!"

JC was allowed inside the chapel with paper and pen, as were all the journalists. He saw Shara Adams, Al Pine, Alex Cochran and Lila Seneff also seated in the pews.

Somehow, the victim's former husband had carved a place for himself in the service. Some mourners resented that. Paul Prospect delivered a short eulogy and stood beside the casket. He was the former and the future CEO of Grizzly Mountain. JC had learned that succession was in the paperwork of the divorce, but only if Marsha died within five years.

JC concluded, watching him at the memorial, that Paul Prospect was an enormous presence. He shook hands with people there, even if they didn't want to shake hands. He smiled into faces that didn't smile back. Prospect didn't care, he didn't do it for them.

He arranged to be at or near the center of attention, everywhere he went. He was six foot two inches tall and very handsome. He was about twenty years older than Marsha and had a thick mane of silver hair and a prominent jaw. He wore a two thousand-dollar suit and a pair of thousand-dollar cowboy boots.

JC met him after the service. Prospect was charming and polite. His smile was just enough of a smile not to be inappropriate, considering the circumstances. Every move he made seemed to be the right one. He was working the house like a politician with an insurmountable lead before the election.

Al told JC, "Prospect could charm an elk out of his hide and have it mounted on the wall before the poor animal felt a draft."

Trip Lake was at the service. He had to peer over a crowd standing in the back. Few knew why, but he thought he belonged at the front of the church. Those seats were reserved for close family and friends.

Trip Lake felt cheated again, as much in her death as when she was alive. He was almost trembling with rage.

There was a man at the service JC couldn't place. He was middle-aged and dressed in a military uniform. JC couldn't quite figure out what branch of service he belonged to.

The man who owned the ski resort's video gambling franchise was also there. He had gotten to know

Marsha when he put his gambling machines inside the bar that Shara eventually purchased. So, Shara knew him, too. Marsha called the video gaming devices "money presses."

The man's name was Bill Peck. His clever logo was on every one of his machines. It was a caricature of a woodpecker's head. Peck called his gambling company "Peckerhead."

After the memorial, the crowd mingled outside in the cold air. Those who flew to Bozeman to attend, complained about the airfare.

Al stood with JC and disclosed that Mrs. Prospect's autopsy showed a lethal level of something called prussic acid. The dose was big enough to kill three people her size.

The medical examiner told Al that prussic acid was an exotic substance known to the military and those in the game of international espionage during the Cold War. The United States had accused the Soviet Union of using it, but there was a common suspicion that spies from the U.S. also had the deadly toxin at their disposal.

"You think she was murdered by a Soviet spy?" JC asked in a disbelieving tone.

"I have no idea who killed her," the forest ranger responded. "We have any number of paramilitary nuts in these parts. It's hard to keep up with them. If it can kill, some of them will want to get their hands on it, stockpile it."

Al told JC that the military officer in the odd-looking uniform was the leader of one of the most active militia groups in Montana.

"I was surprised to see him here," Al said. "He and Marsha didn't get along very well. He wanted her to hire his militia members as security for the ski resort. She wouldn't have anything to do with it."

"This is sort of new to me, "JC admitted. "Do they all live together in some fort?"

"They're serious, JC," Al cautioned. "They live in this camp in the woods that's like Valley Forge. I don't know how many people they have up there, but all they seem to do is shoot guns and sit around the campfire talking about how they'd love to take down the government."

"Is this 'General' or whatever he is, is he a suspect?" asked JC.

"Maybe Marsha should have taken him more seriously," Al said. "She thought he was a nitwit. But I suppose you could say he has a motive, and he's got a bigger arsenal than the local National Guard."

The crowd outside the service was dispersing. They hurried to the warmth of their idling vehicles. In that crowd, Marsha Prospect's killer turned and muttered, "This isn't the way I wanted it to end."

15

The sky still had a gray overcast to it in the afternoon after the memorial. JC was in his 4x4, rocking his way down a rutted, snow-covered road in the woods. He was twenty miles north of Sierra.

JC had been surprised at how easy it was to find a telephone number for the local paramilitary group. He'd made an appointment to see the "Brigadier General" who ran the operation.

To meet the leader of Benedict's Brigade, JC at least expected a few secret passwords and a ride in the trunk of a car, blindfolded.

"Quite the contrary," the Brigadier General would tell him. "We enjoy popular support here. The public is on our side." That was his story, anyway. JC wasn't allowed to bring a cameraman along for the visit.

Before JC spotted the first sentry, he saw a Sierra County deputy's patrol car sliding over the icy road, coming toward him. It was Cochran, with Al in the passenger seat.

"Good luck," the deputy said to JC. "They wouldn't let us in." The law officer wasn't sure exactly why but suggested that they'd return with a warrant. The two cars went their way. JC continued toward the compound of the militiamen.

He suspected that he was getting closer because he spied two sentries in the woods. They were wearing camouflage pants and jackets. They appeared to be armed with some sort of military-style rifles.

A heavy wooden gate prevented JC from proceeding any further. A sign overhead welcomed him to "The Last Square Mile of America."

After some radio communication between a uniformed guard and parts unknown, the gate was raised and JC drove through.

This "Valley Forge" was not as stark as he'd expected. There were two dozen comfortable log cabins scattered about the grounds. Some had mothers and children in front of them. They had happy faces. They were playing and making snowmen.

JC drove past a handsome A-frame dining hall sitting on a hill. It had huge picture windows and smoke was coming out of the chimney. In the distance, he could hear gunfire from one of the firing ranges.

An escort on foot waved JC's car to a parking place in front of a cabin that was larger than the others. The escort stuck his head in the door of the building to announce the new arrival. He took a step backward to allow JC to enter. The escort departed, closing the door behind him.

Logs were burning in the fireplace in the modest cabin. The front room was an office furnished with a drab green metal desk and file cabinets. Despite the fire and a couple of desk lamps, the room was dark. One of the two men in camouflage fatigues stood quietly in the shadows of the corner.

The other man sat behind the desk. He was somewhat overweight and looked familiar. He remained seated as he introduced himself, "Mr. Snow, I'm Brigadier General John Smith."

"You were at the memorial this morning," JC stated, "Did you know Marsha Prospect?"

"We had some business dealings," the general responded. "I take an interest in my community, Mr. Snow. It was my duty to be there."

The general seemed to be about fifty years old. He had a big round head and big ears, though the buzz cut might have just made it seem that way.

His complexion showed the scars from acne and his teeth were yellowed. But his boots were shined and his uniform was crisp and starched. He wore a star on each side of his collar.

Following their visit, a background check using files at the library in Sierra would tell JC that John Smith never rose above the rank of corporal in the U.S. Army. Now, he was the charismatic leader of four hundred men and women who thought an armed rebellion was possible in their lifetime, maybe even desired.

Members would come for a week or two at a time, like going to camp. They could practice their skills at the firing range and swallow the latest propaganda. Then they'd return home to spread the gospel.

They opposed taxes, gun control, government dominating the use of the land, and pretty much anyone who disagreed with them. There were few conspiracies they didn't clutch to their breast.

Al had told JC that while General Smith's members made vague references to the dire consequences for opposing them, police experienced few problems with the bunch.

There were exceptions, JC was informed, like the guy who refused to pull over for a minor traffic infraction. The driver paused only long enough to tell the officer that he wasn't subject to the police department's laws. Slowly, the driver proceeded to his house, exited his car and entered his home, locking the door behind him. The standoff lasted for two days, never a gun drawn or a threat issued. The suspect would occasionally shout out of his window, "You have no jurisdiction here!"

Eventually, his friends on the Internet assured him that police do have some jurisdiction. The man emerged and was sent to jail for six months instead of the forty-dollar fine, if he'd only pulled over as requested.

"Why wouldn't you let the sheriff's deputy into the compound a while ago?" JC asked the general.

"Oh, Cochran is harmless enough," the general told him. "It was the government man."

"The government man?"

"The U.S. Forest Service guy, or whatever he was posing as," the general said. "For all we know, he could be the man who killed Mrs. Prospect. Grizzly Mountain is on U.S. Forest Service land. It is clear that the federal government is systematically revoking our permits, bankrupting our ranches and confiscating our land."

JC had a feeling that the general was just warming up. This is what his audiences paid to see.

"Every day, they are taking back our property and putting further restrictions on the land they can't get their hands on," the general continued. "It is part of a federal plot to return this country to tyranny. That's why we are here, Mr. Snow. We don't intend to allow that to happen."

"That sounds a bit paranoid, General."

"And you, Mr. Snow, sound a bit naïve."

The general sat at attention, his eyes riveted on the reporter. He was waiting for the next question. JC thought he saw a tiny sneer on the general's face, or was that a smile?

"What do you know about the method used to kill Marsha Prospect?" JC asked.

"Prussic acid? Excellent choice, if you want to get the job done," the general replied with assumed expertise. "It is effective and deadly. Hard to detect."

"I thought that was why you came," the general told JC. "You want to know if I killed her."

"And?" JC asked.

"I'm afraid I can't be of much help. No, I did not."

The other militia member had been standing in the corner the entire time. He hadn't said a word.

General Smith chose this time to introduce his silent partner as Captain Steve Hemingway. His blond hair was unruly and he hadn't shaved in a number of days. There were dark rings around his eyes. JC didn't think it was lack of sleep, that's probably just what he looked like.

Hemingway's camouflage fatigues were neither ironed nor particularly clean. He was trim and his long thin muscles looked hard. He was the only one JC had seen in the compound who looked like the killing machine they all seemed to aspire to be. JC instantly came up with a nickname, "Spook."

JC asked the general, "Do you have prussic acid on the grounds here?" The general returned a look saying, "I wouldn't tell you if I did."

JC admitted, "I'd never heard of the stuff. A metal tube was found at the scene, dented. Any idea how it works?"

"He crushes it."

To JC's surprise, that was the voice of Spook.

Captain Hemingway continued, "The toxic gas is concentrated in a cartridge. When broken, the gas pours into the surrounding air. If someone is close, they won't survive."

"In 1957," Hemingway said as he became more animated, "Soviet spies used prussic acid to kill an activist named Rebet. His death was diagnosed as a heart attack. Prussic acid causes the instant constriction of blood vessels. It mimics a heart attack."

JC was scribbling notes in his small notebook. He thought that Hemingway was getting excited. Did he like discussing murder?

"Upon death," Hemingway continued, "the body relaxes, including the blood vessels, and evidence of the murder disappears into thin air."

Spook offered another example, "A year later, another Soviet dissident was murdered the same way. This time, tiny shards of glass were found in the skin on his face from the exploding ampule. That's why they knew to look for prussic acid in his lungs. In the 1950s, this was a popular way to kill for covert killers with access to the material."

"Wow," JC muttered.

General Smith interrupted, "That will be enough, Captain. That will be all."

Without a salute or even a "Yes, sir," Captain Hemingway let himself out, leaving JC and the general alone.

"He gets excited when he discusses the arsenal of freedom fighting," General Smith said with a grin.

JC had another question: "I understand Marsha Prospect refused to employ your people at Grizzly Mountain."

The General responded, "She made a silly business decision. Grizzly Mountain was more than a woman could handle. She was in over her head." JC wondered if he'd see a single woman in uniform here. Wives could accompany their husbands, but did the women really get to play army?

"Did I kill her? Was that my motive?" the general asked with a grin. "Did you come to arrest me, Missus Snow? I'm disappointed in you. I expected you to be more clever."

JC noted that his manhood had been disputed. "Very cutting," he mumbled.

"What?" the general asked. He rose from behind his desk to escort the reporter out.

"Very cunning," JC replied with a laugh he shared only with himself. "You're very cunning." Then the reporter asked, "Why did you let me visit you today, General?"

"Because we like your reporting, Mister Snow."

"So, my manhood has been restored. Who do I pay?" JC noted.

The general ignored the remark. He told JC, "You're not as honest as we'd like, but compared to your liberal brethren, you don't close a blind eye to government corruption."

The general had apparently seen a series of reports JC broadcast regarding extravagant government spending and, at times, corruption. JC knew that the stories struck a chord with viewers. He just never considered that some of those viewers were armed and dreaming of revolution.

"Besides, "added the general, "We don't want to give you an excuse in your next report to say we dodged you, or let you suggest our silence was a guilty plea."

The general was holding an invisible microphone up to his chin as he mocked the vision of a television reporter looking into a camera.

"Very grown up," muttered JC, not caring if he was heard or not.

Another hand gesture by the general, toward the door of JC's car, suggested the interview was over.

And as JC pulled away, he looked in his rearview mirror and saw General Smith jotting something into a small black book. Maybe JC's license number.

Following JC's live report for the television station that evening, he went for a four-mile run. It was dark now at Grizzly Mountain.

His warm breath turned to steam as it hit the air. It was the dinner hour, and most of the resort's guests had exhausted themselves with another day of skiing and snowboarding. A horse-pulled sleigh trotted past JC, taking its riders to their dinner destination. There was the sound of fiddle and guitar music in the distance.

There were thousands of people out there in the darkness. Each was pinpointed by a tiny light on the hillside. The glow was supplied by a porch light, or a fireplace or a living room lamp.

MURDER ON SKIS

Some of the resort's visitors had come from across the country. Some had come here years ago and never left. Some were having the time of their lives. Some were probably even falling in love. One of them was getting away with murder.

16

His burgundy ski boots snapped shut in his bindings. The sound resembled a mouse trap being triggered.

JC had been gate training with local racers at Grizzly Mountain. Adult racers trained when they could, and that wasn't enough. They had jobs, many had families to come home to.

Was it so different for the Olympic racers, seventy years ago, JC wondered, when they were really amateurs? Today's adult ski racers found time to practice when they could, not when they should.

But for an unknown number of days, JC's job was at the Grizzly Mountain Ski Resort. This was a lifestyle he could get used to.

JC had informed viewers in last night's live shot of the confusing trail of evidence left behind by Marsha Prospect's homicide. He showed video of the large crowd exiting her memorial service. And he reported that investigators had no idea who committed the murder.

JC had been surprised to find a wide selection of disturbing books at the library and bookstore in Sierra. They provided details about how to assemble homemade weapons. And offerings on the Internet seemed unlimited. It was something he thought should be classified "Top Secret." Instead, this narrowed the list of suspects to anyone who can read.

JC would need to prepare another report for tonight. But at the moment, he found himself at the top of the mogul run named after Marsha Prospect. He skied there deliberately, knowing the body of the unidentified woman had been found there.

JC often liked to experience being at the site of an event he was reporting on. He just wanted to feel what it was like. He thought it was probably the same reason people liked to visit old battlefields.

Below him, there were skiers scattered across the bumps in various stages of duress. It was a difficult run.

They'd been eager for the challenge but found out too late that they lacked the skill to master the moguls.

One of the hill's victims was brushing snow out of her hair after an eggbeater of a fall. Another was attempting to become reacquainted with one of his skis, which had stopped to rest about twenty steep yards up from where he was currently climbing to his feet.

There were names in ski lore for the best of the tumbles. A "yard sale" described the separation of a skier from his complete set of equipment, skis, poles, maybe a hat.

A "face-plant" was just what it sounds like, only hurts more. At best, a skier would emerge from a face-plant with goggles raked down their face and now filled with snow. The same snow covered their face and helmet.

The worst was a "starfish." That involved a yard sale and a cartwheel. It required high speed, so the momentum sent a skier cartwheeling downhill while shedding skis, poles and perhaps gloves. The G-forces extended arms and legs until the skier looked like a starfish doing revolutions down the hill.

However disastrous, a certain sense of achievement comes with these performances by skiers. They were certain to get cheers from the crowd on the ski lift, and companions would remind the victim of their acrobatics for days to come. Total and coerced capitulation to the elements was a badge of honor.

JC stood at the top of Marsha's Moguls and looked for a line through the bumps. He also wanted to avoid the carnage. He had been taught by some Austrian, on the day he finally mastered moguls, "Follow the fall line." The fall line, his mentor told him, was the path an orange would take if you rolled it down a hillside.

JC pushed off and barreled almost straight down the treacherous hill. His skis bounced off the side of one mogul and then off the next. They recoiled off the tops of others, giving him a little "flight time". He dropped back down to the snow and absorbed the impact in his legs. His powerful thighs were shock absorbers, and he thought to himself, I guess my knee is all better.

He stopped near the end of the bump run. He thought he spied a familiar rear end attached to a skier inverted in the snow. JC recovered one of the victim's skis and side-slipped down to the crater. He smiled to himself.

"I see you're standing there on one ski," JC told the woman. He held up the other ski in his hand. "Have you considered trying two?"

"Very funny, JC Snow." Shara Adams was getting herself righted.

"It happens to the best of us," JC offered in a kinder tone. He handed her the ski. There went his heart, racing again.

Out of the woods trotted the big Labrador, Jumper. "Isn't he supposed to carry brandy or something?" JC inquired.

After piecing her back together, JC, Shara and Jumper bounded down the slope together. JC noted how good a skier Shara still was. Her hair bounced off of her shoulders below her helmet. She skied with confidence and daring.

JC followed her, with Jumper leaping down the hill nearby. Of course, from the chairlift, Jumper was the crowd-pleaser.

At the base of the mountain, JC and Shara stepped out of their skis in front of the lodge. They exchanged big smiles that all skiers shared at the end of a run.

"You haven't changed," Shara said as she brushed more snow out of her hair. "You're still an amazing skier." She looked into his eyes. He stopped breathing. It wasn't voluntary.

JC packed a snowball and threw it as far as he could. Jumper was in close pursuit.

"You know the great thing about skiing?" JC offered his theory, "I was such a dork when I was a kid, too tall and hopelessly uncoordinated. I was the last kid picked for every team at gym. I wasn't a great skier, either, but every time I fell, I was allowed to get up and try again. That's what's special about skiing. If you fall, you can always get back up."

"You said you used to be a dork?" Shara asked with a serious face. "Who says you still aren't?" and she started to giggle. He laughed, too.

They found themselves only inches apart. She continued to look at him and thought to herself, the boy she once loved had grown into a man. There was wisdom in his eyes now.

They both had nervous smiles on their faces, uncertain what to do next.

Out of nowhere, a furry ninety-pound projectile leaped on the two of them. Jumper was eager for attention. He was licking their faces.

"Good grief," exclaimed JC, "I got tongue! Did you teach him that?"

Shara responded with a laugh and punch to JC's ribs.

He wanted to kiss her. But a crowd was pushing past them, eager to get into the lodge for lunch. It wasn't the time or the place. And thinking that she could read his mind, he was a little embarrassed.

"I guess this story is going to keep me here awhile," JC told her.

"Good," she said quietly, and she turned to walk to the lodge. When she looked over her shoulder, he saw that smile that only belonged to him.

They both had places to be. JC walked in the other direction. He changed out of his ski boots and headed for his car. He had an appointment to see Paul Prospect.

His phone rang. It was Al. "Where are you?" the ranger asked.

"Just got off the mountain," JC responded.

Al found that amusing. "And taxpayers accuse us of being goof offs? Anyway, we identified that woman who the grooming machine uncovered."

"Buried in the snow?"

"Yep." That was followed by silence. JC could hear pages flipping. Al was back at his desk. He was preoccupied with the report.

"Do I have to guess?" JC finally asked into the phone with sarcasm. "Amelia Earhart?"

"Right, how did we miss her airplane? It was right there," Al answered as he was peering down at a pile of paper. "Sorry, I was reading the file on her."

Pine turned his attention back to the phone, "No, she's a local woman. Her family didn't even report her missing. She told them she was moving to California. They're not a tight-knit family. They didn't think anything of not hearing from her for a couple of months. Her name's Sally Decker, thirty-seven years old."

"Does she have anything to do with Marsha Prospect?"

"Not that we can tell."

"How did she die?"

"M.E. thinks she froze to death. Maybe she got banged up when she crashed on her snowboard." Then there was more silence.

"What?" JC asked.

Al sighed into the phone, "Well, she was frozen. The body was left out to defrost. Now, some big shot in Los Angeles tells us that we may have destroyed evidence by not letting her melt more scientifically."

"Still a snowboard accident?" JC inquired.

"We think so." Al let JC digest that for a moment. Then the ranger's tone brightened. "But, at least we know who she is."

Then Al added, "Hey, what are you doing tomorrow?"

17

The murder victim's ex-husband was sitting behind Marsha Prospect's desk when Mrs. Seneff led JC back into the office. All the drawers were open and he was surrounded by cardboard boxes and a trash can. Most of Marsha Prospect's personal items seemed to be piling up in the garbage.

Mrs. Seneff excused herself and exited the room. She gave JC a displeased look that said, "The body isn't even cold yet ..."

One day after her memorial, photographs of Marsha Prospect that had been on the wall of the office were replaced with photographs of Paul Prospect. The theme hadn't changed a lot. There were pictures of Paul Prospect with movie stars and a couple of presidents.

But there were nuanced changes. There were pictures of Prospect with a few women of stunning beauty. "They're the centerfolds for June, July and August," Prospect told JC with a childish grin.

"Some will think that I'm doing all of this in a hurry," Prospect continued as he waved his arms around his new office, "but there is business to conduct. I feel more comfortable in my own element." Then the silver-haired business magnate flashed a charming smile. "Besides, I can't be expected to work while being stared at by the woman who took me to the cleaners in divorce court, can I?"

Prospect was invoking a tone that inferred this was a conversation only men would understand. JC hated that crap. He knew that Paul Prospect mistreated his wife for thirteen years. That had nothing to do with manhood. JC was uncomfortable with Mr. Prospect's notion that they would belong to the same club. Any club.

It reminded JC of the locker room after football practice in high school. There was a circle of guys who made lying about their sexual conquests a regular routine. JC came to learn that the only guys really sharing intimacy with their girlfriends were the ones who weren't bragging about it.

One photograph of Marsha Prospect, a face shot, seemed to peer out of a cardboard box, witnessing all the changes to her office.

Paul Prospect, sitting behind the desk, told JC that Grizzly Mountain needed a lot of work.

JC asked, "Like what?"

"All of it," Prospect responded. "This is my mountain again."

He told JC something the reporter had already learned: "The divorce settlement says in the event of Marsha's death, the ownership of the ski resort reverts back to me."

That's why you're a suspect, JC thought to himself. In fact, JC was thinking that if Paul Prospect had handled his ex-wife's memorial arrangements, it might have included balloons, streamers and a clown for the kids. Prospect knew that he was literally better off, financially, with his wife dead.

Prospect could hardly hide his delight. But he quickly changed his demeanor when he realized he was gushing too much.

"I've seen you on television," Prospect said, changing the subject. "You're very good. In fact, I could use someone like you. Sometimes I just don't say the right thing to the press at the right time."

"Thank you, but no thanks," JC said. It probably wasn't a real offer anyway, JC thought. But if it was, he'd just passed up a chance to probably double his salary.

JC had met people like Paul Prospect before, from billionaires to powerful U.S. senators. They believed that their money or influence could sweep anyone or anything out of their way. JC took Prospect's "job offer" as a demonstration of a very rich man flexing his muscles.

But JC also knew the tactic often worked. It could cause someone who was provided a glimmer of hope of joining Prospect's empire to do Prospect a favor. Maybe it would be a member of the municipal zoning board, or someone with a say in an environmental review of a development Prospect proposed. Maybe a member of the news media could choose to say nice things instead of not-so-nice things in a newspaper or on TV.

The telephone rang. Prospect gestured JC toward the couch decorated with bears and elk. While the businessman made a lunch date with someone on the other end of the phone in New York, JC picked up a copy of Grizzly Mountain's annual report. Profits were up in Marsha's first year at the helm of the ski resort. JC had heard they would be up again at the end of this season.

Paul Prospect had the Midas touch, but he had just repossessed a property that was worth even more than when he lost it.

When Prospect got off the phone, he had a sour look on his face.

"Bad news?" JC asked.

"No, not that. I just found another picture of this punk. Do you know who this kid is?" Prospect pulled a photograph of Trip Lake out of an open drawer and showed it to his guest.

"Beats me," JC lied.

"It's clear to see what Marsha was doing with all her spare time," Prospect said through clenched teeth. "God, that kid could be her son."

JC tried not to smirk, remembering all the stories he'd heard about Mr. Prospect stalking college girls hired by his ski resort.

Prospect was still seething about the photo when a look of discovery came upon his face. "I know who that kid is! He'd still be in the brig if it wasn't for me."

"Excuse me?" JC suddenly cared about what this loathsome bore had to say.

"I was doing a deal at Fort Drum in New York," the businessman said. "This Trip Lake had gotten into some trouble while he was in the Army, right out of high school."

JC thought about the coincidence. Trip Lake had belonged to the same unit Prospect's father had, when the founder of this resort learned to ski during World War II. By the time Lake enlisted, the Tenth Mountain Division had abandoned its role as a skiing unit and moved to Watertown, New York.

"So, Lake isn't in the army for long when he realizes that he's not cut out for that stuff. He got into some trouble," Prospect explained. "My old man was in the Tenth. So, somebody asked me to pull some strings so Lake could have a soft landing back in civilian life."

The tumblers were working in JC's brain. So, Trip Lake had Army training. And in the Army, they train you to kill. JC voiced his thoughts to Prospect.

"That's the business they're in," responded Prospect. "Say, you don't think this pretty boy had anything to do with Marsha's death, do you?"

JC said that he didn't know what to think. But he was concluding to himself that for a nice a woman like Marsha Prospect, there were a number of people with a motive to kill her. Trip Lake was one of them. So was Paul Prospect.

18

It was a massive beast. The thick fur on its head and shoulders made it look even larger and more menacing. It lumbered through the deep snow, making a loud puffing noise.

The roar coming from the animal's nostrils reminded JC of a steam locomotive making a slow advance down the rails. JC had ridden a train like that as a child, visiting Colorado.

Only moments ago, JC and Al had been cross-country skiing north on the path through the woods near a feature called the Fountain Paint Pots. But along came this bison plodding south on the same trail.

The humans departed from the path and surrendered as much real estate to the monster as possible, but the colossal animal also left the path and slowly marched closer to the pair. As the bison exhaled into the freezing air, it looked as though he was breathing fire. The two men feared and admired him, in that order.

"It's an older bull, maybe ten years old," the forest ranger quietly reported. "You can tell by the size and curve of his horns. He's about twenty-five hundred pounds."

"What's he doing here?" asked JC.

"There are about four thousand of them here in the park."

"No, I mean 'right here,' not 'why is he in Yellowstone National Park!'"

"When there's deep snow, they like to follow trails already cut by skiers. It's easier to walk. But we seem to make him nervous," Al calmly deduced.

"He's nervous? What about me?"

Al snickered a little. "Do you know how many park visitors have been killed by buffalo here? A lot. It's usually the visitor's fault. One summer, a guy wanted the bison to stand next to his child for a snapshot. So, the father gives the animal a little kick." Al was snickering again. "That bison gored the guy and was back to grazing in the grass so fast, he didn't miss a bite. These are not animals to be fooled with."

"Thanks, I feel better about this dinosaur walking toward me. Any advice?"

Al calmly and quietly told JC, "Bison can outrun a horse, so don't do that. Maybe climb a tree. They can't do that."

JC thought that Al was enjoying this encounter a bit too much.

"By the way," Al told him, "that giant muscle behind his head, that's called the dorsal. Very good meat."

That confirmed it, JC thought. Al's having too much fun. "Really," he tried to fake dry wit. "What part of us is he considering eating?"

"No worries, he's a vegetarian," Al said as he nodded his head toward the animal.

"Seriously, do we have a plan here?" JC asked.

Al was distracted by the animal. "Well, that's not a good sign," he declared. "He just licked his nostrils with his tongue. That really does mean he's nervous."

The two men continued to back away from the ski trail until they were on the edge of a steep gully.

In the distance, they could hear the paint pots boiling. JC though it sounded like spaghetti sauce cooking. Then, the animal raised his tail.

"Well, we'll know his intentions soon," Al announced. "When he raises his tail, it means he's either going to charge ... or discharge."

JC and Al began looking over their shoulder for a safe spot to jump into the gully. But the animal stopped with his dark eyes still trained on the two men.

Then the frightening monster raised his tail almost straight into the air and a steaming stew dropped to the snow behind him. The feces could have filled a bowling ball bag.

That being his uncontested declaration of triumph, the huge animal gave the pair a final look, swung his head, and slowly walked away down the ski trail he now solely owned.

"I guess we scared the shit out of him," JC feigned bravery. JC was trying to disguise his elevated sense of alarm. "By the way, bison or buffalo?"

"Technically, bison," Al informed his friend while keeping his calm eyes on the animal as it disappeared down the path. "But it's also fair to call it an American Buffalo. They didn't call the old cowboy 'Bison Bill Cody,' did they?"

"And it's not Bison, New York." JC's nerves were calming. He wasn't a stranger to bison or the wilds of nature or even Yellowstone. He knew of the danger the animals could present, but that was the first time he'd been cornered by a grumpy one.

Al was in his element. These were the days he'd dreamed of when he chose his major in college. On this day, he was assigned the task of inspecting the border of his forest district for snowmobile tracks intruding into the national park. Al asked JC if he wanted to come along.

Al's district shared borders with the national park on this side. Snowmobilers were allowed in the national park, but only on a few roads. It was an effort to protect the park's delicate ecosystem. Al conducted his inspection on skis.

JC was happy to take the excursion, but he also had a number of questions to ask Al about the murder investigation. They hitched a ride into the park's Geyser Basin on a Bombardier snow coach. It was owned by one of the tour guides who take vacationers into the park during the winter months. The firm was happy to help rangers when there was room left in their coach.

Instead of tires, the snow coach had treads like a tank to stay on top of the snow. Al said Bombardier made the best ones. "This one was built in 1953. It's worth it to salvage for parts. They just don't make them like this anymore."

They'd pulled their skis off the back of the vehicle along the Firehole River. "Personally, it's the best time to be here," Al said. "They had about four million visitors here last year, and outside of snowmobilers, almost none of them come in the winter. But look at it!"

They skied as Al pointed out more bison, elk and birds of prey. Al noted when they were surrounded by the remains of two million-year-old volcanos, "That's why Yellowstone is Yellowstone. The last volcanic eruption spewed ash over six hundred miles, and it left behind the park's geysers, hot springs and mud pots."

JC marveled at flowers in bloom near the geysers. The air temperature was approaching zero.

"This place is so cool, it's ridiculous," the forest ranger muttered.

JC and Al intended to ski the Geyser Basin, looking for renegade snowmobile tracks, and then hitch a ride back to the West Yellowstone park entrance from the visitors center at Old Faithful.

"Look both ways for renegade bubbleheads," Al hollered to JC as they skied single file. When they stopped to take a drink from their water bottles, they recounted tales of arguments between skiers and snowmobilers. Sometimes they became more than arguments. JC could remember a few news stories when those disputes ended in fistfights or gunshots.

"And then there are SPORS," Al told JC: "Stupid People On Rental Sleds." Al said he had been called to rescue snowmobilers after collisions with trees and other snowmobiles. Some of them were fatal.

JC had piloted snowmobiles and thought they were a lot of fun. Al owned a number of them. His wife and his oldest boys rode with him. But he never hopped aboard one after a night of drinking. He said he'd been called to scenes past midnight where a snowmobiler had driven with a wide-open throttle into the side of a barn, or a grove of poplars. "Can't fix stupid."

"Before the laws changed," Al recounted from his earliest days as a ranger, "the West Yellowstone entrance to the park looked like Dodge City, with snowmobiles flying up and down the main drag. It was kind of cool, but the biggest problem was the air pollution from so many sleds."

They skied through the odor of rotten eggs. "That's the Grotto Mud Pot," Al said, without stopping. It was a hole in the ground the size of a Cadillac. JC thought it looked like it was filled with boiling Cream of Wheat.

A few miles later, the forest ranger stopped at the edge of the snow and popped out of his skis. He kneeled on dirt alongside a steaming pool and took the temperature with a surface thermometer he carried in his breast pocket. "They asked me to take some samples, since I was going to be here. Routine stuff, but with climate change ..."

Al said the spot where he was kneeling was known to park rangers as a safe one. Snow melted near the hot spring and the ground was visible.

"The danger is posed by what you can't see. The ground may look stable, but in some places, there's such a thin crust that you fall through and boil like a lobster," Al told JC. The ranger was writing the temperature reading in a small book. "It happens to animals from time to time," Al continued, "even a tourist or two. This one's about two hundred degrees. There's a one hundred percent fatality rate for anyone who falls into these things."

"You know about geyserite?" JC asked, thinking he might know something about the park that Al didn't.

"Yep. It's a bacteria found along the edge of some of these hot ponds," Al replied. "It's believed to be one of the oldest and purest substances on earth. Somehow, criminologists use it in DNA fingerprinting. They used some from here in the park in the OJ Simpson murder trial."

"So, its official," JC capitulated. "You know everything there is to know about every inch of this park."

"And then some, Brother," Al said with a smile, as a snowflake landed on his hand. He looked up at the sky.

Al snapped back into his skis and they pushed off. "Let's pick up our pace," he told JC, as more snowflakes fell. And then more.

"The forecast only called for brief flurries," JC said as he followed Al at an accelerated tempo. "This is more than a flurry."

"Yeah," was all Al replied.

The snow was falling harder and the wind was picking up. The reality of the two skiers being caught in a blizzard was becoming a more frightening prospect than being cornered by that bison.

"Let's ski a straight line for the Old Faithful Visitors Center," Al shouted over the wind. JC could hear the sound of snow hitting the hoods they'd pulled over their heads.

They'd scampered only another half mile when the storm gained intensity. They stopped and gave each other a worried look. Their heavy breathing was forming icicles around their mustaches. They squinted to prevent the fast-moving snowflakes from stinging their eyes.

"Can we reach Old Faithful?" JC panted.

"Probably not," Al admitted. But they were getting cold just standing there. They both were becoming concerned about hypothermia. First, confusion would set in, and then they'd probably freeze to death.

Al's bearded face still reflected calm.

"You're going to be the calmest corpse they've ever seen in the morgue," JC exclaimed. However, his own concern was elevated.

The ranger was staring into a vast white snowfall.

"What are you doing?" JC shouted to Al.

"I'm looking for a road," he responded. "If we're where I think we are, we may have a prayer."

"And if we're not?" JC reluctantly inquired.

"You don't want to ask," Al replied.

Now, they both squinted into the storm, looking for a feature in the snow-covered landscape. Al instructed JC to look for something so flat that a man-made road might lie beneath it.

The light was so dull, and the snow so uniform, the landscape looked like a single white canvas. It could be hopeless.

"Is that it?" JC shouted, pointing.

Al looked in that direction and a little grin returned. "You're not just a pretty face, are you?"

Al instructed JC to follow in his ski tracks as he pointed in the direction of the road, "That's Excelsior Geyser. Make sure you follow me. It's still a ways off."

They had to ski hard through the storm. A cloud of steam prevented JC from seeing the actual geyser as they skied past. Then Al stopped.

They were almost at the road. "It should be safe here," Al told him. "From falling through the crust, I mean."

Al had taken off his skis and was using them to dig through the soft snow. Out of breath, he signaled for JC to do the same thing. Side by side, they dug with the thin skis until they reached the ground.

"Keep digging," Al said.

"Are we digging our graves?" JC offered with morbid wit.

Al stopped digging and leaned on his ski, motioning for JC to do the same. They would take a minute to catch their breath and then resume.

Al bobbed his head in the direction of Excelsior Geyser. "It used to be the biggest in the world, until it blew itself up. There's a lot of plumbing under here. And it's steam-heated."

They continued to dig until the depression resembled a shallow foxhole. Al stopped pawing at the ground with his ski and dropped to his knees. He pulled the thermometer out of his pocket and jabbed it into the earth. Snowflakes bounced off the back of his jacket.

When he pulled the thermometer out, a smile covered his face. He held the dial up to JC. It read 85 degrees. JC's face was beaming too.

"There's a place nearby," Al shouted, "where I brought my wife's family on Thanksgiving. I wrapped a turkey in an oven bag, buried it, and when we came back from our hike, the bird was cooked. We ate Thanksgiving dinner right there."

JC and Al were settling into their foxhole, covered by their jackets as blankets. They would not only survive the night, they'd sleep in relative comfort.

Al's smile had grown, "Man, you've gotta be a dope to freeze in this park."

19

They were still alive.

The first rays of sunlight woke them up. The snow had stopped. They shook the accumulation off their jacket-blankets and watched the sunrise.

They'd spent some of the night talking and then slept. They talked about their shared ancestral roots in Scotland. JC was from the Lindsay and Crawford clans. Al was a Stewart.

Al spoke about his childhood in West Yellowstone. He recounted playing in the national park with his brothers. They didn't grow up thinking of it as a tourist attraction. It was their backyard. "Good thing you didn't have to mow it," JC said.

Al had tried to phone his wife, Soozie, once he and JC had found a place to safely wait out the storm. But his cell phone couldn't get a signal.

"They'll be worried sick," he said. "But she'll figure I was busy rescuing other stranded skiers. She'll think it's funny that I was the stranded skier this time … when she's done being mad."

Al loved his life here. He said it was a great place to raise his four sons. "They are wild animals. They live outdoors. There is nothing they won't climb or jump off of."

Every winter, Al dressed up as a mountain man and fired a muzzleloader into the air to start Yellowstone's big cross-country ski race.

Now, as the sun rose, the storm was only a memory. There was a clear sky overhead. A few buffalo grazed near Excelsior Geyser, where the grass was exposed.

"Makes you wish you were one of them, doesn't it?" Al said, "Then you'd never have to leave."

JC began to rise and said, "Well, if we don't leave soon and call your wife, she'll finish digging this hole and bury you in it."

"I believe you're right," Al responded. "Let's ski to Old Faithful. We'll use a phone there and hitch a ride out."

It was a magnificent ski trip over the fresh white snow. It sparkled in the sun's reflection. The hot air from the geysers hit the cold air and the plume of steam looked like skyscrapers.

When they saw Geyser Hill and Old Faithful moving closer, they were almost disappointed that the adventure was coming to an end.

As they arrived at the cluster of buildings, they heard a National Park Service ranger's voice: "Good God, Al. Your wife is a saint!"

Ranger Mick Berns continued her happy belligerence as the two men stepped out of their skis. She told them that park rangers had been alerted to keep their eyes peeled for the missing pair. NPS hadn't launched a search during the snowstorm. It was a big park and they didn't really know where to look.

"I radioed headquarters that I'd found you as soon as I saw you skiing this way. Maybe I'll get a medal," Ranger Berns laughed.

"We figured that your survival instincts would serve you well," she said as they exchanged a hug. "Now, call your wife so she can quit worrying and start getting pissed."

"Mick" was short for Michelle. She was a beautiful blonde who made her uniform look like something worn on the runway of a fashion show. Her hair was short, her legs were long, and the windburn on her face disclosed the long days she spent outside.

After introducing JC to Mick, Al pulled on the heavy wooden handle of the door into the Visitors Center and advanced to a telephone. That left the remaining pair to trade some barbs at Al's expense. And at her prodding, JC provided details of their survival overnight.

Al emerged through the door of the Visitors Center. "That woman of mine knows me too well. She says she wasn't even going to start worrying unless I missed dinner tonight."

Ranger Berns told JC, "This isn't the first time he's tried to scare us. He's not easy to kill, so we've just quit trying." She gave Al a friendly look.

JC and Al caught a ride to West Yellowstone on the first snow coach of the day. Then, they drove north on Route 191 toward Grizzly Mountain, in the ranger's Forest Service truck.

On the edge of Sierra, Al pulled into the parking lot of a steakhouse named "Bronco Billy's." It was open for breakfast. "Bronco Billy" Peck was behind the cash register and greeted the two exhausted men as they entered the restaurant.

Bronco Billy was a football All-American thirty-five years ago, at Montana State. He came out from behind the counter and showed the pair to a booth. It offered soft leather seats framed by old barnwood.

The restaurant had a low ceiling and its wooden timbers were exposed overhead. The walls were knotty pine. A fire roared from fireplaces in both dining rooms.

Trophy animals from Bronco Billy's hunting triumphs hung from every wall. There were heads of antelope, elk, moose, bear, buffalo, bighorn sheep and mountain goat. Assorted fish were mounted on the walls, too. Outside, there were two full rows of pickup trucks parked. Bronco Billy's did a good business.

As they worked on an order of eggs and buffalo steak, JC said to Al, "Did you take another look at the first aid box that rode up with Marsha Prospect? There's got to be something in there that looks like a trigger and a charge. I was talking to one of those guys with Benedict's Brigade. He seems to know a lot about this stuff."

"Who's that?" Al asked with a mouthful of food.

"Spook," responded JC.

Al gave him a glance, "Really, that's his name?"

"That SHOULD be his name," JC chewed steak through the words.

"Do they give him a Merit Badge for that?" Al asked. He told JC that they would have a warrant to look around the militia's outpost by the next day.

"You still don't know who killed her?" JC asked.

"Nope, do you?"

"Nope."

"Good morning, gentlemen." The greeting came from the man pouring JC and Al fresh coffee. It was Bill Peck Junior. He was the son of Bronco Billy.

Al introduced Junior to JC. "I recognize the TV star," Peck said. "They've been worried about you. They said you might be lost in the storm."

"Oh crap!" JC excused himself to use the pay phone. His cell phone was dead. "I need to call the TV station. I missed my live shot last night."

Bill Peck Junior would sometimes help out at his father's restaurant. Really, it was a social call. Junior had his own money.

He was the president of Peckerhead, the video gambling franchise. He was unmarried, socially awkward and would never achieve his father's popularity. But he was thirty-seven years old and already believed to be a millionaire. He was a geek getting rich, while the popular guys were getting girls.

Peck had a clever mind. His video gambling games found in bars and restaurants across Montana had a biting humor.

The automated voice in the machines was sarcastic and even insulting while updating the status of the game. When the machine wasn't in use, the voice heckled passersby, challenging them to a game.

JC came back to the table after talking with his television station in Denver. "They inferred that I'd be a better story if I was dead," he said. He thought they were joking, but he wasn't sure.

"They made a big deal about me missing last night," he told Al and Peck. "It's going to be a boring conclusion to the story." JC mimicked a broadcaster's voice: "Breaking news! Never mind, he's alive. Forget all the nice things we said about him."

"Fame is fleeting," Al chipped in.

"Tell me about it," JC said. They were all grinning.

They invited Peck to join them at their table. He did.

"Anyway, that's my big story tonight. They're going to interview me and I'll give them EXCLUSIVE details about our brush with death." There was a jaded emphasis to his use of the term "exclusive."

"You want to join me?" he asked Al.

Al almost spat out his food as he started to laugh. "Rather I died out there."

"It will be exclusive, won't it?" Peck asked sincerely.

"Yeah, but don't get me started on my industry's hype and clichés," JC told him. Peck was clearly glowing at being included as an insider by a television star.

JC mimicked the deep broadcaster's voice again: "You know, Al hasn't changed his underwear for two days!" They all chuckled. JC continued his parody, "Oh, that's right. That's not exclusive. That's not even unusual."

Al responded with a mock laugh, and countered with his own resonant TV voice: "Mr. Snow, how many times did you pee yourself when that buffalo was staring us down?"

JC responded to his interviewer, "Sorry Mr. TV man, as your audience knows, peeing myself is not that unusual ... and certainly not exclusive."

They smiled at each other and finished their food. Then Al turned his attention to their guest: "Didn't you just build a new house?"

"Yeah, on the hill outside Sierra." Peck told them a bit about the layout of the house. JC determined Peck was smart and had a big ego. Maybe he had good reason for the ego. He could talk intelligently about everything from computers to building to international banking.

JC also noticed that he had a big head, literally a massive cranium. As Peck continued to speak, JC was thinking that it was quite a bit larger than the average scale of a human head.

Talking later, Al agreed, with a snicker. "Did you size up his mouth?"

"Literally a very large hole below his nose," JC said. "I think a pigeon could build a nest in that thing."

Al let out a loud snorting laugh at the suggestion, before saying, "Not nice."

"No, not nice," JC admitted.

At the breakfast table, Peck had inquired into the status of the Marsha Prospect investigation. "Everyone knew she always took the first ride on the gondola in the morning. Isn't that why the emperors in Rome had food tasters?"

Peck immediately looked apologetic for his small joke. "Sorry, that was in bad taste." He laughed at his pun, too.

After breakfast, Al drove JC back to his hotel, and he provided the rest of the story about Bill Peck Junior.

He said that Peck was putting a lot of pressure on Marsha Prospect to install more video gambling machines in her ski lodge. The games inside Shara's Sheep Ranch were making a tidy profit, he argued, why not put some in the hallways of the hotel, and maybe the cafeteria? Al said that Marsha had refused the overtures.

Al also told JC that while Peck was a good businessman, he was haunted by his relationship with his own father.

"He had his father's muscular build," Al said, "but he has none of his dad's athletic skill. He wasn't a very good football player and he's the worst hunter I've ever seen. I just don't think he likes that stuff."

Al provided the full narrative. "Bronco Billy has been living off his reputation as a football star in these parts since I was born."

But Al said that Junior grew up to be a huge disappointment to his dad. "It's not like the kid was doing anything wrong. He was good at schoolwork and preferred to stay inside to read a book. But Bronco Billy saw the other kids outside playing ball and learning to be ranch hands. That drove Bronco Billy a little nuts. He'd ridicule his son in front of others."

"You said he's not married?" JC asked.

"Junior? No. A lot of people believed Junior had a crush on Marsha Prospect, and then Shara Adams."

Al thought that father and son had grown to accept their relationship, over the years. But Bronco Billy still looked at his only child through disappointed eyes. And Junior had finally arrived at his own response to his father's rejection: "Fuck you." Though he would never say that to his face.

20

Harvard Harrison was blown to bits. There were still pieces of him missing. Harrison was the unfortunate soul who was hit by an explosive, fired by a ski patrol cannon on January second.

The projectile was intended to knock loose a cornice. Harrison is believed to have trekked right into the shell's landing spot.

The Sierra County medical examiner told JC that they found Harrison's head in one spot and his severed arms in two other locations. The lower half of his torso was relatively intact, partially protruding from the snow slide created by the explosion.

"If he didn't leave a trail of blood, we'd never have found a lot of him," the doctor shared. "We haven't found most of his spinal column. There are parts of him that probably don't even exist anymore."

The medical examiner's name was Bob Platz. He was a lifelong resident of Sierra County. He was in his early seventies. He had a red face and his legs were giving him trouble. He was stubbornly getting used to the glasses his aging eyes required him to wear. Sometimes he'd laugh at himself. He was getting old.

Platz had told JC, over the telephone, to meet him in Livingston. The doctor said that he had business to attend to there. "Meet me at the Mustang Restaurant," Platz said. "It's on Main Street. You'll find it."

Dr. Platz was already sitting at a table when JC arrived. "Try the Montana Meatloaf," the ME told him. "It's their specialty."

Dr. Platz was the definition of a modern Montana resident. He loved living in Big Sky Country. There was nothing he enjoyed more than a day of hunting or fishing. He had a tireless work ethic.

His old-fashioned bedside manner was even practiced on the dead who reclined on the stainless steel table in front of him.

Doctor Platz said that Harrison's injuries were consistent with what he had been told, that the victim took a direct hit in the back from an explosive fired by the ski patrol cannon. "What are the odds?" the medical examiner asked, shaking his bald head.

"How do you know he was hit in the back," JC asked, "if you can't find his back?"

Platz told him that they found pieces of Harrison's backpack. It clearly had been close to the detonation.

"If Harrison had been hit from the front," the M.E. reflected, "some of the pack probably would have been thrown from his body. What we found of the pack really amounts to some charred yellow and black ribbons."

The blast that killed Harrison was intended to knock loose a cornice before the snowy ledge triggered an avalanche. The ski patrol at Grizzly Mountain fired the cannon at threatening snow accumulations practically every morning. They did it before the ski slopes opened.

Ski Patrol Director Elise Du Soleil had told JC that it didn't even have to snow the night before. The powerful winds blowing over the Rocky Mountains constantly moved snow along the peaks. "A ledge could be bare when you went to bed, and when you woke up, it could have a ten-foot drift on it."

Deputy Cochran had let JC read the investigation notes about Harrison's death. They said that Harrison showed up at the ski resort in early December. He was alone and didn't make many friends. He didn't work. He didn't indicate where he got his money. And didn't indicate if he was staying for the winter or for the rest of time. He just kept showing up at the gondola. He had become a familiar face to the operators.

Investigators noted that Harrison arrived earlier and earlier in the morning to take a ride to the peak. Then, he would climb over the back of the mountain and ski the steep and challenging out-of-bounds areas. He always wore his yellow and black backpack. In it, he carried a small shovel that stuck out of the top of the pack.

The small shovel is sort of a trademark of backcountry skiers. It comes in handy if you have to dig yourself or someone else out of a snowslide. That's in the event you survive the snowslide.

The few who remembered having conversations with Harrison, including the gondola operators, got the impression that he didn't have much experience as a backcountry skier. They say he was clumsy at times and unprepared at other times.

He appeared to be more adept at playing the video gambling games at Shara's Sheep Ranch. He was a regular at the bar during the evenings.

Some of the barmaids who served him drinks noticed that he carried a small notebook. They said he discreetly scribbled notes onto its pages while he sat at the gaming machines.

The staff also noticed that he always left, at the end of the night, with more money than he arrived with. He'd pay his bill with his winnings but still have forty or fifty dollars left.

After parting with Dr. Platz, JC returned to the ski village. He decided to make a trip to the Sheep Ranch. He wondered what the staff knew that wasn't in the sheriff's notes.

It was the middle of the day in the middle of the week. The bar wasn't very crowded.

"Yep, I knew who he was," a bartender named Kit told JC. "But he wasn't chatty. When he walked in, he'd order a drink, walk to a video gambling setup and sit down. He'd play for a while, order another drink and play some more. And when he got up, he'd pay his bill and leave."

"Was anyone with him?" JC asked.

"Never."

JC ordered a beer. He needed to give the bartender time to feel comfortable talking to him. JC asked about the mahogany bar. "It's a real relic of the Wild West." Kit passed along the history that had been passed along to him.

JC asked about all the great skiing he must enjoy as a ski resort employee. Kit replied, "Don't ask me, I don't ski."

A big smile grew across the bartender's face. He liked telling this story. "I grew up about fifteen minutes from here and I've skied once in my entire life. I tried it with some high school friends. Nearly killed myself and said, 'I'll see you in the bar,' and that's where they can still find me." The bartender laughed at his own story.

Then JC steered the discussion back to his reason for being there. "When someone wins a lot of money on those video gambling machines, do they tip the bartender?"

Kit half smiled and half sneered. "It's happened as many times as I've skied." JC nodded his head, appreciating Kit's threading his stories together.

Then the bartender leaned toward JC and lowered his voice. "But listen to this ..." He told JC that two nights before Harrison died, he'd hit on the poker machine and won a pair of eight hundred-dollar payouts. "He won eight hundred dollars on a two-dollar bet, twice. In the same night!"

The bartender looked over both shoulders, as if he wanted to see if they were being overheard. Then he said, "And then the next night, he did it again, only seven hundred-dollar payouts. Twice! That raised some eyebrows."

"Do you think he was cheating?" JC inquired, also with his voice lowered.

"You're not the first one to wonder. I just wish he'd shared his secret with me. Instead, he took it to the grave," the bartender replied with a smile.

"Did you ever see the notebook?" JC asked.

"A couple of times, a supervisor told a waitress to go tell him that it's frowned upon to be taking notes about the gaming machines. Harrison would tell the waitress that he was just writing to his family. But it wasn't a postcard, it was a notebook."

Still, JC thought that Harrison's winnings were putting a small dent in the money split between Peck, Mrs. Prospect and Shara, with the state getting their cut. Those machines earned thousands of dollars each night.

JC gave his beer one last swallow. He expressed his thanks to Kit and left a good tip.

"But what if he was just testing his system before going for a big score?" JC was quietly holding a conversation with himself as he walked out of the bar's door into the cold daylight. "And what if someone had figured out what Harrison was doing?"

21

There wasn't a cloud in the sky, but this house felt like it was under one.

JC knocked on the door. It was a two-story wood frame pressed against the side of the mountain.

A man in his forties answered the door. He didn't say a word. He was powerfully built with thick bones and big shoulders. His hair had fallen out on top and his face looked both tan and pale at the same time.

His name was Greg Jones. He was one of the two ski patrollers blamed in the death of Harvard Harrison. JC had been told that Jones was the one most likely to talk. The other was angry at the news media, police, his employer and anyone else who crossed his path.

JC introduced himself to Jones. The sad-looking man tried to gently close the door while saying, "I'm sorry, I'm not giving any interviews."

JC caught the door with his hand, "Mr. Jones, what will it hurt? I can't say you'll gain anything out of talking to me, but I don't think it will make things worse. Right now, your accusers are having a feeding frenzy."

Jones held the door still. He looked at his uninvited visitor. JC asked, "Don't you have a hard time believing you shot a guy in the back with a cannon from a half mile away?"

"Every day," the defeated-looking ski patrol member replied, and then let out a loud breath of air, as though another piece of him was escaping with it.

He opened the door and allowed JC to enter. The blinds were down. It was dark in the living room. Jones gestured for JC to find a seat on the sofa by a coffee table.

Du Soleil had told JC that Jones was her second in command. He'd been on the ski patrol at one mountain or another for twenty years. He'd been at Grizzly Mountain for eight.

Jones offered JC some coffee. He accepted and Jones walked into the small kitchen to pour it. "Elise has been good about the whole thing. What is she supposed to do?" Jones said from the other room.

He returned with JC's coffee and asked, "Cream or sugar?"

"No, black. This is fine." JC took a sip. He'd had worse coffee.

Jones sat on a chair by the coffee table and picked up an official-looking piece of mail. It had the letterhead of an attorney's office. "Now, the other shoe drops," Jones exclaimed without expression. He looked very tired.

JC inquired, "Is Harrison's family suing you?"

Jones nodded. "For everything I own, ever will own and anything I ever hoped to own."

JC sipped his coffee, letting everything in the room slow down. He asked in a subdued voice, "What on earth happened that day?"

Jones exhaled again. He rubbed his face with his hand and began. "The clouds were really low. The mountain was socked in sometimes, then sometimes there would be openings."

It was during those openings, the ski patroller claimed, that they could see a lot of new snow piled on a ridge above the chutes called "Hoppel's Horror."

"We had to knock it loose," Jones continued. "Little did we know that Harrison had talked his way on board a gondola a half hour before opening. We hit the chutes with two rounds. I guess one of them nailed the poor guy."

JC asked if they could see the target they were shooting at. "Off and on," Jones recalled. "The clouds would break, and then you could see it and set up your shot. That cornice had to go."

JC couldn't accept the probability of it, even as the man in front of him recounted how it happened.

"I swear to God, and I will go to my grave believing that I saw both rounds make powder marks on the snow," Jones tone was begging someone to believe him.

"So, did you check the snow for the black powder marks?" JC asked

"We couldn't," Jones answered in a deflated tone. "The charge triggered even a bigger avalanche than we expected. All the snow moved. That happens a lot."

"So, who let Harrison on the mountain early?"

"No one's admitting it," Jones told him. "Can you blame them? I think I know who it was, though."

JC waited for the disclosure. It didn't come. "Who?" he asked.

Jones looked at JC and smiled a little. "If I tell you and then you report it, then that poor guy gets his name added to this." Jones was holding up the letter informing him that he could expect a lawsuit. "I don't wish this on anybody. It was a mistake, that's all."

JC could remember hearing the cannons roar in the mornings. He enjoyed the sound. It was just another neat thing about ski mountains.

"How was his body found?" JC asked.

Jones searched for words, sort of swinging his arms as though he could catch them with his hands. "The cloud cover was pretty thick, I told you. But I thought I saw the two rounds hit, so we didn't know there was anything wrong. I will say, the second one produced a hell of an echo or something. It sounded like three blasts."

Jones said that they wondered if all that noise indicated they'd triggered more avalanches, so they decided to go up and take a look. "When we got up there, we skied about one hundred yards down the slope, and there he was. God, it was awful."

"What are the odds?" JC heard him saying to himself softly.

"Tell me about it," Jones said back to him, as his eyes sunk to the carpet.

JC asked Jones if he thought he'd ever be allowed to continue his work as a ski patrol member.

Jones took a deep breath, "I don't know if I'd even want to. This is a lot. Some souvenir hunter even stole my jacket. He took it right out of my locker."

"Really?" JC's eyebrows were raised.

"What?" Jones asked.

"Nothing," JC fibbed. He didn't know what a missing jacket meant, but it made his gears spin.

Thanking the dejected man for speaking with him, JC headed across the dark room for the door.

But the reporter turned and asked, once more, who Jones thought allowed the skier on the gondola early.

"Off the record?" Jones asked. The reporter agreed.

"I think it was a guy named Trip Lake. He was showing up to work late a lot. We think he was shacking up with some woman. Anyway, he was losing track of time a lot. We'd caught him letting people on early before, and he didn't even know it. He'd lost track of time and thought the mountain was open."

Then Jones had a look of remorse on his face. "Who am I to judge," he said. "Maybe he took a liking to Harrison and was trying to give him a break."

Or, JC thought to himself, was trying to get the guy killed.

22

Harvard Harrison's strange demise was still on JC's mind. He was sitting at the bar at Shara's Sheep Ranch.

"Maybe Trip Lake killed Harrison to get even with Marsha Prospect," he suggested to the owner of the Sheep Ranch. It was his college girlfriend, Shara Adams. "Marsha dumped him," JC suggested, "so he got even by making a mess out of her mountain. The fact that it was Harrison may have been random."

JC took another bite of his hamburger and continued to list the possibilities. "But say Trip Lake did want to murder Harvard Harrison, for whatever reason. Say he choreographs everything, lets him on the gondola early, hopes the ski patrol guys fire a shell at him ..." JC dabbed his chin with a napkin. "How did he steer Harrison to that exact spot, and how did that cannon fire such an accurate round? Into the clouds?"

Shara reached for JC's plate and grabbed a French fry. She offered her own version: "Maybe he was only counting on the avalanche killing Harrison. Or maybe he paid the ski patrol guys to hit him."

Shara was behind the bar, sipping some bottled water with a twist of lemon. She was wearing a dark blue turtleneck sweater with "Grizzly Mountain" written across the collar.

"That would still make the murderer a pretty lucky guy," JC said, after a pause to swallow.

Shara brushed her hair behind her ears and told JC what she knew about Harrison. "He was here most nights. He'd buy one drink at the bar and spend about an hour at the poker machine. He was a bright guy. I think he was a computer nerd. He said he had an Ivy League education. I thought the whole backcountry skier thing was just an effort to get out of his routine. He didn't strike me as a daredevil."

"Harvard?" JC inquired. Shara gave him a puzzled look. He thought he was stating the obvious, "Ivy

League education. His name was Harvard. He didn't go to Harvard?"

A burst of laughter and a big smile covered Shara's face, "Oh, yes he did!" They both shared a laugh now.

"Sorry, I've still got my mind on work. OK, I've got to think," Shara said, remembering more about her dead customer. "His parents gave him that name because they had high hopes for him. He said that they are really smart, too. But he said they were pushy. He said he wasn't above cheating at school, if it would get his parents off his back."

Shara grabbed some more fries off of JC's plate. "The funny thing is, he said he didn't have to cheat. He told me that he did it to prove he was so smart that he could beat the brilliant faculty who were supposed to catch that type of thing."

"Hmm, like an evil genius. But I don't get it," JC interjected. "He barely spoke to anyone. Was he shy or was he arrogant?"

"Oh, he was really awkward around people," Shara answered. "But if you got to know him a little, you could tell that he thought he was pretty cool."

"What do you call that," JC pondered aloud. "Delusions of grandeur? Narcissist?"

Shara asked, "Don't you remember your psychology class in college?"

"Not really," JC was shaking his head. "I was just trying to hook up with the girl who sat next to me."

"That was me," Shara answered, teasing a curt reply.

JC made a face as though it was a dim memory. "How'd I do with her?"

"It was slim pickings. You were about as good as a girl was going to get." A big smile emerged on her face.

JC shifted his weight as he leaned on the bar and looked toward the gaming machines. "Can you cheat those things?"

"They say you can't," she answered. Shara emerged from behind the bar, carrying her bottle of water, and they walked into the corral surrounding the video poker games.

JC sat down in front of a machine and asked her to show him how to play.

"Money talks," she told him. He looked at her for a moment, then sighed and leaned over so he could squeeze his hand into his pants pocket and pull out his wallet. He slipped two dollars into the slot.

"Pleasure doing business with you," she grinned. She leaned on the machine and led him through the steps.

The sight of her breasts pressing against her sweater was arousing him. "I can't see the screen, those things are in my way," he said, giving her an innocent look.

"Oh my gosh!" she offered with the sound of mock scandal in her voice. "Stay focused!"

"Yes, ma'am," he responded obediently, before murmuring, "Harlot."

"Pervert," she murmured. Their eyes met. Both of them were smiling.

She was beautiful, he thought. She was only a foot away from him. He could smell her perfumed scent. He wanted to kiss her. He wanted to make love to her. But it wasn't the place or the time, again. He let out a deep breath.

"What?" she asked, smiling from above.

"Nothing," he said and paused. "So, what do I do now?"

She looked at him from the corner of her eyes with a small grin. "OK," she said with a determined change of energy, "Pick your game." He picked five-card draw and the screen displayed the hand he was dealt.

He followed her instructions until the animated voice inside the machine sarcastically whined, "Loser!"

JC looked at Shara with a frown. "You cost me two dollars."

"Oh, did I mention," she took a sip from her water, "you never win at these things."

JC rolled his eyes.

"I saw Harrison win," Shara offered. "Actually, I saw him win a lot. I've never seen anything like it."

She told JC that Bill Peck's machines had been taken to the cleaners by some guy playing his VGMs up in

Kalispell. "I think he was playing poker. He just kept winning. He won like thirty thousand dollars in one night. Peck went ballistic when he was told about his losses the next day, but by then, the guy had left town."

"Did the guy cheat?" JC asked.

"When you win," Shara told him, with some mischief in her eyes, "and you wouldn't know this because you didn't win ..." JC just swiveled his head in mock disgust.

"When you win," she continued, "the machine gives you something that you redeem at the bar. You get a ticket with printing on front and back so it can't be counterfeited. If it's a big win, we open the back of the machine and see if the records match what the ticket tells us. They have to match."

Shara looked at JC and asked, "Do you think Harrison cheated?"

"I wouldn't bet against it," JC responded.

"And you sounded like," she hesitated, "you think Harrison was murdered?"

"I wouldn't bet against it," JC repeated.

23

It was clearly the sound of a gunshot. Its echo in the dark woods made it sound like there was more than one. But one was enough.

JC and his news photographer, Fred Shook, scrambled out of their news car. JC crouched for cover. Fred galloped on all fours to the back of the car. He blew on his cold hands, opened the trunk and grabbed his camera.

Police lights were bouncing off the dense forest and the deep snow. All the cars, including the news car, were sort of lined up in two single-file lines, where a road was plowed.

In the flashing police lights, JC could read the sign overhead that declared this "The last square mile of America."

Shook was already recording images with his camera. JC spotted Al Pine, crouching behind a patrol car. JC headed his way, covering about twenty yards in a crouch.

"We've got trouble," Al informed him. "Keep your head down. Those screwballs have already taken three shots at us."

"Did they hit anybody?" JC asked.

"No," responded Al, "but all hell's been breaking loose. They beat up a guy last night. He's a new forest ranger. It was his first day on the job."

"Why did they beat him up?"

"Who knows with these guys," Al responded. His eyes had turned from surveying the scene to lock on JC's. "I'm just not sure how crazy these guys are."

Al slid to the ground with his back pressed against the fender. "Then, today we tried to serve that warrant to search the grounds. We want to eyeball their arsenal. Besides, General Smith still won't come talk to us about Marsha Prospect's death. We invited him. This seems to be his answer."

JC noticed that Al was wearing a holster and a handgun. That was out of the norm for Al.

"These guys are probably the only people in Montana who know what prussic acid is," Al said as he glanced past the bumper of the car. "We've got to see what they have in there. The investigation is going nowhere, and the killer could be standing on the other side of that gate."

"Are you going to storm the place?" JC asked.

"Naw, we didn't even return fire. Nobody's been hurt, and we'd like to keep it that way. We don't need another Waco, Texas."

Al told him that they were going to wait outside the gate and see what happens. He said, "This could go on for days."

The forest had returned to nature's quiet. Chatter between law officers were kept to a relative whisper. In the distance, the howl of a coyote could be heard. Closer, there was the occasional hoot of an owl.

Then, the rumble of a truck crashed through the silence. It was still out of sight. JC turned to the forest ranger, "What do you have, a tank?"

Fred, the news photographer, scurried over to join JC and Al. JC introduced the two men. "This is my photographer, or my videographer. Though, they're using digital now. What do I call you, Fred?"

"A photographer," Fred responded, almost with a straight face.

He tilted his head toward the approaching clatter and the beams of light crawling over the snowbanks. "That's our truck," Fred said to JC. "They want a live shot."

"Of me being killed by a sniper when you shine a spotlight on me?" JC asked in a slightly disbelieving tone.

The photog returned a knowing chuckle in agreement. "You're not going to change their mind," he told the reporter.

"I know," JC responded in a resigned voice.

"What the hell ..." could be heard from some of the armed law officers, as they heard the racket and then saw the huge satellite truck emerging down the plowed road. It was tall enough to break some of the thin tree branches overhead.

"I'll handle it," Fred told JC, as the truck lights illuminated the positions of the law enforcement group. Then it stopped with a hiss of its air brakes.

Fred hurried into the woods, outside of the reach of the truck's lights, and then made his way in that direction. The truck driver would ask where he was supposed to park, and then proceed to scan the dark sky for a satellite that would carry their signal to Denver.

"Seriously?" Al said as he looked at JC and the enormous vehicle.

"Mine is not to ask why, but why not?" JC responded. "But you notice that it hasn't drawn any gunfire from the compound?"

Al lifted his head and took note of it. "The guards are probably on the radio to their general," Al said. He climbed to his knees so he could see over the hood of the patrol car. "And knowing what a glory hound he is, he's going to think this is a pretty good turn of events."

"Any publicity is good publicity, as long as I spell his name right. Something like that?" JC asked.

"Exactly like that," Al told him.

Police officers, positioned behind trees, were waving their arms at the truck to turn off its lights. Terms like "idiot" could be heard. JC winced. He knew that he was, at least, guilty by association.

JC pulled himself up and made his way back to the truck. As he passed a group of law officers in camouflage, one of them asked, "Is that yours, asshole?"

"Well, sort of," JC replied sheepishly.

The driver of the satellite truck was also the engineer who would beam the signal to their television station. Fred had already cautioned him that live rounds had been fired. "This ain't my first rodeo," was the unconcerned engineer's reply.

His name was Jimmy Vazquez. He was part Crow Indian and part Mexican. He had a dark handsome face framed by a trimmed beard, no mustache. He pulled on his work gloves and proceeded to uncoil cable and get on with his business.

JC and Fred knew that Vazquez wasn't afraid of bullets, but they were careful to wipe their feet as they entered the truck to edit a piece for the news. Vazquez couldn't stand dirt on the carpet of his truck. Behind the driver's cab, there was a metal ladder leading to a compartment that shared a crude editing bay and the equipment needed to feed a live image via satellite. The room was the size of an average chicken coop.

Deadline was quickly approaching. Vazquez easily found a satellite signal, but Fred would have to do a quick job of editing and feeding the footage he'd shot. JC was furiously writing a script into his notebook. He'd voice it live, covered by the footage that was being pieced together.

They didn't have time for distractions when Deputy Cochran appeared in the editing bay door. "Oh no," the deputy's voice boomed. JC thought Cochran definitely emphasized the "No" part.

"Hi Alex," said JC, "We're tight on time here, can we talk after our live shot?" JC was already turning his focus back to his notebook.

"There isn't going to be a live shot, not here," the deputy proclaimed. His tone was a little scary. He didn't sound like he was worried about hurting JC's feelings.

The reporter lifted his head and locked eyes with the lawman. "They're shooting at us here," Cochran reminded JC. "We do not need our men and women getting shot so you can entertain the folks at home while they start their second glass of wine."

"Wow, you're hard on our audience," JC said in a joking fashion. But the deputy was not going to be coaxed into breaking from his "cop mode." Fred's eyes never left the monitors in front of him, but he laughed at JC's effort, nonetheless.

At that moment, JC heard Vazquez's voice: "JC, they say they're going to drive my truck out of here, if I don't." JC looked into the driver's cabin and could see two deputies climbing aboard the half-million-dollar truck.

JC knew he had to salvage the situation, fast. Fred was still editing. The reporter didn't see much hope of achieving a clear victory with Cochran, and he saw two deputies staring at the instrument panel from the driver's seat. They looked like they had every intention of putting the truck in reverse and seeing what happened. That is, if they found reverse.

"OK, where do you want us?" JC surrendered.

"I don't want to see you!" Cochran barked.

"Me personally, or the truck?" JC inquired. Cochran stared in disbelief at the reporter.

"I don't want to see you!" Deputy Cochran sternly repeated, and he marched away.

JC rubbed his eyes, maybe hoping it would all go away. "We don't have time for this," he said.

He looked for Vazquez. "Jimmy, can you disconnect the cables and back out of sight, just over the hill?"

"I'll try," Vazquez responded.

"OK, I'm done here," Fred declared, telling JC that the editing was done and he could feed it back to their TV station.

"Nice," JC complemented his photographer. "Thank God they sent you on this assignment. If we can run the cable back over the hill from the truck, can we stand where our audience can see the flashing lights and the gate over my shoulder? From there, we can tell them what's going on. Sound good?" The photog agreed.

The live shot hit the air on time. There were images of sheriff's deputies, forest rangers and state police wearing bulletproof vests and kneeling behind trees and patrol cars. Some had their weapons aimed at the outpost's gate.

JC told viewers that gunshots had been fired from the compound, and about his conversation with General Smith the other day. He also reported that the Forest

Service was investigating a possible connection with an attack on a forest ranger the night before.

JC concluded his broadcast saying of the militia members, "They are well-fortified, well-armed and, frankly, comfortable. This could be a long stalemate. I'm JC Snow, reporting live from twenty miles outside Sierra, Montana."

24

"Nice job, don't get shot out there." It was the voice of a TV producer in the control room back in Denver. He was in JC's ear as soon as he finished his live report and tossed back to the anchors.

JC responded, "You mean don't get shot unless Fred is rolling on it, right?"

"Right." The producer made sure JC heard him laughing. No point in hard feelings.

JC and Fred then turned to help Vazquez coil cable and clean up after the live shot.

Deputy Cochran walked over through the snow, not looking any happier than the last time they saw each other. "He wants you to come in," Cochran reported with a half scowl on his face.

JC wasn't totally surprised. He half expected the invitation. JC asked, "Smith?" The deputy nodded.

Cochran disclosed, "We've been talking to him over the telephone for the last hour and getting nowhere. He must have a television in there. He watched your report, just now. Anyway, he wants to talk to you in there."

JC looked at the deputy, waiting for the "but" part.

The deputy obliged, "We can't stop you, but we can't assure your safety either. If you get in trouble in there, I don't want any of my people getting killed trying to rescue you."

Minutes later, JC was walking toward the gate with his news photographer. Cochran, nearby, pulled his ear away from a portable telephone, the one he was using to communicate with General Smith. "He says, no cameras."

JC countered, "Tell him, no camera, no visit by the nice reporter."

Deputy Cochran returned to the telephone and spoke at a volume too low for JC to make out. After a couple of minutes, Cochran put down the phone and walked over to JC. It was "nice Cochran" again. "He said OK, you can bring in your cameraman. Have fun, boys."

JC paused and thought of old movies about the Wild West. "Wait," he said to the deputy, "doesn't the undertaker want to get our measurements first?"

Cochran understood the reference. He smiled. "I would if I was him."

JC was glad he was with Fred Shook. JC knew Fred wasn't afraid of a little adventure. Shook had just celebrated his fortieth birthday. He was losing his salt-and-pepper hair on the top, but he was in good shape, muscular.

Fred had been an outstanding athlete in high school. Now, he had a wife and three young children. Back in Denver, when Fred was called by the TV station in the middle of the night to go shoot a house fire, sometimes he'd bring his oldest son. The boy often was waiting by the car door before Fred even got to the garage.

Now, JC and Fred stood at the gate of the outpost, as a camouflaged sentry walked out of the darkness. He was carrying a semiautomatic rifle, pointed at the ground. He raised the gate.

JC could see the headlights of a Jeep approach. The car reminded him of the old Willys driven by U.S. troops during World War Two and the Korean War. Despite the cold night, the Jeep had no top. The driver was exposed to the elements. JC could see the driver's breath. Then, he could see the driver's face: Spook.

Fred loaded his camera in the back and climbed in. JC climbed in the front passenger seat. The camouflaged sentry disappeared back into the darkness and the Jeep pulled away.

They were taken to a different cabin this time, with a staircase leading up a hillside. JC realized that it was the A-frame dining hall they'd passed on his last visit.

The room was empty of people. There were just tables, chairs and a large, stainless steel kitchen for food preparation. On the walls of the dining room hung the heads of elk, bear and wolf. There were also military-looking shields and banners. The room resembled what you'd expect from a hunting lodge at West Point.

General Smith walked into the dining room, wearing an ironed uniform. It looked like he'd just put it on. He wanted to look "the part" on television, JC thought.

About five others, dressed in camouflage, followed the general into the room. They'd be his backdrop. The general shook hands with both journalists. Fred quickly set up a light and placed his camera on a tripod.

The interview commenced. Smith explained why he wouldn't let the police or forest rangers into the compound. "They don't have any jurisdiction here. It's our land," the general declared. "We didn't kill that woman, and they don't have any evidence to the contrary."

"Benedict's Brigade," JC said. "That's an interesting name you've chosen for your militia. Benedict Arnold?"

"He was a patriot," Smith responded, "Do you really know the truth about Benedict Arnold?"

It happened that JC was familiar with the soldier whose name was synonymous with treason. JC was raised in probably the only portion of the country where there were others who thought Benedict Arnold was a hero, rather than a traitor. Saratoga County, New York.

"He fought bravely for the American cause at the Battle of Saratoga," JC told the general, who smiled his approval, "but he turned against his country when he didn't receive the rewards he felt he deserved."

Smith's face turned dour. "He was betrayed by General Washington! He was betrayed by Congress! Just like the American people have been betrayed by those tyrants in Washington, D.C.!"

JC watched as General Smith turned and made direct eye contact with the camera. "That's why we won't let the federal government come here. This is 'The Last Square Mile of America.' They cannot just walk onto any piece of land and arrest innocent people any time they feel like it."

The general continued to speak, mostly ignoring JC, to address whoever he thought would be watching the interview when it was aired on TV or posted on the TV station's website.

JC listened as the militia leader vaguely accused the U.S. government of carrying out mass shootings and bombings and then contriving evidence to blame others. He accused Washington of secretly developing the power to activate tornados and turning them loose on the Midwest.

The general catalogued outrageous conspiracies and paranoid plots. He even accused the U.S. government of trying to kill him.

"Do you have any evidence of this?" JC inquired.

"Plenty," the general responded.

"Can we see it?" JC requested

"No, I won't give the government a chance to see it and corrupt it," the general replied.

"Did your people beat up that U.S. forest ranger last night?" JC asked.

"Outsiders are taking our jobs," the general protested. "I don't know who assaulted that man last night, but ..."

"Did you order it, General?"

"No," the general raised his voice. "But I can't blame men with women and children to feed, if they feel they have to fight for their piece of God's green earth! This is a tough place to live, Mr. Snow. The winters are hard and so are the people who live here. They don't need to take orders from outsiders. Someone here should have that job."

"Someone here in the compound?" JC asked.

"Yes, someone who understands what it's like to live here," said Smith.

JC remembered what Al Pine had told him about the new ranger. "The man who was attacked last night met the qualifications to be a forest ranger," JC asserted. "He has a college education. He has expertise in forestry and wildlife management. Do you have someone here meeting those qualifications? Someone who was passed over for the job?"

The reporter had noted that General Smith scoffed when JC mentioned the victim's college education. "You don't need college to manage these woods when you've grown up in these woods," the general said.

"So, you punished him?" JC asked.

"What are you getting at, Snow?" The general's response was angry.

"Did you punish Marsha Prospect, too?"

The reporter's question caused Smith's eyes to narrow. The general sneered as he said, "I told you before, that job was too big for a woman. She should have stayed in New York City and played with her husband's money."

"Marsha Prospect was from Montana," JC reminded him. "Right down the road from here."

Smith paused to think. He knew he was being cornered. He knew that his recruiting opportunity could unravel.

"Mr. Snow, thank you for coming by and hearing our side of the story." Smith struggled to regain the appearance of composure. "Our followers come from all walks of life. We're not all hayseeds, as you suggest. We even have a member with a Ph.D. in biochemistry." JC immediately thought to himself, Spook.

General Smith had already wheeled around and was heading for the exit of the dining hall, followed by his camouflaged entourage.

After packing their equipment and proceeding down the stairs in the cold air, JC and Fred were driven back to the gate by a militia member they didn't recognize.

But as the Jeep rocked over the packed snow, JC saw an open door in a cabin, illuminated by the fireplace burning inside. In the doorway stood a man with unruly blond hair. Captain Steven Hemingway, Spook.

25

JC's exclusive interview with General Smith was featured on televisions across the country. As the standoff at the gate of the compound continued, the story gained national attention.

There hadn't been any more shooting since the first few minutes, when law officers served the warrant. The two sides just stood their ground, staring across the gate at each other.

JC visited the site the next evening. He was sitting in the snow next to Al behind a patrol car. They were sharing Chinese food. JC brought it from town.

If militia members on the other side of the gate did not have anything to do with Prospect's death, Al told JC, then this had become a distraction from the murder investigation.

All efforts by law enforcement at this gate were aimed at ending the standoff peacefully. Politicians in Washington, D.C., were watching now, and they didn't want to be embarrassed. They also didn't want to turn General John Smith into a martyr for the militia movement.

Sierra's remote location, and the remote likelihood of a quick resolution, prevented a large news media presence from crowding into town. Most television stations and newspapers would use the material furnished by the few crews already on the scene, like JC and Fred.

Decisions in newsrooms, in the modern economy, concerned more than the value of a story to its viewers, listeners or readers. Cost was a crucial variable. And it was costly to send a crew to the middle of nowhere. It required money for room and board and perhaps satellite TV time. Most newsrooms decided not to do it.

Besides, more and more TV newscasts had determined "If it bleeds, it leads." And no one was bleeding on either side of that gate at the militia compound.

JC knew that as quickly as events in Sierra had gained a national audience, that short attention span would swivel to a fresh shark attack on the coast or a shooting spree at a shopping center. Only Montana and viewers in the Rockies demanded daily updates on the murder investigation and the holdout at the militia compound.

JC and Fred had just worked out a rotating work schedule with their local TV network affiliate in Bozeman. Each crew took turns watching the standoff or being "on call." So, they all didn't have to be on hand or "at the ready" twenty-four hours a day.

JC had already finished his broadcast for the evening news that night. After sharing Chinese food out of a box with Al, JC was taking the night off.

JC told Al that he'd paid a visit to the forest ranger who'd been attacked the other night. "He's a tough guy. He really got walloped, but he says he reported for work the next day?"

"Yep, Keith Evans," said Al. "He seems like a good guy. He went to Missoula."

"That's what he said," JC responded. "University of Montana. Great forestry and wildlife school, right? That kind of blows a hole in General Smith's theory that Evans didn't 'know these woods.'"

"Yep," Al said.

The two men turned to small talk and conspiring to compete in a ski race during the approaching weekend.

Munching on a spring roll, Al told JC that investigators had carefully dissected the cardboard box found in Prospect's gondola car. The ranger said that they didn't find anything resembling a trigger to detonate the prussic acid: "We have the one cartridge. There has to be something else, if we're right about what happened."

Al also informed the journalist that a search of murder files across the country hadn't encountered a single killing using prussic acid in decades. "It's rare stuff," Al told JC. "Our killer is in a class by himself."

"Is it possible that some old Soviet spy had a grudge against Marsha Prospect?" JC asked.

Al shook his head. "One of the benefits of working in a remote area is that outsiders, even in a tourist attraction, stand out. People would remember an old guy with a Russian accent."

JC used his chopsticks to corner more rice and shrimp. He informed Al that Marsha Prospect's secretary insisted that the murder victim didn't own the tape recorder found on the gondola.

"She was murdered by that gas," Al reminded JC, "not the tape recorder."

"Yeah, but then whose tape recorder is it?" JC asked.

Al gave JC a look telling him that he didn't have an answer.

"I also have a funny feeling that Harvard Harrison was murdered," JC told Al.

Pine raised his eyebrows with a full mouth and a look of surprise. "Any proof?"

"Nope," JC replied.

For a while, the two friends ate their food in silence. Then Al asked, "So, what's happening with you and Shara?"

"Nothing," answered JC. "What's supposed to happen?" It was a half-truth. Increasingly, JC was having a hard time keeping Shara Adams off his mind.

"I never understood why you guys broke up," Al offered.

"She left to marry a guy in New York City," JC responded. "It's common courtesy to break up with your boyfriend before marrying your husband."

"She may believe that she made a mistake, you know," Al told him, "Besides, you might show a little interest."

"Is this what you do on the side?" JC asked a little impatiently. "Find husbands for mountain brides?"

Al smiled with a bit of mischief on his face. "Yep."

26

The phone rang while JC was driving away from the compound. It was his news director in Denver.

"Nice job tonight," the news director told his reporter.

"Thanks," JC said, wondering what the real reason for the call was.

"How much longer do you think this is going to last?" JC was asked.

"The standoff or the murder investigation?" JC asked.

"Both, I guess," his boss responded.

"Honestly? There's no telling," JC reported. "There's no primary suspect in Prospect's murder, and this standoff could still be going on until the spring."

"Well, we've just got to watch our spending. I've got a budget to stay within."

JC was silent. He didn't know what the budget was, or even which budget his manager was referring to at the moment.

"I wouldn't want your job," JC told him.

"Really? I was just about to offer it to you. Oh well, never mind then." JC could hear the snicker over the phone line.

When JC returned to the Bearly Inn, after dinner with Al, it was beginning to snow. He went for a run anyway. He was wearing a thick sweatshirt with a hood. "Colorado State University" was stamped across the front. JC's legs felt strong. There was no lingering sign of the twisted knee.

The snow was collecting on his dark hair that protruded from under the hood. He made his way along the roads of Grizzly Mountain. He passed the lodge, where skiers were relaxing in steaming hot tubs after a tiring day. He ran by stores that were still open for the night. He ran into the darkness. It led him up roads past slopeside mansions, their lights illuminating the landscape.

He began running faster and the snow began falling harder. He ran along a frozen lake with its shore lined by rocks. At the end of the lake, he could see a new, two-story log cabin. Smoke was rising out of the chimney.

He found himself at the top of the stairs that led him to the log cabin's small porch. It was covered by a red tin roof, like the rest of the home. He leaned against a wooden post to catch his breath.

He wondered what to do. He stared at the doorbell. The snow was melting in his hair and water was trickling down his face. His heart was pumping.

He had not rung the bell. But Jumper was making a fuss on the other side of the door. The black lab stood on his hind legs, peering out the window panes. Shara Adams opened the door and saw JC standing there.

She watched his chest rise and fall. She saw his wet hair and a confused look on his face. Then, without a word between them, she wrapped her arms around his waist, pressed against him and reached up until her lips met his.

She welcomed his passion. She ran her hands across his broad back as she kissed him. He ran his hands through her hair.

He heard a trembling voice escape from his own lips, "Hi," and he saw a smile that had been saved for him.

She took his hand and pulled him inside the door, closing it behind them. She was wearing a white wool nightshirt that only fell halfway down her thighs. He thought his heart would explode.

Still holding his hand, she silently led him into the back of the house, to her bedroom. She stared into his face and saw the boy she loved long ago, looking back at her. She closed the door behind them.

Jumper lowered himself to the floor, resigned to sleep at the foot of the bedroom door.

27

They woke up in each other's arms. The sun was pouring over JC and Shara through lace curtains and frost on the window.

Jumper had joined them during the night, happy to sleep next to the bed.

JC rose and primed the automatic coffee maker. He turned on the radio in the kitchen. If anything had happened at the Brigade's compound overnight, he'd hear it on the news at the top of the hour. For the moment, he was told that he would be enjoying a golden oldie from the disco days.

Shara emerged from the bedroom as she tied a knot on the belt around a thick terry cloth robe. She let Jumper out the back door, anxious to begin his morning routine.

"If there is a God, you'll find another radio station," Shara sleepily declared as she gave JC's arm a pat. He handed her a cup of coffee.

"Disco was tone-deaf," she declared. Her thoughts lingered and she said absently, "Marsha felt the same way. We think it went back to our awkward adolescence."

"Well, Marsha must have gotten over it," JC told her. "She was listening to a tape of disco music when she died."

"No way, not Marsha," Shara insisted. "She would have jumped out of the gondola first."

JC stared into his coffee cup. "What is it about that tape recorder?"

JC told Shara that the news was coming up and he wanted to hear it. So, for a while longer, they tolerated the singer imploring his "baby" to dance with him.

JC asked Shara, "Who else knew about Marsha's taste in music?"

"She didn't make it a secret," Shara shared. "She even sponsored a 'Disco's Crap' promotion at The Sheep

Ranch earlier this winter. It was so fun. People were into it. Bill Peck even showed up, unannounced, and gave away a bunch of stuff."

"Nice. Like what?" JC asked. He was making conversation as he sorted through the cupboards looking for something to eat. He was famished and mostly ignoring everything else.

"Prizes promoting Peckerhead. Tee shirts, water bottles, hats and stuff," she told him. "You know what?"

JC realized there was now silence. The "you know what" apparently required an answer. "What?" Well done, he thought.

"That was the night before Harvard Harrison was killed," Shara said as she handed JC a cup of yogurt she pulled from the refrigerator.

"I remember that he got something from Peckerhead. Oh yeah, he won a water bottle. So did I." She reached into a cupboard and pulled out a plastic water bottle with the Peckerhead logo on the side.

JC was admiring the clever logo on the yellow bottle. It was a woodpecker with an evil grin.

There was scratching at the kitchen door. It was Jumper, finished with his morning duties outside and now desiring breakfast. Shara let him in and placed his bowl on the floor, already prepared.

"Oh my God," Shara remembered. "That was the night Trip got into such a terrible fight with Marsha."

JC was being more attentive now, with yogurt attending to his empty stomach. "What were they fighting about?"

"She'd just broken up with him," Shara answered. "I walked into the kitchen to get some margarita mix and I saw him choking her."

"Choking her?" JC repeated.

"It was the scariest thing I've ever seen," Shara continued. "I thought he was going to kill her. He was going berserk. I started hitting him on the back with a cooking pan and he stopped. He took off. She said she was OK, but I could see how frightened she was."

"Did you tell this to the police?" JC asked.

"Not then—Marsha begged me not to. And then when police interviewed me after Marsha was killed, I'd forgotten." Shara stared at the floor, as though she were trying to envision that night. "As soon as he left the kitchen, she collapsed in tears. It was so scary, so sad. She said that he had never done that before. He just went crazy when she broke up with him."

JC watched Shara silently sip her coffee. Minutes passed. Then she looked at him. "Do you think Trip did it?"

"I don't know," JC answered as he shook his head. "Think like the police think. As a rejected lover, he had the motive. You saw him demonstrate that rage. He is also the one who put the cardboard box in the gondola where she died. And I don't know what to make of the tape recorder, but does it make sense that Trip knew something about her taste in music?"

"No doubt," Shara responded.

"Did you know that he was in the Army?" JC asked her.

"Trip?" Shara asked in genuine surprise.

"He was young," said JC as he nodded his head. "So, he may have learned something about that toxin that was used to kill her."

The tumblers in his mind were turning again. "I have to go," he said.

He pulled on his sweatshirt. He pulled Shara by the collar of her thick robe until her body pressed against his. He stared at her dimples and into her eyes. He really didn't want to go at all.

He kissed her and slipped out the front door, the same door he slipped through so nervously only twelve hours before.

28

Snowboarders were soaring high in the sky above the half-pipe. JC pulled his 4x4 up to the ski-bum compound. A group of young people held their boards in their hands and stood at the top of the semi-circular tube built out of snow. They enthusiastically cheered stunts performed by the man or woman currently in the pipe.

Their fashion sense included baggy, mismatched clothes and handkerchiefs pulled across their helmeted faces. JC figured that offered protection from the sun, and the cold when temperatures dipped.

A new arrival they just called "Shredder Dude" had the half-pipe buzzing. JC was told that the guy could "rip it."

JC walked into the center of Fort Affordable and saw the one they called "Ski Fish." He was leaning against a picnic table and smelled like marijuana. Ski Fish said that Trip Lake wasn't there.

"Why do you keep bugging him?" Ski Fish asked JC. "How about leaving him alone? He's been through a lot."

"I respect what you're saying," JC tried to assure the skier, "but there's a murder investigation going on. A decent woman lost her life to a calculating killer. Trip Lake is an important witness."

"Well, why don't you leave it to the police?" Ski Fish asked. "You're not a cop, you're a TV reporter."

"What have you told the police?" JC asked.

"Sheesh," Ski Fish responded. He looked like he was going to spit. "I don't tell the cops shit."

"Well, there you go," JC answered. "Some people would rather talk to me. If it gets the killer arrested in the end, I feel pretty good about that."

JC asked the skier if he'd ever heard Trip Lake say anything that might incriminate him in Mrs. Prospect's murder.

"I've heard no such thing," Ski Fish replied. He slowly shook his head from left to right to left.

"Did you see Trip on the morning of the murder?"

"Nope."

JC asked if Trip had kept a cardboard box around the compound.

"Nope."

"Do you know if he had a small tape recorder, pocket-sized?"

"He did not."

"Are you bullshitting me?" JC asked the skier.

"No, I am not."

JC asked, "Did he ever talk about his time in the Army?"

"Really? He was in the Army?" Ski Fish honestly seemed surprised and interested. "He never said anything about that."

"Anyway," the ski bum told JC, "there's nothing wrong with that. You guys are too much. You look at us like we're freaks. Now, when something bad happens that has nothing to do with us, we're the first ones you look at. Get your ass out of here and leave Trip alone."

"Listen, it's not my job to disturb your fantasy," JC quickly replied, "but no one here thinks you're a freak. You're good skiers and snowboarders and you don't seem to break any major laws. I kind of like you. You're wasting your martyr complex on me."

Ski Fish was silenced. He didn't know how to respond.

"Did you know Trip Lake had an affair with Marsha Prospect?" JC asked.

Ski Fish raised his eyebrows but said nothing, at first. "So, it's true? That explains some things, like where he was every night."

"Don't you wonder why Grizzly Mountain even let you live here?" JC asked as he waved his arm around the surrounding encampment.

Ski Fish didn't answer, but JC could see that he was making his point.

"I think your friend could be in some serious trouble," JC told the young man. "He ought to get an attorney and talk to the sheriff."

"He didn't do anything, man," Ski Fish said quietly.

JC walked away, casting his eyes on the performers in the half-pipe. But his mind was elsewhere. He was asking himself why he didn't think Trip Lake did it, when all the evidence pointed to the lift operator.

The reporter climbed into his car and pulled onto the road. It had been eleven days since Prospect's murder. JC needed to meet Fred Shook and Jimmy Vazquez at the satellite truck in the ski village. He had to talk to Al and Cochran, too.

Trip's guilt or innocence wasn't something JC could report to viewers until police had drawn the same conclusion. If JC reported it, and Lake was innocent, there would be no defending it in a certain lawsuit.

JC drove into the center of the ski village and searched for a place to park. He had to pull into a parking garage. One other car pulled in and found a spot near him.

JC pocketed his keys, heading for the exit of the garage. He heard steps approaching him from behind, but when he looked over his shoulder, a man wearing a dark ski mask and an army fatigue jacket was upon him.

Something hit JC hard in the back. A baseball bat? A crowbar? JC stumbled to his knees. He tried to breathe but it hurt.

The masked man walked in front of JC and clenched his fist. But JC was able to spring from his knees and tackle the offender. It was something he'd learned playing football. JC drove his shoulder into the man's stomach as they crashed to the ground. The masked man wheezed.

JC was moving slow. His back hurt and he was wobbly. He wanted to be the first to get to his feet.

JC felt a crashing blow to his ribs. As he collapsed to the asphalt floor of the garage, he saw that the blow had come from a second attacker. He was wearing a mask, too. It was stretched out at the neck and hung loosely over the mugger's head.

JC noted that the mask was black with red circles around the eyes. The men picked him up and leaned JC against a trash dumpster.

One of the attackers aimed a punch at his victim's face, but JC ducked. The attacker screamed as his fist hit the dumpster's metal side. "Fuck, I think I broke it!" wailed the goon to his accomplice.

The second assailant didn't miss. He hit JC in the face, first with one fist and then the other.

JC was still standing, only because he could lean against the dumpster. One of his attackers was dancing about in pain, holding his broken hand under his other arm.

The second masked man, still holding a baseball bat in his hand, stuffed a piece of paper into the pocket of JC's jacket.

They were gone as fast as they had appeared. JC heard the squeal of their car tires. He was still leaning against the dumpster, folding his arms across his ribs. He smelled the garbage in the dumpster and had a sick feeling in his stomach.

He didn't move for what could have been a minute but felt like an hour. Then, he slowly reached into his pocket and pulled out a piece of paper. It said, "Leave Trip Lake alone."

29

"Slow and steady," JC mumbled to himself as he inched his way into the driver's seat of his car. He searched for a way of sitting behind the driver's wheel that didn't cause more pain.

The process was repeated when he had to climb out of his car in the parking lot of the Bearly Inn.

Inside his motel room, he was able to slowly lift his arm to reach the ibuprofen, fill a glass with water and raise the glass to his lips. Then, he gingerly reclined onto his bed.

Hours later, he woke up to the sound of knocking on his door. He saw that it was still daylight out. The knocking continued, but he was slow to reach the door. He squinted into the daylight, folded over by the pain in his ribs.

Al and Fred stood in his doorway. Both had been looking for him. He was overdue to meet his TV crew. But that was momentarily forgotten by the forest ranger and the news photographer, as they surveyed the bruised man stooping before them. "I haven't felt like this since New Year's Eve," JC tried to joke.

His face was red from the beating. He was still wearing his disheveled clothing. Fred said, "Holy shit." Al asked, "What happened to you?"

"I got a fist-o-gram," JC said unsteadily. He headed back to sit on the bed and grunted when he landed on the mattress, "Ouch."

"You need to go to Urgent Care," Al said.

JC slowly shook his head. "No, what will they do, put my ribs in a cast?"

He told them what had happened. "In broad daylight," Al noted and shook his head.

"In a dark garage with nobody around," JC noted, "and ski masks."

"Did you get a look at them?" Fred asked.

"Did you recognize any voices?" Al inquired.

JC shook his head, "They didn't say much."

Al said he'd file a report, but there wasn't much to work with.

JC handed the note to Al. "This doesn't look very good for Trip Lake," Al declared.

"Why put it in writing?" JC slowly contributed, but it was as much a statement as a question. "It sure points a finger at Lake. Why do it if you're trying to protect him?"

Al gave JC a look, acknowledging the logic, "Amateurs?"

Al and Fred departed after a while. JC was told to rest for the remainder of the day. Fred said that he'd call the TV station and tell them what happened. They could get back to work tomorrow.

JC followed their advice and quickly fell back asleep.

He had no idea how much time had passed when he heard another knock at his door. Again, JC slowly rose and looked through the peephole in the door. He turned the door handle and Trip Lake was standing there.

Lake entered the room as he examined JC's red face and pained expression. "You look better than I thought you would. You're pretty tough," Lake told him. "I didn't do it," he added.

JC looked at the handsome, if slightly ungroomed, young man and asked, "Which? This?" pointing at his face. "Or Marsha Prospect?"

"Neither."

JC lowered himself into a chair at the room's only table. Lake was still standing, anxious to present his defense. "I didn't tell them to beat you up. I didn't even know they were going to. If I had known, I would have stopped them. They were my friends, though. I apologize. They thought they were doing me a favor."

"Who were they?" JC asked.

"I'm not going to tell you," Lake answered. "They're not bad guys. You can turn me over to the police, but I'm not going to tell them, either."

JC stared at Lake. He didn't have much stomach for revenge. The young man looked as though he hadn't shaved in a week. He was wearing a sweat-stained baseball cap over dirty blond hair.

"I'm leaving Montana anyway," the gondola operator told JC.

"Where are you going?" JC asked.

"Utah," Trip responded. "Nobody knows me there. The powder is unbelievable. Maybe Alta, it's quiet there. Just ski."

"Leaving Montana isn't going to make you look like less of a suspect," JC advised him. "If you run, they'll come after you. And they'll be convinced you have something to run from, like Marsha Prospect's murder."

"I would never kill Marsha. I loved her ..." Lake's voice trailed off as he finished the sentence.

"Would you choke her?" JC asked in an accusing tone.

Trip Lake had the word "no" on his lips. But he didn't say it. "You already know, don't you?" JC just stared at him.

"That's the worst thing I've ever done," Lake said in a defeated voice, "I can't forgive myself." He looked JC in the eyes. "But she forgave me. How does she do that?"

"I don't know," JC said softly, and turned toward the small refrigerator in his room. He slowly got up and removed a bottle of cold orange juice. He silently offered it to Lake, who refused. Gestures hurt JC's ribs less than sucking in the air required to speak.

JC sat down and poured the juice into a glass. He pointed Lake to a seat at the table. "You had the motive. She broke up with you. You pushed her around. You loaded that box into the gondola. It probably played a role in killing her. If I was on the jury, I'd convict you."

The color drained from Lake's face as he heard the facts pointing toward his guilt. His throat was suddenly dry. He reached out, indicating that he'd now accept some juice. JC hadn't taken a sip from his glass. He pushed to toward Lake. JC could drink from the bottle.

Lake swallowed. "Look, you told Ski Fish all this complex stuff was used to kill her. It sounds like it took

194

a lot of planning. I wasn't around the gondola complex planning Marsha's murder. I showed up late to work. That's probably why the ski patrol guy gave me the box. He caught me outside the building. He didn't even have to go in. That's probably why nobody saw him besides me."

"Why were you late? You weren't sleeping with Prospect anymore," JC said.

Lake disclosed that he had spent the night with another woman.

"And she would tell me that she kept you occupied the night before the murder?" JC asked.

Trip nodded. JC requested the woman's name. Lake responded, "Shara Adams."

JC's heart dropped to his stomach. He tried not to show it on his face. There was silence. He didn't want to talk anymore. He drank from the bottle.

"Do you know how to get in touch with her?" Lake asked. JC nodded. "And you'll tell the police, after talking to her?" Lake asked. JC swiveled his head toward Lake and nodded.

Lake stood, preparing to leave. "I'm sorry, again, for what happened to you. They're good guys. They made a mistake." And Trip Lake disappeared through the door.

30

"He says you're his alibi."

JC had pulled his 4x4 up to Shara Adams' log cabin. He held his ribs as he dropped his legs down to the ground. It hurt to swing the car door shut. It hurt to walk up the stairs. He used the rail to pull him up.

Shara opened the door with a smile on her face. But it quickly faded as she saw the red welts on his face and his stooped posture.

JC walked past her kiss and entered the living room. "What's wrong? What happened to you?" she asked with worry in her voice.

"I just spoke with Trip Lake," JC said.

A knowing look came over her face. She'd gone from fearing the worst to witnessing its arrival.

"He says you're his alibi," JC stated, his back still to Shara.

"What?" Shara didn't know what else to say. She knew what Trip had told him, and she knew it was true. She didn't want it to be true, and she didn't know what else to say.

JC turned his face to meet her gaze, "His alibi." He said it with a bit of impatience. "He tells me that he couldn't have set up Marsha Prospect's murder that morning because he was in bed with you."

Tears formed in Shara's eyes. It was the blunt way JC delivered the information. She covered her mouth. She felt sick.

"Is it true?" JC asked quietly. His eyes looked at her, but they were emotionless eyes.

She nodded her head, "Yes." There was fear in her voice. She was afraid of what that admission meant. JC looked away.

She approached him with her arms ready to embrace his shoulders, "Oh JC, I'm sorry. It was stupid."

He let her touch him. He longed for her touch. He didn't want any of this to matter, but it did. He didn't move.

"We were both vulnerable. I was upset. He was upset. It was just once, and we both knew it was going nowhere. We said as much, that morning."

"You don't owe me an explanation," JC didn't look at her as he spoke.

"How did I know that you were suddenly going to appear, after all this time?" She knew, as the words left her mouth, that she was delivering a defense that hadn't been requested.

"You walked away from me once," JC said when he finally allowed himself to look at her. "Why did I think you wouldn't walk away again?"

Without another word, JC headed for the door and closed it behind him. He never looked back. If he had, he would have seen Shara peering through the lace curtains as he climbed into his car. She was crying.

31

"It was pretty brutal. They didn't tell me to take self-defense classes when I studied journalism at CSU." JC was trying to make light of his discomfort, as a live interview with his anchors at the TV station in Denver wrapped up.

The anchor and co-anchor had taken turns, asking JC for details about the attack. He'd answered them while trying to add a bit of levity. During the interview, he sat on a chair with the ski resort as his background. It was compelling TV, for a talking head.

He had glanced at the social media page he maintained, so viewers could communicate with him. He knew he'd need a few hours to answer all their "get well" messages.

"We're glad you're getting better," one anchor said as the interview came to an end. "Speedy recovery, JC," the co-anchor chimed in.

A few days had passed since the assault. He was a little less uncomfortable. He had been convinced to visit a doctor, who confirmed that his ribs were bruised, not broken. "And no concussion, so it's mostly good news," the doctor had told him.

He was offered prescription painkillers. JC refused: "I'll just take ibuprofen."

"Good for you," the doctor responded.

JC walked away from the satellite truck on the wood-plank sidewalks that gave the ski resort some of its Old Western charm. He thought that the center of town probably resembled a Montana settlement 150 years ago. The sidewalks had a wood-shingle roof over them, so shoppers could move from store to store without being impeded by snowfall. But 150 years ago, the streets would have been mud, and the potholes could have been knee-deep.

It was on one of those wood-plank sidewalks that JC spotted Paul Prospect. He was dressed like a cowboy, but a billionaire cowboy. He wore blue jeans, but they probably cost five hundred dollars. His jacket was made of bearskin. He didn't skin the bear, he probably paid thousands of dollars for it.

Prospect touched off the ensemble with impressive cowboy boots, a spotless cowboy hat, and a stunning, fur-wrapped young woman on his arm.

The two men stopped to exchange polite greetings. Prospect introduced the young woman as a new employee at Grizzly Mountain's public-relations office.

"How are you getting reacquainted with your ski resort?" JC asked him.

"Oh, it's a toy, Mr. Snow." He made himself sound terribly important to the pretty blonde on his arm.

"This will be a gold mine again," Prospect told JC. "Marsha didn't ruin it, but she didn't do anything to help realize its full potential. She just wanted something to play with."

But JC had read the financial reports. He knew Marsha Prospect had actually improved the standing of the ski resort. JC was coming to understand that one of Paul Prospect's talents was self-promotion. If Paul Prospect thought it would inflate his image, he'd say it, whether it was true or not.

Prospect turned and whispered something into the ear of the young lady wearing the new fur coat. "Nice meeting you, Mr. Snow," she said with a smile. And she disappeared into a store across the street.

"So, have they determined who murdered my ex-wife?" Prospect asked JC.

"They're open to suggestions," JC responded.

"We both know who killed her," Prospect said as he locked his handsome eyes on JC's.

"Who is that?"

"Trip Lake. I'm sure he was after her money," Prospect told him.

"He has a pretty good alibi," JC told the billionaire. Remembering the details of Lake's alibi gave JC a sick feeling.

"Something wrong?" Prospect asked.

"No," said JC as he tried to regain his focus.

"Well, if you want to scoop the papers on this one, you stay on Trip Lake's trail." Prospect said it as if he were sharing inside information. JC knew that he wasn't.

"You had a lot to gain," JC said to Prospect, without any sugar added. And he watched Prospect's self-serving grin fall from his face.

"Mr. Snow," Prospect said frostily, "I was in New York City, remember?" Prospect gave JC a look suggesting the reporter was stupid. Stupid and inferior.

"You have the resources to get the job done, even if you were on Mars," JC responded without any kindness.

Prospect was agitated. Billionaires don't need to take lip. JC could see the man was struggling to keep his cool.

The resort owner began to rant. "The entire sheriff's department has surrounded a campground full of guys playing soldier with real guns. You have a penniless hobo who was sleeping with a woman way out of his class. You have a two-bit gambler who thinks my ex-wife was the only thing standing between him and turning Grizzly Mountain into the next Las Vegas. But you want to put me on trial for murder?" Prospect was raising his voice, "Mr. Snow, what makes you so smart and everyone else do dumb?"

JC hardly heard the end of Prospect's performance. Instead, the reporter asked, "Peck wants to turn Grizzly Mountain into a casino?"

"In the worst way," Prospect responded, trying to regain his composure. He wasn't a man who got where he was using street brawls.

"How do you know?" JC inquired.

Prospect sighed, weighing whether he wanted to share the answer with the journalist.

"I'm meeting with Peck about the idea tomorrow," Prospect decided to disclose. "We were on our way to making the deal when Marsha got the divorce and took the mountain away from me."

"Did Peck try to strike the same deal with Marsha?" JC asked.

"I told you," Prospect looked JC in the eye. "She was in over her head. She didn't want anything to do with the idea. She didn't care about the money. That's not important to some people, I guess. Maybe if they're given everything, they don't know how hard money is to earn."

Prospect turned his head and saw the blonde crossing the street in their direction. She had a new shopping bag in her hand.

The billionaire turned back to JC. His cheerful demeanor had returned, at least for show. He said, "Mr. Snow, I hope you think about what I said. I must be going."

With that, the blonde wrapped in fur took Prospect's arm and they strolled away. The young woman looked over her shoulder at JC and gave him a happy, "Bye."

JC instinctually waved his hand in her direction. But he was a bit bewildered. If Trip Lake didn't do it, was there someone with even more to gain from Marsha's death than her ex-husband?

32

JC's skis drifted up to the wand in the start house. They were slippery. They had a fresh coat of race wax.

His ribs had healed enough so that the pain could be masked by ibuprofen. As long as he didn't fall. "So, don't fall," JC told himself.

He was wearing a green and gold speed suit left from his college days. It was torn in a couple of places. There were some blood drops in other places, but he liked all of that. He reached over the wand and stabbed the snow with his poles.

"Racer ready!" shouted the starter. "Three, two, one," the starter cried in cadence. JC bent his knees and sprang out of the gate, slapping the timing bar aside with his shins. He made a loud grunt as he exploded onto the race course.

Desperately pushing at the snow with his poles to go faster, he gained speed passing the first three gates. Then, it was "wings up."

He crouched into a tuck. He rose to attack two sweeping turns before disappearing over a lip to negotiate a blind gate. He rolled forward on his toes and roared down the steeps.

He was full of adrenaline. The wind ripped at his face. He was confident. Every gate was where he expected to find it.

He tucked past the last three gates on the flat and crossed the finish line. He stood and kicked his skis sideways, to scratch to a stop. He was in the corral now, fenced in by plastic netting. He knew he was fast.

JC had a smile on his face, even as his legs begged for oxygen. He felt his ribs throb a little. "Did they bother you?" Al asked.

"Not until I was done," JC told him, smiling. His head was bobbing, as his body demanded air. He wiped spit off his lips.

A friend of Al's approached and said, "Hold still!" She snapped a picture of the pair and asked for their email addresses. "I'll send it to you!"

Al's time was slightly slower than JC's. "But not by much," Al told him. "Do you feel me breathing down your neck?"

"It's the lump in your pants that I'm worried about," JC joked.

They climbed onto the chairlift to retrieve their coats and ski pants. They had chucked their extra clothing aside, like all the other racers, when they stripped down to their speed suits at the start house.

As race officials moved gates and reset the course, the racers were informed that the second run would commence after lunch and a quick inspection.

Al was wearing a white Lycra racing suit with black spots. He looked like a dairy cow. Fellow racers would bellow, "Moooo," as he entered the start gate. He thought the whole thing was funny.

They were racing at the Big Sky Ski Resort, not far from Grizzly Mountain. Television News anchor Chet Huntley had been the inspirational co-founder, before he died too soon.

From the top, they could see an outstanding cross-country skiing resort down the road. It had produced U.S. Ski Team members. Years ago, one of the women on the national team had been kidnapped by a father and son searching for a "mountain bride." Her rescue had been heroic and violent.

JC and Al put their pants and jackets on over their racing suits and skied down to the lodge for a quick lunch.

At the bottom of the hill, JC spied a familiar face sitting in a log chair by an outdoor fire. It was Ski Fish, Trip Lake's friend.

JC was almost certain that Ski Fish had been one of the masked muggers the other night. Ski Fish was now sporting a plastic cast on his hand.

"You shouldn't go poking that thing where it doesn't belong," JC said, as he rapped his knuckles on the plastic.

Ski Fish was startled. He looked at JC nervously. It made JC's ribs feel good. Nothing more needed to be said. JC continued into the lodge to get some food.

Al and JC tried not to talk business over lunch. This was their "day off."

Al broke the rule only once, to tell JC that the standoff at the militia compound had been relegated to "caretaker status." No shots had been fired since the first night. Law officers weren't anxious to go in, and the militia members weren't anxious to come out.

The forest ranger and reporter both agreed that General Smith was winning a public relations war every day the standoff continued. It signaled "defiance" to his sympathizers. JC and Al turned their attention back to the ski race.

Whoever invented ski racing decided that the sport was inherently unfair because it was held outdoors. For reasons only nature could explain, the snow might be fast for one racer and slow for the next. That could be decided by whether the sun was out or not, or the wind was blowing or not.

The answer, in the eyes of this wise inventor, was to make the racers ski two runs. Then, perhaps, the sun and the wind would be a problem for one racer during the first run, but another racer during the second run. In the end, it would all come out even. Sometimes, it worked out that way.

There are exceptions: Downhill and Super-G races are only one run. They're just too dangerous. You were lucky to finish one, without crashing.

The day continued to be clear and pleasant. The chairlift carried racers to their second run. JC was quiet at the top of the course. He was on his knees as he applied a powdery wax onto the base of his skis. Other racers around him were performing similar rituals.

He wasn't joining in the banter with other racers. He had a serious look about him. He was remembering how his last race ended, "On my ass."

Racing was a great cure to whatever was bothering JC at any time. He wasn't thinking about Marsha Prospect or Shara Adams or Ski Fish, right now. He was thinking about the race ahead of him. His body tingled slightly with excitement.

The race had started, and the bib number of the racer in the start gate signaled to JC that he would hear his name soon.

He pushed his tools back into the pocket of his ski jacket and peeled off the down parka.

He pulled on the zippers that ran the length of his ski pants, the type especially preferred by racers. They spilled open, allowing their removal without catching on the skier's bulky boots. All that covered him now was the thin, tight, green and gold speed suit.

"How're they turning?" JC asked as he slid next to Al.

"Like they have a mind of their own," Al responded with a grin.

They tapped their ski poles together, in the traditional sentiment among racers at the top of a course. It meant "good luck" to each of them.

There was a cowbell clanging as JC approached the start. Someone yelled, "Come on, JC!" More onlookers and racers joined in.

He kicked out of the start gate with a grunt. He built up speed past the first few turns and was a bull in the next few. He crushed the gates. The slap of his shoulder against the cold plastic was audible.

He carved through the flat in a tuck and left the ground as he soared over the lip.

The rest of the race course seemed to unfold before JC in slow motion. He knew where to be and where to look for extra speed. He was having fun. At the bottom of the course, observers would say he was in "The Zone."

Wherever he was, he arrived there first. He emerged from his tuck after crossing the finish line and worked to get his skis stopped before hitting the back of the plastic corral. He was breathing hard, but happy with everything he had done on the way down.

"I'll take it," JC told congratulatory onlookers who lined the finish area. Already with a smile on his face, he looked over his shoulder for the clock. The digital readout reflected his time, and next to it, "1st Place."

"Mooooo ..." could be heard as the next racer hurtled down the course. Al in his cow suit looked fast. But he'd have to settle for second place.

The two racers shared a beer next to a fireplace after the awards ceremony. JC's drink was poured into an engraved vase presented for his victory.

"You're slowing down, JC," Al told him. "In the old days, you'd have beaten me by more. This may be the last race you ever win, ever." He emphasized "Ever."

JC laughed, "You can't just let me enjoy this, can you?"

They both checked their phones. In email, they had received a copy of their picture together, taken by Al's friend.

JC and Al had been joined at the fire by a crowd of men and women who had also raced that day. They were packing their gear up, windburned faces still covered with smiles. They'd all have heroic and humorous stories to tell. From the fastest racer to the slowest racer, they all admired each other's courage and passion. They made plans to see one another at the next race.

This was why JC told anyone who would listen, "Ski racing is the best sixty seconds in life."

33

Darkness had fallen, as JC slipped into the bindings of his cross-country skis. The bright half-moon and clear cold night had energized him.

He left his car at the side of the road and began to follow a creek bed into the woods. His skis barely made a sound as he moved forward.

He was dressed in black wool pants and a black fleece shell. He hoped that he wouldn't be easily seen. He wore gaiters over his shoes so the snow wouldn't get in. A small dark day pack carried water, an energy bar and small tools.

He skied for nearly an hour before dim lights appeared up ahead. He could make out the silhouettes of a few cabins and the A-frame dining hall. There was no road back there, so JC knew the woods would be absent of guards at the militia outpost.

Al told JC that he suspected a cache of weapons was stashed in a basement beneath the dining hall.

The compound was quiet. There was singing coming from a distant cabin.

JC buried his skis under a thin layer of the soft snow. He was behind the dining hall and began to search for a way into the basement.

The basement was cut into the hillside. He found the door was locked. He'd have to learn another way inside the walls. They were made of stacked concrete blocks.

JC spied an air vent. It covered a hole he thought large enough to barely squeeze his shoulders through.

There were a couple of screwdrivers in his day pack. He removed six screws from the vent and it lifted away from the wall. JC dropped his daypack into the room and crawled through the opening.

He stood still for a moment, allowing his eyes to adjust to the dark. Grasping a penlight in his daypack, he flipped it on. "Holy shit," he whispered.

There were dozens of boxes with printing stenciled on the sides, military-style. The tape sealing some of the boxes had already been broken. Inside those boxes, JC saw long guns he recognized, and some he didn't recognize.

JC thought that some looked like M14s. Some, he thought, looked like an Uzi he'd fired when doing a news story on attempts to regulate guns. There were probably hundreds of guns, judging from the number of boxes. There was even a crossbow sitting on top of a box.

There were boxes of ammunition stacked to the ceiling of the cluttered room. "Good Lord," he muttered, as he saw a box labeled "grenades."

The room smelled faintly like a gardening center. Fertilizer? JC walked through the room and found bags of it piled against one wall. There were also oil drums with markings he couldn't make sense of.

On one side of the dark room, he came across a workbench. JC shined his light on bottles and boxes lined on a shelf over the bench. There were also boxes on the floor below. He smelled sulfur. He was standing next to a drum stamped "black powder."

On one end of the bench, he saw an assortment of small clocks and timers tossed haphazardly in an open box.

There were flasks, test tubes and a pair of scales. There were containers marked "potassium nitrate," and something that looked like a still.

JC pulled a piece of paper out of his fleece pocket. He'd copied something out of a book he purchased in Sierra. The paper read, "potassium ferrocyanide" and "calcium chloride." He'd found those names among the ingredients needed to make prussic acid. And he found the same names on labels in front of him.

JC pulled out his phone and took pictures, fearful that the flash would be seen. Then he traced his steps back to the open vent and grabbed his day pack.

But as he pushed his shoulders out the vent hole, he was blinded by light. Someone was training a flashlight on his eyes, at close range.

He felt cold metal pressing against his forehead. It felt like a gun.

"I could decorate all four walls with your brains, Mr. Snow," said the muted voice behind the flashlight.

"And then what," JC responded. "Spend the rest of the night washing brains off the walls?"

"Good point," the voice said. "Get back inside, raise your hands and take three steps backwards."

JC pulled his head back into the room and did as requested.

"Now, turn around," the voice demanded. With JC's back turned, he heard what sounded like a man crawling through the vent hole.

"I trust," the voice inquired, "that you're not armed with anything mightier than the pen?"

"I have enough trouble shooting myself with that," JC responded.

"I guess you can turn around," the voice instructed.

JC did so and stared into the face of his captor. It was Spook.

"Did you find what you were looking for?" Captain Hemingway asked.

"I guess I found more, I wasn't looking for you," JC said.

"Funny," Spook said, actually showing a bit of a grin.

"This was very brave on your part," Hemingway told the reporter. "How did you get past our sentries?"

"I distracted them with a trail of doughnuts," JC said. He tried not to show his fear. "It works for cops, too."

Spook walked toward the crossbow. "You know, this doesn't make much of a mess." He fit his handgun into his belt and picked up the medieval weapon.

Hemingway cocked his head and pointed the crossbow toward his captive. Spook's eyes looked like they were sparkling. Then, he lowered the weapon.

"Relax, Mr. Snow. These morons aren't your murders. They can barely slaughter the English language." And

Captain Hemingway told him, "You can put down your arms. What did you hope to find?"

JC dropped his arms and reached back to feel the seat of his pants, "Well, it looks like this is laundry night."

Hemingway laughed aloud. Then he raised his own index finger to his lips, "Shhhh."

"I don't mean to convince you otherwise," JC inquired in a whisper, "but why aren't you going to shoot me?"

"Why should I?" Spook replied. "I'm not a murderer any more than anyone else in this place. These guys are idiots, but they're not murderers. I wouldn't be here if they were."

"Then why are you here?"

Spook looked at JC with a face that almost seemed bored. "I like to play with their fireworks." His arm made a sweeping gesture across the room. "You've just seen some of it. And I get to play with it all." A smile had creased his face.

JC remembered General Smith bragging about a militia member with a Ph.D. in biochem. JC didn't know that having brains made Hemingway any better than the rest of the misfits living in the compound.

"Were you part of the attack on that forest ranger?" JC asked.

"I told you," Spook said with a very serious look. "They're idiots."

Hemingway turned and walked away from JC, as though he didn't have the stomach for that particular topic. He turned again and sat on a set of steep stairs.

"Where do they go?" JC asked.

"The stairs? To a pantry in the dining room. They have to come down here when they need this." And he rapped on a small metal door that looked like a fuse box. "So, what did you find?" Spook inquired.

"I think I found the ingredients for prussic acid," JC said in a voice that challenged Hemingway's innocent pretense.

"I know," Spook confirmed, "but most of them don't." He said that most of the other camp members didn't know how to mix a martini, let alone a deadly vapor.

Hemingway was quiet, as he looked like he was weighing what he would and wouldn't tell. "You know, the Nazis and Communists used to murder each other with it." JC figured that he was talking about prussic acid. Then Hemingway said, "But the spies liked it, because when you're done cooking it up, there's nothing left but a harmless blue residue. You could dye your shirt with it."

"Alright," JC asked. "If someone here didn't kill Marsha Prospect, then who did?"

"I don't know." Spook ran his hands through his long blond hair, as though he were trying to concentrate. "Tell me what you know."

"Seriously?" JC asked in surprise.

"What have you got to lose?" the militiaman asked.

34

The strange man with long blond hair and dark rings around his eyes listened intently as JC proceeded to diagram the mysterious death of Marsha Prospect.

Spook never changed his expression. He had a slight smile on his face and seemed to devour the details. He brushed his hair with his hand.

"Where did you find the tube?" he interrupted.

JC told him that a couple of gondola operators found it jammed in the doorway.

"That's where it rolled, after the fact," Hemingway said. "She probably was holding the recorder, dropped it as she began to feel its effects and it broke open. The canister rolled away."

Hemingway stared at the floor. He seemed to be witnessing the murder with his own eyes. He looked up at JC. "It was squeezed inside the tape recorder. Did you look inside the tape recorder?"

JC told him, "I didn't. I don't know if anyone thought to take the tape recorder apart."

"You might be surprised by what you find," said the militia captain. "Maybe one of the cops found it open, and stupidly put it back together. They probably wanted to see what was recorded."

JC thought Spook was deducing the events with a touch of arrogance, but also a touch of brilliance. "So, the evidence isn't what's on the tape at all. It's what's inside the recorder," JC said.

"Sometimes," Hemingway offered, "we can't see the forest for the trees." He told JC to open the tape recorder. He said they'd find remains of a second tiny tube. "It's called a 'tilt trigger.' It would have just enough charge to rupture the tube containing the gas."

"The tube they found wasn't very big," JC told him.

"It doesn't have to be," Hemingway pointed out. "A drop of prussic acid will kill you. If I put a drop on your dog's tongue and he licked you, you'd die. Of course, your dog would die, too."

Hemingway stood and walked to the workbench. He fondled a couple of beakers, wondering to himself what JC had seen. "You'll probably find some liquid, most likely mercury, in that detonator tube."

"What your killer did is this," Hemingway said as he turned to JC and casually leaned against the workbench. His arms were folded. "He pushed 'play' on the tape recorder and put it in the box. The box was loaded onto the gondola. The first five minutes or so of the tape were probably blank, so the tape was running the whole time."

"Then a song starts to play," Hemingway had a small grin on his face, somewhat appreciating its evil. "Maybe the killer chose a song his victim recognizes. If a husband wants to kill his wife, maybe he chooses their wedding song."

JC listened, thinking it was interesting that Hemingway was using a husband and wife as an example.

"The victim reaches into the box," the captain continued, picking up his tempo as though the story was reaching the "big finish". "She wants to see where the song is coming from. As she picks up the small recorder, that tilts the tube containing the mercury. The mercury pours into the loaded side of the tube and detonates. And that sprays the prussic acid. If the victim is close enough to hold the recorder, she's close enough to breathe a fatal dose."

Hemingway paused for effect, "And the curtain drops." Hemingway had his arms spread out now, like a theatre performer ready to take his bow.

JC stared in disbelief. Spook just smiled, pleased with his performance.

There was silence, which Hemingway terminated, abruptly informing JC that he was free to leave. "But I have one condition. You have to promise not to reveal what you've seen in this room."

"That's a tall order," JC responded. "Is this stuff legal?"

"You might be surprised to learn that most of it is," Hemingway told him.

"Since you're the one with the gun and the crossbow, I don't have a lot of currency to negotiate with," JC said. "But the deal is off the moment someone gets hurt with this stuff."

"Agreed," Hemingway nodded. "I don't think anyone here is that crazy. Right now, the feds aren't coming in. We'd be crazy to give them an excuse, like Waco."

Spook gestured his head toward the vent hole. Time to go.

JC picked up his day pack and headed for the opening. On his way out, he even felt Hemingway give him a boost from behind.

"There is another condition I'd like to secure from you," Hemingway whispered as he poked his head through the hole.

"What's that?" JC asked quietly.

"Don't get caught leaving here," the captain had a slight smile on his face.

"Agreed," JC answered with a similar smile.

"Hey, one more thing," Hemingway whispered to JC as he was about to turn and depart. JC was all ears.

"Some of my toys have been disappearing," the captain told him. "I've been burglarized twice this winter, once around New Year's and once … about a week before Mrs. Prospect died."

He tilted his head and gave JC a look. He was emphasizing the importance of his information. JC wondered if this was the message Spook had intended to deliver all along. Maybe it was the reason he allowed JC to crawl into the basement. Spook was watching him from the start, JC suddenly knew.

Hemingway had more to say about the burglaries. "I'd suspected that someone here at the compound got into them." Hemingway instinctively looked to his left and right. "Now, I'm not so sure. I think if you find the thief, you'll find your killer."

JC nodded silently in agreement. Then it was JC's turn to share a suspicion of his own. He rested his elbows on the hole in the wall. Hemingway watched with curiosity.

"How would you blow up a guy on a ski mountain?" JC asked. "Just blow him to smithereens?"

"The same way," Hemingway said and gave JC a look to see if he understood.

JC shook his head slightly. He didn't know what Spook was getting at. "The same way as what?"

"The same way as he did it," Hemingway responded, but he saw that his conclusion still hadn't clicked with JC.

"That one, I was sure of," the militia member said. Hemingway told JC that the first time he knew someone had stolen some of his ingredients from below his workbench, was about a week before the backcountry skier died. "When I read about his death, I knew that avalanche gun hadn't hit him with a shell. That was preposterous."

He told JC, "I knew that somehow the stuff stolen from this basement, which were all the ingredients you needed to build a bomb, I knew it had something to do with that guy's death."

"Did you tell the police?" JC asked.

Hemingway shook his head no. He scanned the basement with a look of pride. "I told you that MOST of this stuff is legal, not ALL of it."

"How do you think it happened?" JC asked the man on the other side of the vent hole.

"Judging by the stuff that was stolen?" Hemingway surveyed the room. "By the way, the guy is smart. He is not your average scout." Hemingway told the reporter that ingredients were stolen to make a bomb and to make a barometric fuse.

That was a technique JC was somewhat familiar with. "Terrorists have used it to blow passenger planes out of the sky. It explodes when you reach a certain barometric pressure, or altitude?"

"Right," Hemingway concurred. "Our killer had to get the skier to carry the bomb with him before he got on the chairlift for the ride up. The barometric pressure falls as you gain in elevation. So, when he reaches a chosen altitude, kaboom!"

"He did it, I'm telling you," Hemingway quietly implored. He didn't take his eyes off JC. "It's the same guy."

"The same guy who killed Marsha Prospect?" JC asked

"It has to be," the captain told him.

JC was trying to think of reasons to doubt the man in camouflage.

"There are not two guys out there, in this little resort, who can dream up, let alone build, a barometric-pressure detonator and a tilt trigger," Hemingway insisted. "And he had to figure out how to keep the swing of the gondola from setting off the charge prematurely. I told you, this guy is smart."

The revelation caused JC's head to swim. But it was time to go, before being seen. He reached into his bag for his screwdriver. "Hand me those screws. I'll put the vent cover back on."

"Don't bother," Hemingway said as he smiled. "I've got to find a way to make this place burglar-proof."

35

The next morning was so cold, the snow creaked when you walked on it. The fabric of JC's jacket and between the thighs of his pants made an audible "swish" when he walked.

If the Grizzly Mountain Ski Resort had a singular image problem, it was the occasional arctic freeze. Mornings like this dragged the temperature down to a wind chill of minus-twenty. Local service stations made a minor fortune jumping cars and selling batteries.

Montana residents all used to have oil-pan heaters, plugged into their garages at night. Newer cars put up a better struggle with freezing temperatures, with the possible exception of mornings like this.

JC was still groggy from his late night in the darkness at the militia compound. Now, he wanted to see if Spook was right.

JC called Al and arranged a meeting with Deputy Cochran. The deputy was holding the tape recorder in evidence.

Al picked up JC in his Forest Service truck. There was bagpipe music blaring from the truck's tinny speakers. "Ah, the Motherland," Al said over the music.

Both men celebrated their Scottish ancestry, on occasion. Al reminded JC of the time they entered the caber toss at the Scottish Games in Colorado. It was a test of strength and agility requiring the competitor to toss something resembling a utility pole. Both laughed at the memory of their ineptitude and listened to more bagpipes.

Then Al said, "We're going to catch this asshole."

"I might be able to help," JC said as he turned to Al. It had been three weeks since Marsha Prospect's murder. Al returned JC's look and disclosed that he was frustrated by his own inexperience investigating murders.

The Forest Service truck pulled up to the Sierra County Sheriff's Office in downtown Sierra. Cochran was waiting for them inside. He walked them back to a quiet room. JC thought it was unmistakably an interrogation room.

"Open it up," JC said, as Cochran held a bag containing the tape recorder.

Cochran slipped on evidence gloves and pulled the recorder from the bag. He easily popped open the plastic recorder, splitting it in half.

"Spook was right," JC said to himself. Inside the workings of the recorder was a small tube, and room for another. He knew that when they conducted a test, they'd find residue of mercury.

"If anyone did open this up, they could mistake that tube for something that belongs in a tape recorder," Cochran supposed. "We're not tape-recorder repairmen."

Cochran pulled another plastic evidence bag out of the box on the table. The tube discovered by the gondola operators was in it.

Cochran seized it with his gloved hand, and it dropped into the empty space in the tape recorder's housing. "A match," he declared, looking up at his two companions.

"How did you know?" Al turned his head to JC.

"I was told I'd find it," JC said, "by the only guy in Montana who can probably put one of those together, besides the killer."

"Where do we find him?" Cochran asked.

"Inside the militia compound," JC replied. The postures of Al and Cochran both sank a little.

"All you have to do is seize the compound, and not get anyone shot while you're doing it," JC said with a smirk. He knew that he had just walked the law officers up to a line they could not cross.

"You talked to him?" Al asked with a look of frustration on his face.

"Yep," JC replied, with enough pride that he felt a bit guilty about it. "Look, there are some places a reporter can go that you guys aren't welcome. You know that."

Both law officers silently nodded in agreement.

"What else did you see? Can we take them?" Deputy Cochran asked.

JC failed in an effort to suppress a little laugh at the suggestion. "They have more guns than you."

"What kind of weaponry are you talking about?" Cochran inquired, in a professional tone.

"I don't know if I'm qualified to answer that. He told me that it's legal, or most of it anyway," JC told them. "By the way, I think I'm violating an agreement not to tell anyone. I'm only doing this so you don't get any ideas. A lot of people would die, on both sides."

The two law officers looked at each other without saying anything.

"Besides, I don't think the killer is in there," JC told them.

"Who's the killer then?" Cochran asked, leaning back in his chair and looking a little weary. He was getting tired of hearing things from a news reporter that he didn't learn from his own investigation.

JC shrugged his shoulders. "I don't know."

Deputy Cochran sat behind the table and Al leaned on it with both arms. It was an old wooden table with plenty of scars. It was the only piece of furniture in the interrogation room besides the chairs they were sitting on, just as old and just as scarred.

Al continued to lean, sort of hovering over the table. "JC thinks Harrison was murdered, too." Al was making eye contact with Cochran now.

"How do you figure?" Cochran asked as he looked at the reporter. And JC told the officers everything Hemingway had told him, without naming his informant.

"There's one way to find out," Al suggested to Cochran. "Do another autopsy."

"His remains are already back in Massachusetts with his family," Cochran said, a little exasperated and looking at the two men.

"Have the M.E. do it there," Al suggested. "We just have to get the family's permission to exhume."

Cochran thought to himself. He scratched the back of his head, "Alright," he conceded. "That'll be the Berkshire County Medical Examiner. Tell him to look for traces of wire and other ingredients you'd expect to find in a bomb, right?"

"Right," Al concurred. He turned to JC. "If he was killed by a bomb, then the murder weapon was buried with the victim. His corpse, what's left of it, would have absorbed pieces of wire and metal and plastic that the bomb was made of."

"They didn't look for any of that here?" JC asked.

For the second time, the forest ranger and the deputy looked a bit sheepish. Al finally spoke up. "Everyone thought the poor guy got hit by a shell aimed at the cornice. They just picked up whatever they could find of the guy, boxed him up and sent him home."

"OK, let me get the request in," said Deputy Cochran as he stood from the table.

"One more thing," Al said as he stole a glance at the deputy and JC. "Why don't we have our medical examiner take another look at Sally Decker."

The deputy nodded his agreement. "The woman found frozen in the snow?" JC asked.

"I know she's still sitting in the morgue. Like I said, not a tight family," Al informed him. "I don't even know that there's a connection, but we may have three murders on our hands. Maybe we should take a new look at everything."

36

"Let's go to JC Snow, live again at the Grizzly Mountain Ski Resort. JC?"

JC heard the anchor toss to him through the IFB in his ear. With that cue, JC launched into his newest report on the investigation underway into Marsha Prospect's death.

He told his viewers that the tape recorder had become a key piece of evidence. He also reported that an autopsy would be performed on the body of Harvard

Harrison. For the first time, it was reported that Harrison's death could be connected.

The anchors back in Denver would follow JC's live report with a quick update on the standoff at the militia post. Nothing new was happening, but Fred Shook had traveled out to the gate of the compound to shoot fresh footage that day.

The night was so cold, JC's lips were becoming clumsy. He was happy to end his report with, "I'm JC Snow, reporting live at the Grizzly Mountain Ski Resort in Sierra, Montana."

JC scrambled back into the warmth of the satellite truck. He unzipped his parka bearing the television station's logo, and pulled a battery pack out of his pocket. It was attached to the wire in his ear.

He handed the battery and microphone to the engineer, Jimmy Vazquez. The phone rang. Fred answered and handed the receiver to JC. It was their news director on the other end.

"JC, nice work again," the news director told him. "But listen, the guys who pay the bills are pulling the plug. We want you to come home."

The possibility of being ordered to return to Denver hadn't even occurred to the reporter. He told his boss that they were getting close to figuring out the story, and their viewers would be the first to hear it. "We're about to break a big story. I told you, the two deaths might be connected!" JC told him.

"You're doing good work out there, JC," the news director sympathized, "but I don't always make the decisions. Sometimes, I have to follow orders, too."

JC felt a fury building inside him. They were making a mistake. He didn't know of anything he wanted to say that wouldn't get him in trouble. "I'll talk to you later," he said tersely into the phone, and hung up.

Fred and Vazquez just looked at the reporter. They'd had a feeling that call was coming. JC bolted out of the truck door.

"Fuck!" he shouted into the darkness. Then, he felt a little remorseful. He never knew when viewers were observing him. Anger never looked attractive in the eye of other beholders, he reminded himself.

JC's cell phone rang. He reached into his pocket as he growled, expecting an annoyed news director to be on the other end.

"Hey." It was Al's voice on the line. "We just got a new autopsy report on Sally Decker."

"And?" JC asked.

"She was a little bit strangled," Al told him.

"Can you be a little bit strangled?" JC asked.

"As it happens, yes," the forest ranger informed him. "The M.E. thinks it's possible that she was choked to the point of becoming unconscious. That would allow her killer, and yes that means we're looking for another killer, to take her up the mountain and dump her in the snow. Let Mother Nature take care of the rest."

"Sounds like you might be looking for a yeti?" JC asked, instantly regretting his flip response.

Al paused, amused but not ready to go there. "Not necessarily. Say that the killer attacked her in his apartment. Then, he puts her on his snowmobile and carries her up the mountain in the dark. As long as the groomers don't see him, anyone who spots the snowmobile's light from below would assume it was a mountain employee."

"Is that what happened?" JC asked.

"It's a theory," the ranger replied.

"And you said it was snowing like crazy that night," JC reminded Al.

"Yep."

"Can you connect it to the other two murders?" JC asked.

"Not right now. Her death doesn't involve the same high-tech aptitude. But you can't rule it out, either," Al told him, and added, "We're at Shara's, why don't you join us?"

Fred and Vazquez emerged from the satellite truck. The engineer had shut the truck down and double checked that the doors were locked. "I've put her to bed. Let's go find some dinner."

"OK, just give me a second," JC told them. He pulled off his gloves with his teeth.

He tapped out a text message to his news director. It said, "3 murders now!"

He turned off the phone and shoved it into his pocket. He joined his crew. As they walked toward Shara's Sheep Ranch, he explained what he had just learned.

When they walked in the door, it felt like walking into a sauna compared with what they had endured outside.

The après-ski party was in full swing. The music was loud and so was the crowd. The three men couldn't help but bump into some tired skiers, and squeeze between others. The air tasted like beer.

Some customers in the restaurant recognized JC and raised their hands for a "high five" when he passed. He did so with a smile.

A trio of beautiful women surrounded him for a quick picture. Vazquez just shook his head and smiled. "This is what you do for a living?"

"Pretty much," JC said back, smiling and shouting over the noise.

He spotted Al at a table, waving his arm. The Yellowstone ranger, Mick Berns, was seated with him. JC tapped his companions and headed them in that direction.

They reached the table and were happy to see some empty seats, saved by jackets and other belongings thrown on them. Al introduced Fred and Vazquez to Berns and said to JC, "You remember Mick?"

JC smiled and nodded to her, "Yeah, she wouldn't look for us when, for all she knew, we were freezing to death." They all laughed at that, as Berns toasted JC with her bottle.

They ordered more beer. Fred and Vazquez chatted with Ranger Berns, only to arrive at the sad disclosure that she had a boyfriend.

Al took advantage of the distraction to lean toward JC and tell him, "Now, we've got reports of burglaries coming in. People are showing up at their weekend homes and finding them ransacked. When did my district become Fort Apache?"

A waitress delivered beers to the table. At the next table, she lowered her tray to deliver exotic drinks. She announced each one, as though the recipients were receiving a prize: "Strip and go naked! Sex on the beach! Brains!" The exhausted skiers with matted hair were suddenly energized. "Whooo!" they shouted. The noise was somewhat piercing to JC's ears.

There were also a lot of Grizzly Mountain employees in the bar. This was happy hour, and that meant free food. Lift ops and cafeteria workers knew the day and hour of every happy hour at every establishment. It helped them stretch their money.

JC saw Bill Peck pushing through the crowd. When he spied JC, he headed for their table and the one remaining chair.

"He brings gifts!" Vazquez declared in a festive mood. Peck was carrying a pitcher of beer and some glasses. He was happy to share with his new friends.

Peck told them that he was just tweaking his video gambling machines in the corner. He said that the new ones had been blowing fuses.

"They tell funnier jokes," Peck told them. "I guess that takes more watts."

They laughed, and then he explained, "Actually, it's the improved graphics. And as soon as the band plugs their guitars and amplifiers into the same wall, the lights go out."

JC looked at Peck and asked, "How many million dollars do you have to make before you stop making your own service calls? Don't you hire people to do that?"

"Oh, I'm just doing it until we work these kinks out," Peck shouted over the crowd. "You know, if you want something done right, do it yourself."

The party kept growing. The director of the ski patrol, Elise Du Soleil, grabbed a nearby table with some staff members. They pushed the two tables together.

Du Soleil sat down with a beer and said to JC, "I understand that you met Greg Jones?" She was referring to her suspended subordinate on the ski patrol who was suspected of accidentally killing Harvard Harrison.

JC nodded and said, "Nice guy." Du Soleil nodded in agreement, showing a sad smile.

Another of Du Soleil's ski patrol members was seated next to her. He was in a wheelchair. His name was Shawn.

His upper body showed large muscles, even under his shirt. He told JC that he was the mountain's first disabled member of the ski patrol. He cruised the mountain on outriggers with a partner.

Du Soleil told JC, "Shawn approached me about joining the ski patrol a couple of years ago. Of course, stupid me, I said 'absolutely not!'"

She started to laugh and looked at Shawn. He started to laugh, too. She said, "Tell them what you told me."

Shawn remembered back to that day and said stubbornly, "I can do anything you think I can't do, and more!"

"So far," Du Soleil added, laughing, "He's right!"

The conversation at the table was interrupted as Shara Adams approached the table. She was carrying a tray with salt shakers, limes and shots of tequila. "My friends look thirsty," the bar owner announced.

For a brief moment, she and JC exchanged an awkward look. They hadn't spoken since JC confirmed

Trip Lake's alibi. The discomfort was broken, though, when Mick Berns shouted, "Saddle up!"

Her boyfriend had just pulled a chair up to the table. He had a look of surprise on his face as Mick hopped in his lap. "See what I've gotta live with?" he grinned to the crowd at the table.

The park ranger opened his lips with her fingers and pressed the lime between his teeth. She pulled open his denim shirt, licked her tongue against his salty bare skin, threw her head back as she swallowed a shot of tequila, and then kissed him on the lips, squeezing the lime between their teeth.

The table hooted and jeered at the couple. Vazquez waved his hand in front of his face, like it was suddenly getting very warm in the room.

Everyone at the table was still roaring their approval as JC's eyes shifted to Shara. She was wearing a thick white sweater decorated with bears. A flashing neon beer advertisement was reflected in her hair.

She sat in a chair next to Mick. Shara caught JC looking at her. He felt helpless. He was shackled by chains of his own making. He wanted to hold her.

When she told him the truth about Trip Lake, he could have been kind. But he wasn't. It didn't have to happen. But he made sure that it did. He wanted to punch himself in the face. He loved her.

He couldn't remain at the table another moment. He stood and made his goodbyes, and he was gone.

The cold air hit his face as he burst out the door. He burrowed his hands into his pockets and was walking down the snow-covered sidewalk toward his SUV.

He heard Al call out his name. JC shrugged his shoulders and kept walking.

"I thought you handled that well," Al said sarcastically, as he caught up.

JC noticed the Christmas lights hanging on young trees lining the sidewalk. He could smell the smoke coming from nearby chimneys. He was trying not to hear Al.

"You're not giving her a chance," Al implored.

They pushed past people walking to dinner, some wearing new cowboy hats. JC was walking as though he were alone.

Then he stopped. "What makes you think she wants a chance?" he asked in an impatient tone.

"For God's sake, she made a mistake almost a decade ago," Al said in a calm voice.

"Two. Two mistakes. She's Trip Lake's alibi," JC told him.

Al scratched his forehead, buying a moment. "That's none of your business," he finally said, somewhat stern.

Al's eyes searched out JC's. "She hadn't seen you for eight years. She's been married and divorced. Trip happened before you even let her know that you were still alive."

There was a touch of frustration in Al's voice as he said, "You're a smart guy, but ..."

The two men were silent as they faced each other. Then, JC uttered, "Don't make fun of my butt."

Al looked at JC and broke into a grin.

JC grinned, too. "OK, I get the point."

They walked to JC's car. Al asked if JC wanted to join his family for dinner the next night, at their ranch. "Soozie wants to eat with someone who compliments her cooking," he said.

"She's a good cook," JC said. "I'll tell her."

"You're such a suck-up," said Al, though he was well aware of his wife's talent in the kitchen.

"Thanks," JC said. The old friends shook hands.

JC rolled down the window of his car as he drove away. "Hey ranger, I'll bet I catch him first!"

Al smiled and shouted back, "That's a bet you will never collect!"

37

"Have you seen that big bull lying by Grayling Creek?" Al was speaking into a handset on a two-way radio in his truck.

"Yeah, I've seen it," answered the voice on the other end.

"How long has he been there?" Al asked after pushing the button to transmit.

"Two days," the forest ranger on the other end responded.

"Doesn't look good," Al said into the mic.

"No, it doesn't," the speaker responded.

Forty-five thousand elk roam Yellowstone Park and the surrounding forest. Al saw his first one of the day from his truck on a road along Grayling Creek. The bull elk was on the other side of the water, alone and lying down.

His rack was huge. Al estimated it was roughly fifteen pounds on each side. The animal's ears were drooping and he didn't move when Al stopped his truck to take a look.

The ranger suspected that the noble giant probably wasn't long for this world. He was among the biggest and strongest bulls last autumn. He spent that time fighting and mating.

Smaller bulls with smaller racks, the ones he was dominating, spent the fall eating and storing up body fat. Now, the rewards were reversed.

The big bulls of autumn were so busy mating that they didn't eat enough. It betrayed them the following winter.

Al observed that this big bull had no snow piled on his back, and yet it was snowing. That meant that the animal had no back fat to insulate him. On a healthy elk, the snow is piled up on his back. This one, the master of the autumn, would die before spring.

As Al pulled away in his truck, he saw some deep tearing scratches in the trees. Al knew that the marks were the work of buffalo, not elk. Elk left smaller scratches.

Al picked up the handset again. He spoke into the mic and asked, "What did the mother buffalo say to her offspring when it was time to push off on his own?"

There was a pause and then the other ranger answered, "I don't know, but I'm already sorry you asked."

Al pressed the red button and said, "Bye son! Get it? Bison?" Al smiled to himself as he bounced down the road.

The truck turned onto a road and followed it to the end of the portion that was plowed. In the summer, the road would continue to a campsite. There was good fly-fishing here. But in the winter, most roads in the parks were allowed to hibernate under the snow.

Past the snowdrift and the "Road Closed" sign, Al could see a herd of about one hundred cow elk. They were grazing in a meadow.

Al pondered the possibility that one of the cows was carrying the offspring of the doomed bull elk he saw. The forest ranger thought to himself, life in nature was simple, beautiful and brutal.

He thought about pulling his cross-country skis out from the back of his truck. But there wasn't a lot of daylight left. He turned around and headed for 191.

In the Gallatin River, he could see a pair of trumpeter swans. They were stirring up the riverbed with their feet and sticking their necks underwater to find some food. He liked trumpeter swans. They mated for life.

Across the river, he saw a small cave in the distance. He stopped his truck, pulled out his binoculars and could barely make out bones in the entrance. He had taken a look at the bones during the summer. They belonged to a bear. The animal probably died in the cave last winter. Smaller animals had dragged the bones out as they nourished themselves on the rotting meat.

Al was heading north. Before dark, he wanted to check on some homes in the hills overlooking Sierra, to see if there had been any more burglaries.

It continued to snow. As the road dropped in elevation and approached Sierra, new construction dotted each side of the plowed pavement.

This was Sierra's dilemma, he thought. Residents here fought to preserve the rural nature of their community. But that only attracted more outsiders who desired to live the same way. In turn, the arrival of more people spurred the development of more stores and strip malls. Land that was once grazed by elk and buffalo was being lost under asphalt.

MURDER ON SKIS

Al slowed down and peered at the homes as he drove by. Some of them were humble, some of them were trailers, but some sold for millions of dollars.

Many of the new luxury homes were designed to look like log cabins. Some were three stories tall. Their rough-hewn exterior walls had logs with mortar between them.

The biggest home of all caused Al to pull his truck over to the side of the road. There were tall, white stone chimneys on each side and big windows to take in the view. It was carved into the hillside above the road. There were sweeping porches on the second level and a small lookout tower on the roof.

Even in the low light, Al could tell that the garage door was open. He couldn't see the homeowner's car, so he pulled his truck into the driveway and looked for signs of a resident, or maybe a burglar.

With no one emerging from the home to greet him, he turned off the engine of his truck and stepped out the door.

He didn't like the look of this. He entered the open garage cautiously, stopping inside to allow his eyes to adjust to the darkness.

Al found a switch on the wall and turned the overhead light on. The room was still. The walls were fresh-poured concrete.

He caught a glimpse of a workbench against the wall facing him. It was made from pine planks, also new. Everything was neat and in its proper place. He noticed a crude chemistry set on one end. There was a scale, beakers, test tubes and a Bunsen burner.

Now, he heard a noise. Behind him. He snapped his head in the direction of the open garage door. His eyes darted from the door to the woodpile to the staircase leading up to the living quarters. Nothing moved.

He wondered if someone was watching him, maybe a burglar. Al instinctively reached to his side for a firearm. "You don't have a gun, moron," he said to himself with half a smile. He didn't like to carry a gun. He thought that it was rarely the right solution to a problem.

He heard the sound again. It came from behind the woodpile. Al took a deep breath and planted his feet facing the chopped wood. "Alright, come on out," he said sternly.

He thought that he could see a bit of the burglar's red jacket. "I can see you," Al declared in a voice full of menace. Nothing moved.

Slowly, Al approached the wood pile. He thought that he'd grab a piece of wood and use it as a club, if necessary. And he was a formidable six foot four, after all.

MURDER ON SKIS

He devised a plan. He would kick some of the logs on the end, causing others to roll and lower the pile. That might expose the man in red who was hiding behind it.

Al clenched his jaw, steadied himself, and swung a muscular leg at the woodpile. The logs began to roll across the garage, just as something dark and quick lunged at him from behind the pile.

Al fell backward. Startled, he let out a scream. His eyes were as big as snowballs as he searched for his attacker.

Their eyes met as Al was rolling onto his knees. The eyes were green, with black vertical slits for pupils.

It was a cat. "A cat burglar," Al said to himself as his worries evaporated. "You've got to be kidding."

"Just take my wallet, but don't hurt me," Al purred as he reached out and stroked the cat's head. The cat did not resist, blinking its green eyes.

Al stood up. He mumbled to himself, "I make a helluva cop."

He surveyed the mess he had made of the garage. He bent over and picked up two logs and threw them back on the remains of the pile. He picked up more, slowly reassembling the woodpile he had disassembled.

He heard another noise. This time, he thought it sounded like footsteps. He still had a split log in his hand that he could use as a club.

He spun to face the staircase and raised the log above his head. Then he froze. He said, "Oh, it's you. OK, you scared me," with a sheepish smile. Slowly, he lowered the log.

The man was wearing a thick down coat. He had a smile on his face.

"Where the hell did you come from?" Al asked, with an embarrassed look.

"You were making a hell of a lot of noise down here," the man in the big coat replied.

Al explained, "I was patrolling and saw your garage door open. You know, we've had a lot of burglaries lately."

"Yeah, I've heard," replied Bigcoat. His eyes were surveying the garage. "Does he break into people's garages and make them messy? That's a dastardly plan."

Al was trying to think of an explanation for the mess that wouldn't make him look like a complete idiot. But then he asked, "Where's your truck? I don't see it parked in the driveway."

"It broke down, right up the road. You would have seen it if you drove any further," Bigcoat told him. "Anyway, I walked back to get some tools." He approached the workbench.

Al walked back to the woodpile. He stooped and looked between the pile and the concrete wall. He saw the red fabric again.

Bigcoat was watching over his shoulder. He needed an insurance policy. He reached for a bottle and a towel.

"Huh, this must have fallen ..." Al was saying, still bent over as he reached for the jacket. Bigcoat's eyes now had a look of panic. He was helpless but to watch as Al pulled a red jacket out from behind the pile. The symbol on the red jacket's back was unmistakable. A white cross.

Al Pine was a big man. Bigcoat couldn't normally reach Al's face. But the forest ranger was stooped over. So, Bigcoat reached from behind Al and pressed a damp white cloth over his mouth and nose.

As Al stood up, somewhat confused, Bigcoat leaped onto the ranger's back, holding on for dear life. He pressed that cloth against Al's face.

Bigcoat had no lie to explain away that jacket. Everything would become clear to the ranger and the other investigators.

Al couldn't help but breathe the chloroform. He staggered for a few steps. His strong arm pulled Bigcoat's hand away from his mouth. Bigcoat slid down the big man's back.

Al was woozy. He leaned against a post in the garage to keep from falling. Bigcoat reached for a split log, and it came crashing down on Al's head.

Al dropped to his knees and then onto his face. Bigcoat stood over him, breathing heavily, wondering what to do now.

A knowing look came over his face.

He rolled Al onto his back. The ranger was unconscious.

Bigcoat walked out of the garage to a snowbank. He returned with a large handful of snow. He dropped to his knees, beside Al.

Bigcoat broke the snow into smaller pieces and shoved them, one at a time, into Al's mouth. More snow was pushed into his mouth, and then more.

Bigcoat's face was emotionless. He squeezed his victim's nose between his fingers and held a hand over the mouth.

Bigcoat looked away, as he felt the body struggle, unconscious but still armed with survival instincts. Too little, though.

The victim's body stopped shaking. Bigcoat studied his victim to be certain that his work was complete. He lifted his fingers off the nose, and then the mouth. Nothing moved. Bigcoat rolled back to sit on the garage floor. He was sweating and exhausted. "Now, what am I going to do with you?"

38

The storm overnight left a new layer of snow on Grizzly Mountain. JC got on his skis early. There wasn't a cloud in the deep blue sky.

He floated down ungroomed runs called Skipper's, Ronn's Rodeo and Old Ephraim.

"Old Ephraim" was what mountain men used to call the grizzly bear.

JC searched Old Ephraim from the top, looking for its fall line. He bounced down the bump run. Then it was time to grab some breakfast and get to work.

Heading into Shara's Sheep Ranch, he paid for a copy of Montana Quarterly. Taking a seat at the bar, he noticed that Kit was working the breakfast and lunch shift. The bartender was already filling orders for alcohol.

The magazine had a cover story announcing Grizzly Mountain and Peckerhead Enterprises had reached an agreement to build a casino at the ski resort.

The article told JC that there were still a lot of details to iron out. The state legislature would have to rewrite some law to allow it to happen. But Paul Prospect was quoted saying, "Good intentions can move mountains."

There was a picture of Prospect and Peck, standing in front of an artist's rendering of the casino. Both men had big smiles on their faces. Again, JC noticed that Peck's smile covered a lot of acreage.

JC ordered some eggs and toast at the bar. He stared at the article, absently fed his face, and wondered whether a casino would have been built if Marsha Prospect still owned the mountain. He thought he knew the answer.

So, he thought to himself, her death proved fortuitous for both entrepreneurs, Paul Prospect and Bill Peck, Jr. And he couldn't help but wonder, was their good fortune left to chance?

JC was still lost in thought when his phone buzzed in his pocket. It was Fred Shook. "You got a call from a

Yellowstone Park ranger. I think it was that one we were drinking with the other night. She wants you to give her a call. She said it was urgent."

JC called the number and was greeted by a volunteer at the Old Faithful Visitors Center. He asked for Mick Berns.

There was a pause. JC assumed Mick was being located. Then she picked up the phone, "Oh JC." She sounded like she was crying. "They found Al this morning. He's dead."

JC squeezed his cell phone until he realized it was about snap in his grasp. He quickly rose from his seat at the bar and looked for a quiet corner. "Are you certain?" he asked, "What happened?"

"They think he got caught in the storm," she said in a trembling voice. "Don't tell anyone I told you. I'll get in trouble ... because you're with the news. But, just come. Police are on their way."

JC continued to hold the phone to his ear after Mick had hung up. He didn't lower it until he realized that he was frozen, like a statue, by the news. He didn't say a word to anyone as he left the bar. He'd forgotten to pay his bill.

He grabbed his skis from the rack in front of the bar and walked to his 4x4, still wearing a red and turquoise one-piece ski suit. He pointed his car toward Route 191.

During the ride, he saw a sheriff's patrol car parked in the driveway at Al's ranch. JC wanted to stop and comfort Soozie, but there would be time for that later. She'd have questions for him, and he didn't have the answers yet.

JC's mind wandered as he drove the familiar route to the national park's West Yellowstone entrance. He'd met Soozie during his senior year in college. He'd introduced her to Al. JC figured that their youngest of four sons was probably only three years old.

JC remembered his conversations with Al when they were waiting out the storm that had trapped them in Yellowstone only ten days ago. Al spoke about his family a lot.

He described his days off. Sunday was his favorite, Al told him. In the fall, the boys would help him, early in the morning, get his gear together to go hunting. They'd beg him to take them along, but they were too young. But when he got home, he and the boys would take over the living room and they'd watch football together.

JC thought about the strange coincidence that Al would be caught in two storms within ten days.

JC arrived in West Yellowstone in about forty-five minutes. There was a snow coach waiting to carry investigators and others to the scene. JC avoided eye contact and climbed aboard. It was best, he thought, if no one knew he was a journalist.

As the snow coach pulled out and headed for the park, JC recognized Al's truck, covered in snow. He also spotted a sign in a restaurant at the edge of town. It wished everyone a happy Valentine's Day.

The snow coach advanced down the road through Madison Junction and turned south, following the Firehole River. Then, JC saw a cluster of parked snowcats, snowmobiles and men and women in green or gray uniforms.

The snow coach stopped. JC again tried to avoid eye contact as they all climbed down the narrow aisle and out the door.

Some of those in uniform, already on the scene, had packed down the snow with their feet. They looked at JC suspiciously as he followed the thin path toward them. He was still wearing his bright ski outfit.

"He's OK, let him through." The voice belonged to Deputy Cochran.

The two men shook hands and exchanged a look of disbelief. As the line of law officers and rangers parted, JC saw the object of their attention. There was a police photographer taking pictures. It was Al's body.

JC suppressed a nauseous feeling. He noticed that there was no blood. Al was lying on his back. The straps of his ski poles were still wrapped around his wrists. His cross-country skis were off, though, sticking straight into the air. The tails were plunged into the snow, like he had put them there.

He was wearing his U.S. Forest Service jacket and uniform. He was wearing a knit cap down over his ears. He was also wearing gloves.

It struck JC as odd. Al preferred to wear mittens when he cross-country skied. And he wasn't wearing gaiters to keep the snow from creeping into his boots.

"Did you notice that?" JC shared his observations with Deputy Cochran. "Just kind of odd."

Al's lips were parted. Snow had gathered in the gap. Cochran said that they had brushed more snow off of him. "A snowmobiler noticed the skis sticking in the air, from the road. When he took a closer look, he found the body."

Cochran said that Soozie had reported Al missing this morning.

"Any idea what happened?" JC asked. He found himself light-headed, but he tried to hide it.

"As far as we can tell," Cochran replied, "he got caught in the storm and froze to death. He was probably out looking for SPORS again."

"Stupid People On Rental Sleds," JC recited, smiling at the code Al shared with him.

"Right, trespassers," Cochran confirmed. "We found his truck at the entrance of the park. That's actually the only thing in my jurisdiction. We're in Wyoming now and on national park land."

JC just stared at his friend's body.

"Anyway," Cochran went on, "we're just helping out. We're working on the belief he hitched a ride into the park after his shift ended. Maybe he just wanted to go skiing."

"In the dark?" JC asked, "With snow already falling? Without telling his wife?"

"It sounds kind of sketchy, doesn't it?" the deputy responded. "There's no sign of foul play, though," he added. "I'm sure they'll do all the tests. But it looks like he froze to death, JC."

"Did you find whoever gave him a ride into the park?" JC asked.

"Nope," the deputy said as he shook his head. "He didn't ski to get here. His truck is thirty miles away."

Deputy Cochran began using his fingers to fidget with his lips, like he was thinking. "You're right JC, this doesn't seem to make a lot of sense."

"Excuse me," a pair of men pushed by, carrying a heavy bag. It was for Al. He'd be zipped inside and placed in a snowcat and removed to the morgue.

JC shook his head as a cold wind whipped across his face. The wind moved Al's bushy beard. JC didn't want to watch his friend zipped away from his life. JC's eyes turned to the horizon. He scanned the distant hills and then closer trees and steam rising from a geyser.

"Wait a minute," JC said softly. Then he said it louder, directing it to the men loading Al into a bag, "Wait a minute!"

JC approached Al's body. An NPS Ranger stepped forward and held his hand out, demanding, "Who are you?"

JC stopped. He wasn't sure how to answer. He looked toward Cochran, who only returned his gaze with confused eyes.

The gray-haired NPS supervisor blocked JC's path to the body and was looking him up and down. He said, "You don't even have a badge! Get back, or I'll have you dragged back to the road, and then arrested."

JC took a gulp but didn't move. He had to think fast. Identifying himself as a journalist would only make things worse.

Then he told the intimidating ranger, "Let me look in his pocket. I'm a friend. I think there's something you'll want to see."

The supervisor still blocked JC's path, but his eyes scanned the faces of the other rangers and law officers.

Cochran closed his eyes and shook his head a little, not enough for anyone else to notice. Then he aimed his remarks at the gruff ranger, "He may have something of interest. He's been helpful to us in the murder of Marsha Prospect."

The ranger's eyes scanned Cochran, a man in uniform. "Make it fast," the ranger told JC, without looking at him.

JC approached the body bag, his friend partially protruding from it. JC dropped to his knees next to Al and unzipped his parka. He reached for the breast pocket of Al's shirt ... and smiled.

The reporter pulled a surface-temperature thermometer from the dead ranger's clothing. JC looked around at his surroundings until his eyes fixed on a slight embankment nearby.

Rising to his feet, JC walked past a few uniforms to the spot and kneeled down. He began digging in the snow. The fresh snowflakes were brushed away easily. Below them, the snow was already getting moist, beginning to melt.

JC plunged the tip of the old-fashioned gauge into the exposed ground and waited. Then, the needle on the gauge began to move.

The needle climbed to eighty-five degrees. It might have climbed higher, but JC pulled it out of the ground and showed it to Deputy Cochran. Then, he showed it to the stern supervising ranger.

"Al told me himself," JC informed the officers who were crowding around him. JC held the gauge out so others could see it.

"Al told me," JC repeated, "only a fool could freeze to death in this park." He looked at Deputy Cochran. "Al didn't freeze in his own backyard, he was murdered."

39

The sound of bagpipes was haunting in the wet chill of the air. They always struck JC that way, sweet and sad.

JC sat with Soozie Pine and her four sons in a wooden pew at the small church in West Yellowstone. She'd asked JC to sit with her. They'd had a long visit as JC returned from the scene of Al's death. On Valentine's Day, he thought to himself.

They sat in a rustic log-and-stone church, overflowing with friends of Robert "Al" Pine. The mourners were a cross section of Montana's population. There were men with bushy beards, wealthy residents of the valley, ranchers, ski racers, resort employees and park rangers.

JC had even received a message from General Smith, expressing regret that he couldn't attend the funeral. He was certain that he'd be arrested if he set foot outside his compound. JC thought that he was probably right.

Soozie had asked JC to address the gathering, to talk about her husband as a younger man, before many in attendance knew him.

JC discussed the love Al expressed for his family and for the place he lived. He shared a story about their days in college.

He spoke of Al's pride in his Scottish ancestry, something they shared. "Al would challenge me. He wanted to prove he was the best Scot. Normally, this battle was fought over a few drams of single malt," JC added with a smile. "And he knew how to win. He bragged that he was the only one of us who had actually skied in Scotland. That was at Cairngorm. He knew that I'd surrender at that moment, and I always did."

Mick Berns caught JC's eye. She was crying. She had on her National Park Service uniform. She had on green pants and an "Ike jacket," matching green tie and a gray shirt, and held a beaver-skin Stetson in her lap.

Al Pine's coffin sat in the front, facing a gold cross hanging over the altar. The simple church had heavy wooden doors to keep the cold and the wind out. The walls were lined with cast-iron radiators. Occasionally, they made a pinging sound during the service.

The vaulted ceiling had heavy beams and chandeliers made from elk antlers. Every seat was filled with mourners. Some men stood, after giving up their seat for a woman. This was Montana.

To JC, Al would think this service was perfect. Father Melvyn Arthur approached the pulpit and asked aloud, "Why does God allow evil?"

The minister stood silent for a moment, allowing those sitting in the pews to ponder the question. Then he said, "One could use the existence of evil to show the absurdity of believing in God. How can a good and wise Creator allow earthquakes, floods and the murder of innocent men, women and children?"

Father Arthur grasped the pulpit with both hands and leaned forward. He informed the flock that God gave mankind the freedom of choice.

"He gave them the freedom to love him or the freedom to sin. He gave them the freedom to make the right choices or to make the wrong choices. Al Pine made the right choice. His killer made the wrong choice."

The priest then asked, "How does this ease our pain, though? How does this make the death of a loved one, Robert Pine, the work of a good and wise Creator?"

Father Arthur dropped his voice to a whisper, "Because this isn't the end. God's world is still evolving."

He raised his voice again, "God's own angels have, on occasion, fallen ... rebelled. God's universe is still evolving. To many people, death appears to be the greatest evil. This is especially true when someone leaves us too soon."

Leaning forward again, Father Arthur's face brightened as he whispered, "But God gives us eternity." The volume steadily increased. "Life is only one chapter of our existence. Robert 'Al' Pine saw the same evolution in his own beloved forests and mountains. Even the tallest trees eventually die. They drop seeds, though, and grow again."

Heads in the pews were nodding. Father Arthur ended, saying with confidence, "A madman can take away a life only once. God grants new lives every day."

The bagpipes began to play again. The mourners followed the coffin out into the cold chill of winter. They quietly spoke, hugged each other and wiped their eyes. JC saw Paul Prospect and Bill Peck together outside. The three men exchanged handshakes.

Then JC said to the two men, "I guess I should extend my congratulations. I read of your plans to build a casino at the ski resort."

Prospect said, with that winning smile he could conjure up, "There's a lot of work to do. We've got to get to Helena and convince state lawmakers this is the thing to do. But it will help pay a lot of their bills, too." Peck nodded in agreement.

JC parted with the men, again wondering if he'd just exchanged pleasantries with a murderer. Or two? Both men, he thought, had gained something from Marsha Prospect's death.

JC climbed into his SUV and watched the crowd outside the church disperse. But his mind was on what were now four deaths somehow connected to Grizzly Mountain.

He thought about the order they followed: Sally Decker, Harvard Harrison, Marsha Prospect and now Al. Spook had convinced JC that the murders of Harrison and Mrs. Prospect were connected. What about Decker? What about Al?

Was it possible, he thought, that there were three different cold-blooded killers roaming the streets of Sierra County? No, he guessed, not in a community without a single murder in thirty-something years.

Did that mean there was a serial killer amongst them? If so, what was their connection with Sally Decker? That was something he was going to have to explore.

JC's phone rang as he was heading back toward Sierra. It was the executive producer from his newsroom. No doubt he was calling on the news director's behalf.

"Sorry about your loss, JC," the E.P. said. "I hear you were close to Al Pine. Any idea what's going on?"

JC shared a small road map of the deadly events happening in Sierra County. And no, he couldn't forecast when an arrest, or arrests, would be made.

"Well, we're still getting hate mail from the accountants here," the E.P. told him. "They want to know how we can justify spending the money to keep a crew in Montana for three weeks."

"How do the viewers feel about it?" JC asked.

"Oh, they love it!" the E.P. told him. "That's why you're getting more time. But I thought that you should know that the clock is ticking. And please, no overtime, OK?"

JC agreed, not really taking his commitment very seriously. His photographer and engineer were staying within their eight-hour work shift. And JC wasn't paid overtime. He was on a salary agreed to in his contract. It didn't matter if he worked twenty-four hours a day, the bi-weekly paycheck would look the same.

JC pulled up at Sierra County Hospital. He wanted to talk to the medical examiner.

Bob Platz was there, his glasses perched on his bald head. "I understand that you caught this," The M.E. said with a smile of acknowledgement. "It was a homicide, alright."

He pushed some paper on his desk aside and reached for a folder with Al's name on it. "It was no accident. He really did freeze, but he had a little help. And that was only a contributor to the death." The medical examiner's face was grave.

He flipped open the manila folder. "Al had a serious gash on the back of his head," Platz disclosed to JC. The doctor pushed an X-Ray toward him. "It drew some blood, but it wasn't the cause of death. It could have knocked him unconscious."

"This is what caught my attention," Platz said as he looked up at JC. Then, he pulled his glasses down from his forehead and skimmed his report. "There are some burns around your friend's mouth." He glanced at JC to see if his choice of words were insensitive. JC's expression hadn't changed.

"Some other bruises, like he'd been in a fight," he muttered. "But here, burns around his mouth," the doctor was pointing to his file. "They were difficult to see because of his beard, but I thought I could faintly smell something."

The medical examiner tossed his glasses onto the desk and leaned back in his chair. "It was the darndest thing. I went about my business, but I kept smelling that subtle aroma. Then I recognized it. That's what tipped me off to what was going on here."

"What was going on?" JC asked.

Dr. Platz handed JC a page on the toxicology. His finger pointed to a specific section in the blood test. "The burns around the mouth told me he ingested something, willingly or unwillingly." The doctor searched JC's face for a reaction.

"He was unwilling, I suspect," the M.E. shared. "It was chloroform! I found it in the blood and in the lungs. I suspect that it didn't dissipate because he was left out in the cold."

"Chloroform?" JC asked. "Isn't that stuff sort of ... antiquated?"

"Well, yes," Platz chuckled. "They don't use it anymore. It's an anesthetic, but it sounds like you already know that. It was discovered in 1831. We don't use it anymore because it takes a long time to take hold. We've found more efficient sedatives now."

"So, someone drops Al with a face full of chloroform and then drags him out in the storm to freeze?" JC asked.

"That's not exactly how it works, except in old movies," the M.E. instructed. "I told you, it works slow.

I suspect that Al's attacker rendered him unconscious first, maybe that blow to the head. Then, if chloroform was applied, it would ensure that the, um, victim would be unconscious for some time. He could sleep for hours."

"Or, forever," JC mumbled.

"But that's not all," the medical examiner offered, "there are signs of suffocation. That's another thing that separates this from simple hypothermia. There are clear marks in his eyes of hypoxia. The cold probably finished him off, but there's also a little water in his lungs." The doctor raised his arms, almost in surrender. "I'm still working all of this out, but it's a homicide. This was no accident."

JC left the hospital thinking over the possibilities. It had been two days, and law officers had failed to find anyone who gave Al a ride into Yellowstone Park. In a small community like this, JC was told that someone should have come forward in a few hours. Someone innocent, that is.

Al could have been carried to the spot where he was found by a snowmobile. The same storm that might have killed Al would also have covered up the tracks of his killer. And he could have come from any direction.

The scenario had a familiar ring to it, JC thought. It was the same theory Al described to explain Sally Decker's death. He said that she could have been carried by snowmobile to the ski run where her body was found. She was left to freeze to death.

Did that mean that whoever killed Al killed Sally Decker? "Why would anyone want to do that?" JC asked himself.

As he pulled away in his car, he continued to puzzle over connections between the deaths. Then his thoughts drifted to the clock his boss had told him was ticking. He wondered how long he'd be allowed to stay in Montana. He thought about Father Arthur's words, "But God gives us eternity."

40

Only two patrol cars from the Sierra County Sheriff's Office were posted outside the gate belonging to Benedict's Brigade. The standoff had been going on for two weeks now. Sentries inside the compound were seen occasionally by law officers on the other side of the gate. They mostly stayed out of sight, but definitely within shooting distance.

The FBI had arrived to assess the situation. They weren't interested in getting involved.

"After Waco and Ruby Ridge," an FBI agent told Deputy Cochran, "we just consider these guys enthusiastic gun collectors. Tell them to have a nice day. Let us know if you need our help."

The FBI departed, aside from one agent. She was left to keep an eye on things. It was, after all, federal land.

After JC's evening live shot in Sierra, he headed back to the home of Soozie Pine. A nine-year-old answered the door. He was wearing a Denver Broncos jersey, Al's favorite football team.

"He said that's how he wanted his daddy to see him from heaven," Soozie told JC with a sad smile.

"Watch your brother," she told the oldest three as she nodded toward the three-year-old.

She led JC into the kitchen and out of earshot. Soozie told JC that she wondered how the boys were going to grow up without their father. "They were crazy about him."

"Al came home at night and talked about what a good reporter you are," Soozie said with a sigh. "He told me that he was learning something about murder investigations from you. That wasn't really what he was experienced at, you know."

Her eyes were red from crying, her voice was hoarse from exhaustion. "He always said that you'd be the one to solve the murders."

Then, before kissing his cheek and walking into the next room to check on the children, she said, "Just look out for yourself, JC. Don't make me come to your funeral, too."

JC left the young widow to care for her family. He pulled the front door closed and headed for his car in the driveway. Only, his path was blocked. Shara Adams was standing there.

He thought that her beautiful eyes offset her sad expression.

He approached slowly, and into arms opening to him. They embraced in silence, unaware of how long they held each other. Soozie Pine watched them from the window.

Shara finally lifted her head from JC's chest and quietly said, "Maybe we should talk." She searched for an answer in his eyes. As she held his strong arms, she could feel his despair.

She knew JC like he had let no other know him. They were both aware of that.

The front door of the house opened and Soozie stood there. Shara asked JC to wait for a moment. The two women hugged and cried a little. Then Shara returned, telling JC that she'd been dropped off and would need a ride back to her home.

"She said that she and I would catch up later," Shara divulged of her conversation with Soozie. "Take me home."

They quietly exchanged stories about Al as JC drove toward the ski resort. They did not discuss their predicament. Neither of them knew how to start.

When JC pulled up in front of the log home on the lake, Jumper was scratching at the windowpane inside the front door. As they entered, his wagging tail drummed a steady beat against the wall.

JC and Shara peeled off their coats. Shara let the dog out into the backyard. She put a teapot on the stove and reached for two cups in the cupboard over the sink.

But JC was blocking her path. She walked into his arms. Their lips were only inches apart and they smiled. "Oops," she whispered. And when they kissed, JC felt a world roll off his shoulders.

They were swept away in an emotional avalanche. They undressed each other, slowly, in the kitchen.

He unbuttoned her long black dress and let it spill, helplessly, onto the floor. Then, he pulled her white tee shirt over her head and unfastened her bra.

She pulled off the jacket of his expensive business suit and folded it over a chair. She untied his tie as he gazed at her. She unfastened his cufflinks and pulled his shirt down over his muscular shoulders.

She folded his pants and put them on the chair, too. They held one another, naked.

"You've got to trust me. I need you," she told him. They never spoke of that evening with Trip Lake again. JC was back where he wanted to be.

41

This was worth the risk. He had questions no one else could answer.

JC was on cross-country skis following a creek bed. It was a path he was becoming familiar with. That made it easier, along with a three-quarters moon that illuminated the snow. He and Al had cross-country skied under a bright moon a dozen times. JC was alone on this trip.

MURDER ON SKIS

The lights of groomers were visible from a distant peak. He knew that would be Bridger Bowl, the great nonprofit resort where the locals skied.

JC wanted to know who killed Al, and he knew someone who might provide an answer.

After leaving his car parked along the road, JC had been pushing through the woods for an hour. He finally began to see lights from the encampment ahead.

This time, he needed to find a cabin that was closer to the middle of the camp. It would be more difficult to advance unseen.

Still, the cabins were side-by-side along the only road in and out. He'd approach from the back.

The camp at this hour was quiet. He didn't see a soul outside. Behind the line of cabins, he stood amongst the trees. He examined the lone windows each identical cabin had in the rear. He was seeking a particular profile.

When he found it, he buried his skis, cautiously worked his way around to the front door and knocked.

The door opened and Spook's face appeared. He had his shirt off and blocked the entrance. He peered at something, or someone, behind the door.

He looked at JC again, expressionless. A man appeared behind Hemingway. They gave each other a kiss on the lips and the man walked out, disappearing into the night.

"Well, now you know my secret," Hemingway said without any sign of embarrassment. "How about one of yours?"

"I'm here, aren't I? You can call the guards at any time," said JC.

"Quite right," Spook said with half a smile. He backed away from the door and allowed JC to enter.

"This doesn't change any ..." Hemingway searched for words.

"I couldn't care less," JC assured him. Spook nodded and reached for a shirt to put on.

The bed was unmade in the one-room cabin. Hemingway walked across the small space to a workbench. He flipped on a light and sat on a stool. His back was to JC. He was inspecting something he had picked up off the bench.

"It's not fun anymore, is it?" Hemingway asked, still looking over his work.

"What?" JC asked.

Spook swiveled his seat to face the reporter. "The game isn't as fun when you lose, when it touches you."

JC was still standing, not pleased with the reference to his friend's death as a game.

Hemingway picked that up. "Come on, you were enjoying yourself, playing detective." He brushed the hair out of his eyes. "You didn't even know the people who died, until now."

JC thought to himself that there might be more than a grain of truth in what Spook spoke. Until now, it had been an adventure with no admission fee.

JC had never met Marsha Prospect or Harvard Harrison or Sally Decker. In fact, he could name a hundred more people whose deaths, over the years, he'd reported in the news. He felt the inhumanity of it, but there was no personal cost at their loss. In fact, he was paid well to tell others about it.

"You gained in stature every time you went on television to talk about it," Hemingway stated. "I've seen you. You're good. You look authoritative, even a little brave for speaking about it"

The militiaman turned back to the workbench. "It isn't a game anymore, though, is it? But guess what ... it is to him."

Hemingway reached for the lamp over the workbench and turned it off. He grabbed a dirty towel and wiped his hands with it, now looking at JC.

"He's starting to enjoy himself," the captain said. "If you don't catch him soon, it's only gonna get uglier."

JC listened as he peered out a window of Hemingway's cabin. There was a thin layer of ice on the glass. JC scratched some of it off with his fingernail.

"So, why can't the cops catch him?" JC asked, turning to face the man.

"Because he's smarter than they are," the captain responded. "He's smarter than you are. But that doesn't have to be the way it is. That's just the way it is now."

JC told Hemingway, "You were right about the tape recorder and the spot for the cartridges inside."

Spook smiled, pleased with himself. "Alright," Hemingway said in a condescending voice, like a mother comforting her child: "Tell Demolition Man everything you know. We'll make it better."

"Demolition Man?" JC asked.

"It's kind of my nickname around here," Hemingway answered, with a mix of embarrassment and pride.

JC told Hemingway everything he'd learned, up to this point. He emphasized the parts he needed help with, like the chemicals. He also told Hemingway that investigators were taking another look at Harvard Harrison's death.

"Was that your idea?" Hemingway asked. "Might there be an alternative notion to the ski patrol hitting that poor sap with a shell from a half-mile away?" Now he sounded quite sarcastic.

"After our last discussion," JC acknowledged, "yeah, I gave them your version."

"Well good," Hemingway told him. "You're not as stupid as you look."

Hemingway got up and began to walk around the small cabin, thinking aloud. "Look, the body of this extreme skier wannabe was the first to be found." He looked at JC to confirm his recollection. JC nodded. "At the time," Hemingway continued, "it made more sense to say Harrison's death was an accident, because that's the only way people died here in Sierra. Vacationers kill themselves here all the time, but no one is murdered."

The captain held up his forefinger, to make his point: "But we have to reconsider everything now, don't we? Because we know that there is a murderer in our midst. And he has an appetite for the exotic."

"So, who are our suspects?" Hemingway asked. "Someone who can get his hands on chloroform, prussic acid, mercury switches and maybe C-4."

"C-4?" JC asked.

"Do they know what blew up the backcountry skier?" Hemingway asked.

"Not right now. The official explanation is still the ... official one," JC answered. "But they're exhuming his body to take another look."

"Good. If it were me," Harrison declared, "I'd use C-4 to make a skier-kabob."

"At the time," JC told Hemingway, "the ski patrol guys thought they heard three blasts. They'd only fired two shells, though. Jones told me that they thought the extra sound was an echo."

"It wasn't an echo," Hemingway said emphatically. "Think about it. It was the bomb going off. They heard the shell, that's explosion number one. They heard another shell, that's explosion number two. Then, they heard the C-4 going off. That's explosion number three."

JC thought about this. It made sense, he thought. But they didn't have proof.

"You say that they think Harrison was hit in the back with the shell?" Hemingway asked.

JC confirmed that.

"Did you say he was wearing a backpack?" Hemingway asked.

"The medical examiner said that they found pieces of it. He always wore one," JC told him.

Hemingway thought for a moment, "That's where the bomb was, in the backpack."

"Are you sure?" JC asked.

"It could have been sewn in his underwear, but I think he would have noticed," the captain said sarcastically. "Someone may have slipped the C-4, with a trigger, into his backpack before he got on that gondola. That's how I would have done it."

Hemingway pointed in the direction of his camp's own dining hall, "There are more rooms in that basement you visited. Do you know how much C-4 is stolen from the U.S. Army each year?"

JC shook his head no.

"Neither does the Army. They think it's about four thousand pounds in the past ten years. But law enforcement has recovered nearly five thousand pounds in the same time. They don't even know how much of the stuff is missing."

Hemingway walked to his workbench and picked up a catalogue. "Anyone can buy black powder for twenty dollars a pound. They can buy detonating cord and blasting caps. This is not expensive stuff!"

JC informed Hemingway that he'd been looking in bookstores and online.

"Right!" Hemingway concurred. "They tell you how to build bombs!"

"It's our First Amendment right," JC said, sort of shaking his head at the same constitutional amendment that assured a free press and free news media."

JC exhaled. Explosives were not in his skill set. "How do I prove that C-4 was in Harrison's backpack when the whole thing was blown up?"

"Not that hard," Hemingway told him. "You said that they're going to do an autopsy back in Massachusetts?"

"Yeah, Berkshire County, where his body was shipped. That's where he grew up," JC informed him.

Hemingway was leaning against the wall of his cabin. His arms were crossed. He told JC, "Bombs destroy everything around them, but they can't destroy themselves."

The man in camouflage became a little more animated. "The bomb leaves traces of itself everywhere. You can find it in the bodies, in the woodwork, the sheetrock, wires, plastic, metal, powder residue."

"Right, bodies are sponges. Al and Cochran told me a little about that," JC said. He winced a bit at the reminder that Al was gone.

"Yes!" responded the teacher, proud of his pupil.

"If the bomb was in a metal can, we'll find fragments of the metal. If the bomb was in a glass tube, we'll find shards of glass," JC offered.

"Without fail," Spook told him.

JC walked back over to the window. He saw four figures walking outside, laughing and slapping each other on the back. They were walking toward an expensive red 4x4 Land Rover.

JC squinted to take a closer look. "Is that Paul Prospect with General Smith?"

Hemingway looked toward the window but didn't move away from his perch on the wall. JC surmised that he'd seen it before. "Yeah."

JC looked at the captain. "What's he doing here?"

Hemingway shrugged. "He comes and goes. He likes to bring his buddies here to shoot guns. In return, he writes the general a generous check."

"What about the standoff, the roadblock?" JC inquired, still disbelieving. He had just skied through the woods for an hour to avoid detection. Prospect drove his Land Rover through the front gate?

"They don't care," Hemingway said, waving his hand in the direction of the gate, the sentries and the sheriff's deputies. "We're getting food deliveries and beer trucks. Yesterday, a guy even came to fix our video poker game in the dining hall. Third time, mind you. Damn things keep blowing fuses. Anyway, the deputies aren't exactly guarding the Berlin Wall."

Hemingway caught JC staring at him. "What?" the militiaman snapped.

"Did you really get a degree in biochemistry?" JC asked.

"Graduate degree. Ph.D.," Spook corrected. "Why, don't think I'm smart enough?"

"You're smarter than me," JC answered.

"Damn straight," Hemingway glared.

"So, why aren't you working in the private sector for good money?" JC asked.

Hemingway snapped, "I don't wear a suit and I don't work for idiots."

JC thought that Hemingway practiced his own brand of conceit. He wasn't pompous like Paul Prospect. But JC could understand how Hemingway wound up in a camp of renegades. Who else would have him?

"So, why didn't you stay in the Army?" JC asked.

"I hate the Army. I just like to blow up stuff," he answered tersely. "And I know what you're thinking, why do I answer to General Smith if I won't work for idiots. "

"Since you brought it up ..." JC replied.

"I don't work for Smith. He can't order me to do anything," Hemingway snarled. "He's a bigger coward than he is an idiot. But he likes having me around. I know how to work his toys. I make him feel powerful."

Hemingway looked out the frosted window. "We take recruits out in the woods and blow up a couple of trees and then they write the general a fat check."

"You're good for business," JC said.

"I'm great for business," Hemingway's smile returned.

"So, here it's like every day is the Fourth of July," JC said. "And you love the Fourth of July."

"You're catching on," the captain said. Then, a look came to his face suggesting he'd remembered something. "By the way, chloroform is extremely flammable. You did say chloroform. And any self-respecting bomb maker has some sitting around."

Chloroform was found in Al's system, JC thought. He wondered aloud, "Could Al have found the bomb maker?"

"Very possible," Hemingway nodded. "And the bomb maker wouldn't have taken that lightly."

"Who is it?" JC asked.

"I don't know," Hemingway responded. "Like I said, probably the guy who burglarized my stockroom."

"But he's not hiding," Hemingway added. "He's showing off. Each murder is done a certain way on purpose."

"How so?" JC asked.

"Look at it," Hemingway answered. "The backcountry skier was a tech geek. He was blown up with a tech bomb. Why not just shoot him with a .22 in the parking lot? It's like the killer wanted to show that he was smarter than the egghead."

Marsha Prospect's murder, Hemingway told JC, might have to do with a particular song that was playing on the tape recorder when she inhaled the deadly fumes. "Do you know what song was playing?" Hemingway asked.

JC shook his head no.

"Your friend, however," Hemingway continued, "he was an expert outdoorsman. Ironic that he was found dead outdoors, isn't it?"

JC saw the pattern. Hemingway told him, "Your killer has a twisted sense of humor. If I wasn't so well-adjusted, I'd be rooting for him. He does have a certain panache."

The captain told JC, if he knew what he was looking for, he'd find the killer's fingerprints all over his victims.

Hemingway said, "Dead men do tell tales."

42

Dr. Platz was accustomed to seeing gruesome things. His role as medical examiner in Sierra County brought him disfigured corpses pulled from airplanes, from the water, the snow, and the foot of cliffs.

There were hunting accidents, skiing accidents, climbing accidents, swimming accidents and plane crashes. There was the rare suicide but rarely a murder.

He treated anyone before him on his stainless steel table as a soul, and someone who had been loved.

Platz found his life fascinating. He loved carrying out his duties as a small-town general practitioner as well as the county medical examiner. Wearing those two hats, he had signed birth certificates as he brought babies into the world. And years later, he signed their death certificates upon their exit.

Presently, he found this phone call with the medical examiner in Berkshire County, Massachusetts, captivating.

"You don't say," Bob Platz said into the speakerphone. He was jotting down notes, even knowing that modern medicine had email. The autopsy report on Harvard Harrison would arrive only minutes after he hung up the phone.

"I didn't know that," Platz told his colleague two thousand miles away. "Flecks of yellow plastic, huh?"

Deputy Cochran entered Dr. Platz's office. They exchanged a silent salute and Cochran sat down while Platz was on the phone.

When the medical examiner hung up, he smiled at the deputy and said, "Thanks for coming down. I figured that you'd want to see this, as soon as possible."

"I do," Cochran replied. "What have you got?"

The medical examiner pulled down his bifocals and started searching the screen on his computer, looking for the email from Massachusetts.

"Here it is. I'll print it out for you while I tell you what's in it," the doctor said.

Platz stood and walked to the printer. It wasn't a long report. He pulled the paper off the printer and handed it across his desk to Cochran.

"You'll see," the doctor said. "They found tiny flecks of yellow plastic embedded in the remains of Mr. Harrison. They also found tiny strands of copper wire."

Cochran looked up from the paperwork. "There's no yellow plastic in the shells the ski patrol fires from its Howitzers."

"No," the medical examiner agreed. He turned his eyes back to the report. "No, and there is also residue that the M.E. thinks is from the explosive, C-4. He asked an FBI agent to come to his office. They both think they're looking at the ingredients of a bomb, not a Howitzer shell. You'll be getting a report summarizing that conclusion, as will the FBI and the ATF."

Dr. Platz would also be calling JC Snow. The doctor knew that the second look at Harrison's death was Snow's idea.

"So," said Cochran, "the ski patrol members are exonerated. They didn't kill this guy?"

"That would appear to be so," Dr. Platz responded, still looking at the report on his computer screen.

"Thanks, Doc," Cochran said as he stood up and headed out of the office.

"Don't mention it," the M.E. responded as he reached for the phone.

"C-4, huh?" JC had been awakened by the call. He was in Shara Adam's bed. She was gone.

The medical examiner told JC that all the ingredients needed to build a bomb were found, in tiny pieces, embedded in Harvard Harrison's body. The doctor said, "That includes C-4. How did you know that?"

"I've got a guy, Doctor," JC said as he avoided identifying his source.

"Smart guy," the doctor said.

43

"It's getting pretty steamy, isn't it?" Kit the bartender asked Shara as they cleaned up after the breakfast rush.

"It sure is," she told him, daydreaming.

"Wait, what are we talking about?" she suddenly asked Kit.

"Well, I was talking about you running that water in the sink until it's too hot," Kit said with a devilish grin. "But what were you talking about? It sounds more interesting."

Shara's face flushed. She was embarrassed. It was true. She was daydreaming about her night with JC. He was still in her bed when she left for work.

The sun was shining through the big windows in the bar. Skiers who came in for a rest had the beginnings of a sunburn on their faces.

They walked to their table with loud clomps as they rhythmically lifted one heavy ski boot and then the other. They were peeling off sweaty layers of clothing.

It was a warm day for late February. A few weeks before, a weather-forecasting rodent had predicted an early spring.

Shara squinted into the bright sun to watch skiers outside her window. She was looking forward to the "Dick and Jane Downhill." The ski race for Sierra locals was coming up tomorrow.

Each year, it was billed as a "battle of the sexes." Men would race against women but the men would be saddled with a time handicap.

Shara was pondering her ski wax. She thought the snow would get wet this afternoon, in the sun, and then freeze overnight. She needed to look at the weather forecast for tomorrow and decide what the temperature would be when the race started.

JC was racing for the men. She wanted to beat him. She'd begun to wage psychological warfare that morning. She'd left a message for him while he was still in bed.

A phone, ringing in the bar's kitchen, jolted Shara into the present. She hustled across the plastic mats on the floor to answer it.

She recognized the voice on the other end, it was Bill Peck. "Hi Bill."

"Hi Shara. I borrowed my dad's pickup truck, but I have no use for the black Labrador sleeping in the back. Do you want him?"

"Oh brother," Shara exclaimed. "I'm sorry. Where are you?"

Peck told her that he was at home. "Take your time, Jumper's sacked out in the back of the truck with the sun shining on him. He looks pretty content."

Shara asked Peck what the fastest way was to his new home. She jotted the directions on a blank order pad that belonged to a waiter. She tore the paper off the pad, grabbed a fleece vest off the wall and pushed her way through the swinging doors leading back to the bar.

"Kit, I've got to go pick up Jumper. He hopped into someone's pickup truck again," she told her bartender as he was washing glasses.

"OK," Kit responded with a smile, not even looking up. He knew the drill.

As Shara climbed into her truck, the driver of a passing pickup honked his horn and waved. Shara waved back. She shook her head. She recognized that truck from a similar escapade of Jumper's last fall.

JC dragged himself out of Shara's bed when his phone rang again. It was the TV station in Denver.

"OK, JC," the voice said. "We gave you time until your friend's funeral. That was out of respect."

It was the news director. "You've got to come home."

"Are you out of our mind?" JC spit back.

The news director assured JC that he was not mindless, "But I'm penniless. I may not be able to pay for another out-of-town story for three years! You've cleaned me out!"

JC argued that the murders seemed to be the work of a serial killer. He shared insights that he couldn't report yet.

Nothing was swaying his boss from his position.

"You sent me here to do a job," JC asserted. "The job isn't done!"

"You've got to come home, JC. I'm pulling the plug," the supervisor said.

JC was furious. "You can pull the plug, but you can't bring me home. You don't have that big an army." The reporter terminated the call. "Uh, oh," he thought to himself.

He squinted past the lace curtains at the bright sun bouncing off the white snow. He allowed his pulse to return to normal. He told himself that he couldn't worry about spilled milk while there was work to do. "The best defense is a good offense," he told himself.

He walked into the bathroom and turned on the hot water in the sink. Steam rose from the wash basin. As it rolled up the mirror, JC could make out writing scribbled on the glass. It said, "Girls shine, boys whine. Xxxoo"

He forgot about the phone call.

44

Loose ends needed to be tied up. How much time had he purchased with his confrontation with this boss? Maybe two days?

JC woke up with a feeling that he knew who the killer was. But he didn't have enough evidence, not even enough to convince himself.

And he couldn't make sense out of Sally Decker's murder. Where did she fit in? Or did she fit in at all?

He shaved and jumped in the shower. He still had wet hair when he arrived at the sheriff's office. Cochran was waiting for him.

They settled into an office that had been set aside for the investigation. Some of the evidence was laid out in plastic bags. Pictures of the victims were posted on a board.

Cochran was glad that the room was empty except for the two of them. He didn't mind sharing ideas with JC, but he didn't like his colleagues listening or even seeing them together. Cochran never forgot that JC was a journalist, and journalists were generally the enemy.

But Cochran appreciated that JC had shared clues he had gathered independent of the police investigation. And Cochran thought the reporter's instincts were a class above those of the law enforcers the deputy was working with.

Cochran and JC sat at more old furniture and shared notes on the bomb that must have killed Harrison. "I'm being told that copper is rather commonplace," Cochran said. "But the yellow plastic might narrow the field."

The deputy changed the subject: "Trip Lake has taken off. He didn't go to Utah, regardless of what he told you. We can't find him."

"Why would he lie to me if he's innocent?" JC asked. "Why would he even leave here? I told him how it would look."

"And it does," the deputy responded.

JC looked at the evidence positioned on top of some battered metal cabinets. There were two metal tubes from the tape recorder, all in plastic bags. The cardboard box placed on Marsha Prospect's gondola was there, too, now also in plastic.

"Did you figure out what song was playing in the tape recorder?" JC asked.

"The best we can figure," Cochran told him, "it was a disco song that had pieces from an old tune about a gambler."

"Really?" JC thought of Hemingway. He was right again. He shared Spook's advice with Cochran, to look for a pattern in the methods of killing, like the murderer was enjoying himself, playing a game.

"You see a pattern in the disco music?" Cochran asked.

"Gamblers like to play at casinos," JC speculated. "And we have two guys who stand to make a lot of money building a new casino." The deputy's face brightened.

"Marsha Prospect was opposed to expanding gambling at the ski resort," JC continued. "Maybe they thought she stood in their way."

JC turned his attention to the murder that had only recently been reclassified as a homicide. "There is something about Harrison. Now we know he was killed by a bomb. We don't know why, but I have a suspicion."

"What?" Cochran asked.

"If I tell you," JC said, "can you check it out?"

"Of course," Cochran answered.

"And tell me the outcome?" JC pressed.

"Oh," the deputy said in a disappointed tone. He thought for about twenty seconds. Then he exhaled and said, "OK. This could really get me in trouble with my superiors, you know." JC smiled, and shared his theory.

"I tell you what," Cochran said in a whisper, like they were conspiring. "Give me an hour. I'll make some calls. Then come back. If you're right, it puts this guy in a bad light."

Now JC had an hour, and he knew how he should spend it. In fact, he thought that it was a visit he should have made weeks ago.

He drove outside of Sierra. He arrived at an area that wasn't particularly pretty. He suspected that the land was cheap. It was covered by scrub brush. The relentless wind had blown the snow somewhere else, exposing dry brown dirt between the struggling plants.

He pulled up to a mobile home. There were some toys scattered in the yard. A lazy dog was tied to a rope and sleeping in a spot warmed by the sun. There were two cars parked, but tire tracks told JC that two or three others frequently parked there.

He knocked on the metal door. When it opened, his face was hit with a wall of radiated heat. It came with odors. He smelled something burning on the stove, and cats, and perhaps urine.

A teenaged girl with dirty hair held the door handle from the inside. JC thought that he was being sized up. He got the impression that the teenager was experienced in slamming the door on an unwanted visitor's face.

"Aunt Clemma!" the girl shouted. JC wondered whether that volume of voice indicated Aunt Clemma was at the other end of the medium-sized trailer or perhaps over the next hill.

A woman shortly emerged from behind the door. She was in her sixties. She wore sweatpants that didn't look very clean, over a bulging midsection. She wore a blouse that had some sauce splattered on it. JC supposed that she was the one burning whatever was on the stove.

JC introduced himself. He told Aunt Clemma that he wanted to talk about Sally Decker.

"Yes?" the woman said without emotion.

"I'm sorry for your loss. Did she live here?" JC asked.

"Thank you, yes she did."

"Is she a relative?" JC inquired.

"My niece," the woman told him. So, JC thought, the teenager who answered the door might be Decker's sister.

JC figured he was probably not going to be invited in, if he hadn't been by now. It wasn't a place he was absolutely dying to enter, either. Aside from the smell, and a room temperature that would roast a side of beef, there were a number of small dirty children sitting on a worn couch. They were watching cartoons. JC knew this was a school day. He wondered why they weren't there.

While JC exchanged small talk with the woman, he scanned the trailer to see what he might learn. He saw a number of envelopes on the nearby counter. They looked to him like they were bills. His experience taught him that bills piled on a kitchen counter were usually unpaid bills.

"Does Sally's mother live here?" JC asked. The aunt's face turned glum, but she didn't say anything.

"She's in jail," one of the dirty children on the couch shouted, and the others joined him laughing.

"How long?" JC asked Aunt Clemma.

"Two years, so far," she told him. That ruled out mom as Sally's killer, JC thought to himself.

"Any idea of who would want to hurt Sally?" JC asked her.

The woman just slowly shook her head no.

"There's my dad!" JC saw one of the boys on the couch point at the television excitedly. The other youngsters started to laugh. One of them scolded him in a child's voice, "He's not your dad." The children laughed harder.

JC recognized the voice coming from the TV. He looked in that direction, but he couldn't see the picture.

"Is that Bill Peck?" he asked the woman.

She glanced at the TV, already knowing the answer. "Yeah, that's Mr. Bigshot," she said with a growl.

"Is that true? Is he the father of one of the boys?" JC asked.

The unkempt woman just laughed, "Wouldn't that solve our problems. Ha! No, he used to date my niece."

"Sally?" JC asked, with renewed interest.

"Oh yeah," Aunt Clemma answered. "They were a hot item in high school. He followed her around like a puppy!" Aunt Clemma laughed at the thought. So did some of the children who were eavesdropping.

"When's the last time she saw him?" JC inquired.

"Oh, years passed," she told the reporter. "But, then he started making a nuisance of himself again. I know it's hard to believe, coming out of here, but she was a looker. She was a beauty. Good figure. Ha!" She patted her own belly. "Don't know where she got that."

JC made a note to himself to find a picture of Decker. He had neglected to. And yes, sizing up the worn trailer, it was hard to believe.

"So, how recently had they seen each other?" JC asked.

"Up to the time she left for California," the aunt told him.

"But she didn't go to California," JC reminded her.

"Yeah, but we thought she did," she reminded him.

"So," JC tried again, "how long before Sally disappeared had Sally seen Bill Peck?"

"Omphf," was the sound the aunt seemed to make. "She'd had enough of him. She agreed to go out on a couple of dates with him. I mean, it would be nice if she married a rich guy." Aunt Clemma waved her arm at what he assumed were unpaid bills.

"But," Clemma continued, "she thought he was kind of creepy. She didn't want to go out with him anymore, but he kept insisting. Finally, she told us she was going to go to California and stay with a friend."

"Did Sally say," JC asked, "how Mr. Peck took the rejection?"

"Oh," the aunt told him, "she said he didn't take it well at all. She said he was mad. It scared her."

"Did he ever hurt her?" JC asked.

"I wouldn't know," the aunt said. "But she said he had a real temper, if he didn't get what he wanted. You know how rich people are."

Aunt Clemma didn't know any more. But JC had heard the answer to his suspicions. As he said his goodbyes, JC pulled a fifty-dollar bill from his wallet and handed it to the woman. "Maybe it will pay one of those," he said, in a kind voice, as he pointed to the pile of bills.

"Oh, it will take more than this," she told him, "but thank you."

45

"Wait until you hear this," JC told Deputy Cochran. They were back in the office with the evidence and the board with the murder victims' pictures. They were alone.

"Peck used to date Sally Decker," JC informed the deputy.

Cochran leaned forward in his seat. His face showed his interest. JC told him the rest: "And Decker's aunt says Peck was angry when Sally rejected him. Aunt

Clemma also said that Sally had told her that Peck had a bad temper."

"Well, then you'll be interested to hear this," Cochran told JC. "You were right. Harrison was gambling on Peck's machines almost every night at the Sheep Ranch."

"And going home with money every night," JC added.

Cochran nodded as he shuffled some papers in front of him, "I spoke with the chief detective up in Kalispell. They think Harrison is the same guy who won a fortune from Peck's machines up there. Then he disappeared."

"Could Peck have known he was the same guy?" JC asked. "If Peck saw him at Grizzly Mountain, he might not have wanted to get taken to the cleaners twice."

"Harrison seemed to have a system. He matches the description of a guy who got run out of Las Vegas last year," the deputy said. "Different name, but it looks like him on the grainy security camera photos."

"So, his winnings at the Sheep Ranch, just fifty or seventy five dollars a night," JC theorized, "might have been test runs, with the big score still to come."

"Peck probably installed some new safeguards after Kalispell, and Harrison was trying to figure out a way around them," Cochran agreed.

JC rubbed his face. "So, if it's Peck, was he acting alone, or did he have help?"

"I'd like to know how he got the ingredients for these bombs," Cochran thought out loud.

"I've got a couple of ideas about that." JC told Cochran about seeing Paul Prospect at the compound of Benedict's Brigade. "That would give him access to all the weapons they have in there, and they have plenty."

"Prospect?" the deputy asked in a disbelieving tone. "Doesn't he have enough money already?"

"What is a prospector," JC shrugged, "if not someone who is desperate to get his hands on something valuable? Prospect could taste that casino."

The reporter also disclosed that there had been a couple of burglaries in that compound, targeting the storage rooms where the militia kept its weapons and more.

"How the hell do you know this?" Cochran asked.

"I told you, there are people who like reporters better than they like police," JC reminded him. Cochran just shook his head.

"Trip Lake could have proved useful, too. He placed that box inside the gondola, and he's got a criminal record," the deputy offered. "He was angry with Marsha Prospect, and he's taken off."

JC agreed. He and Cochran were on the same page. "One more thing," JC asked. "Do you have a picture of Sally Decker?"

Cochran reached into a file. He handed JC a black and white photo, probably from a newspaper. A lovely woman was smiling back at him. JC thought that Aunt Clemma was right, Sally Decker was very attractive.

JC departed from the sheriff's office thinking about one suspect he wasn't willing to divulge: Spook. He'd been a valuable source of information and JC just didn't think he was the killer. JC had to acknowledge, however, that no one had a better skill set required to commit the murders.

As far as JC was aware, law officers didn't even know that Captain Steven Hemingway existed. JC wanted to keep it that way, hoping that he wasn't protecting a psychopath.

JC called Fred Shook, his photographer. JC asked, "Have you heard from the TV station today?"

Shook said, "Yeah, why?"

"Do they want anything from us tonight?" JC asked.

"Yeaaah," Shook replied, like that was a stupid question. It didn't sound like Shook had been informed of the battle JC had waged with their boss a short while ago. JC concluded that the news director had surrendered, this time.

JC gave Shook a shot list for their story that night. They could report new discoveries in the investigation, but they couldn't report all of them.

JC was walking toward the Sheep Ranch. He and Shara had said that they'd squeeze in a couple of ski runs together.

JC had decided, after his battle with the brass, that he'd better skip the skiing. He'd try to share lunch, though.

"I owe you some money," JC said as he walked in. Kit was behind the bar, feeding the lunch crowd. Business was only moderate. It was mid-week. The "long weekend" crowd would be arriving in a day or two.

JC handed Kit the cost of the breakfast that he had walked out on days ago. Kit smiled a little and took the money. He knew that was the moment JC had learned that Al was dead.

"You just missed her," the bartender said. "She went to pick up Jumper. Hang on, let's see where she went."

Kit motioned for JC to follow him into the kitchen. They pushed through the swinging doors. Kit asked the cooks and dishwasher if they knew where Shara went to retrieve her Labrador Retriever.

The kitchen staff shook their heads. Many were from other countries, here for the winter on work visas. JC wondered what ski resorts would do these days if it weren't for the international help.

One said, with a heavy accent and imperfect English, that he saw her take a phone call and scribble something down on some paper.

JC asked where the paper was. The cook pointed to the pad, sitting on a food prep table beneath the wall phone. The top page was missing, but there was a piece of blue carbon paper exposed.

"I wonder if these are the directions that she jotted down," JC said and held the pad up for Kit to see.

The bartender stroked his thick mustache as he read the scribbling. Then he shrugged, "Sorry."

JC pulled the carbon off the pad and smiled. "Can it be that far?"

Kit shook his head, "Nah, somewhere in the foothills over Sierra."

"I can follow the directions," JC said. "I'll take a ride out there, maybe buy them both lunch."

"That dog will follow you home if you buy him lunch once," Kit warned with a smile.

JC drove as he followed the directions on the carbon paper. He didn't know this side of town. The sun was shining. Melting snow was seeping out onto the road. The sunshine was heating the cabin of his SUV, too. He reached for a water bottle he'd grabbed at Shara's house.

It was a yellow plastic water bottle with the Peckerhead logo on it. He sucked on the plastic straw.

He remembered that Shara told him she had been given the bottle from Peck, at a promotion in her bar.

Harrison had won one. That was the night before he died.

JC thought about the unsolved burglaries at the militia compound. Hemingway had told him that guards let someone into the compound to fix their video gaming machines. Peck's gaming machines.

The machines were in the dining hall. The fuse box was in the basement, the same room where lethal ingredients to make bombs had been stolen.

"Peck even told me he was doing his own service calls," JC said to himself.

"Yellow flecks of plastic," JC remembered the medical examiner saying, recalling the results of Harrison's autopsy. JC slowly pulled the water bottle away from his mouth, a yellow water bottle.

"He switched Harrison's water bottle that morning," JC said to himself. "One with water exchanged for one with the explosive. Easy to do, if Harrison left his backpack for only a moment. A trip to the bathroom, the cafeteria for an egg sandwich. Maybe to go buy a lift ticket. People leave their gear unattended at ski lodges all the time."

A disco song about a gambler. JC thought, "Wasn't that the song Cochran said was playing in the tape recorder?" Marsha Prospect probably was standing in the way of the casino, a place where gamblers go.

"Is he our man?" JC wondered.

JC's phone rang. It was Kit from the bar, "Hey JC, I suddenly realized where those directions on the carbon lead. I do construction during the summer. I helped build that place. It's Bill Peck's new house. Really nice."

"My God," JC blurted. He wasn't going to lose Shara again.

46

Shara was following the directions that Peck had given her over the phone. She was looking forward to taking a peek at the new home. She'd heard that it was stunning.

Peck had no intention of harming Shara Adams. He was having a marvelous day. His problems had been blown away like a summer breeze, he thought with a chuckle.

Peck gave Shara the creeps. He had badgered her to put more games in the bar. She'd refused, but he wouldn't take no for an answer. He seemed to take it so personally, she thought.

She even felt that Peck had a bit of a crush on her. He seemed lonely. But the thought of kissing Peck's big mouth made Shara shudder as she drove toward the mountain house.

She pulled her pickup truck into the driveway of the shining new log mansion. "Wow," she said to herself. "He's this rich? Well, money can't buy class."

She parked behind a faded blue pickup truck with too many dents to count. She climbed out of her own truck and stuffed a tennis ball into her fleece pullover.

Slowly, a furry black head with sleepy eyes rose above the tailgate of Peck's pickup. Shara could hear the dog's tail wagging, banging against the metal bed of the truck.

Shara patted her dog's stomach and gave him a kiss on the forehead. Then the sleepy animal rolled back on his side in the warm sun.

"Hello?" Shara called. There was no answer.

The house was cut into the hillside. It had large timbers and stone. The living quarters were on the second floor, above the garage.

Shara carefully walked into Peck's garage through an open door. She expected to find him there, but the space was empty.

She spied a wooden workbench. Some of it looked like a chemistry lab, she thought. There were glass flasks, rubber tubes and a Bunsen burner. There were also pieces of metal pipe and an assortment of powders and liquids in jars.

She figured that it must suit the needs of a tech geek.

She heard a door open to the stairs leading down from the living quarters into the garage. "Bill, is that you?" she asked.

Bill Peck appeared, climbing down the stairs. He had a smile on his face. He was pulling on a big down jacket.

"Hi," she said with her best smile. "Thanks for calling." She looked over her shoulder and out the garage door.

There, Jumper slowly rose to his feet in the back of the faded truck. He yawned and stretched. Then he placed his front paws over the tailgate and the rest of him spilled out into the driveway.

Shara turned her attention back to Peck and said, "He does this all the time." Jumper stood in the doorway, looking at them. He was holding one of Peck's work gloves in his mouth.

"Oh brother," Shara said to Peck. She shouted at the dog, "Jumper, drop that!" The dog obeyed.

Shara, rather impressed with her command over her animal, walked over to pick up the glove and hand it to Peck. "He wants us to play with him. He wants us to chase him. Sorry."

Shara made small talk before intending to depart. "Are you going to race in the Dick and Jane Downhill?" She doubted that he was. Residents of the valley all knew that Peck had none of his famous father's athletic ability.

He told Shara that he did not think that he'd be participating.

Jumper was now nosing around the woodpile behind Peck. Shara was keeping an eye on her pet. She couldn't think of much trouble he could cause in a woodpile.

The black Lab began pulling something out from behind the stack of logs. Shara interrupted Peck's story about skiing and shouted, "Jumper, drop it!"

Peck looked over his shoulder and thought to himself that in all the excitement, he hadn't moved the jacket.

The dog was now standing next to the wood pile with a red down jacket in his mouth. The coat had a white cross on the back.

Shara recognized it in an instant. She turned to Peck, confused, "You're not on the ski pa ..."

Peck wheeled and grabbed Shara's arms. He pulled her against his body and into his control. She couldn't move, and it frightened her.

Shara was thinking of all the pieces of the murder investigation that JC had shared with her. "The ski patrol jacket ..." She said it as she looked into Peck's twisted face. His teeth were showing. Spit was oozing out between them.

Shara pushed Peck away to gain just enough space. She raised a swift knee between his legs. He groaned and she escaped his grip.

She began to run. All she heard was the sound of her heavy breathing, but that was disrupted by the crack of a single gunshot.

"The next one goes in his head," Peck shouted.

Shara stopped and looked around for Jumper. He had been running after her. He stopped when she stopped. The dog was lying down, scared but unharmed by the gunshot.

Shara slowly turned to face Peck. "You have no idea how good a shot I am," he said. "What else is a boy to do, growing up when he had no friends?"

Peck slowly approached her. The rifle was still trained on the dog. "I like Jumper, I really do," he said. "It would be a shame."

"You know," he stated, "I've fired my guns here any number of times. No one has ever inquired as to its origins. No one has ever called to see if I'm alright."

He spoke confidently. "I guess they think gunfire in these hills isn't unusual. Maybe they think I'm sighting my rifle for hunting season."

Peck began to laugh. "Oh, you heard that I don't like to hunt, didn't you? I just don't like to hunt with my father." Peck smiled at the irony.

Peck grabbed Shara by the wrist. His grip hurt her. He stroked the skin of her neck with the rifle and muttered, "What am I going to do with you?"

Shara heard Jumper growling. He was behind Peck now, slowly approaching in a crouch and showing his teeth.

Peck heard it, too. He released his grip on the woman, swung and pointed his rifle at the dog.

"No!" Shara shouted, just as the gunshot echoed through the valley. But she was able to strike Peck's arm as he pulled the trigger.

The bullet struck a timber in the garage. Shara wrestled with Peck. She kicked him and reached into her pocket to grasp the tennis ball.

She threw it across the road. It rolled down the hillside into some woods. She shouted, "Jumper, get it!" The dog disappeared down the hillside in happy pursuit.

Peck pushed Shara to the driveway from behind. He fired off two shots in frustration, but the bullets harmlessly hit a pair of lodgepole pines.

"OK," Peck growled, "the doggy can live, but he'll be an orphan." Peck reached down and grabbed Shara by the arm, jerking her to her feet.

She looked at Peck's face. She'd never seen a face like that before. Full of anger. It was hardly human, she thought.

"I did something nice for you," he said with spit spraying from his large mouth. "Now you're going to do something nice for me."

He pulled his hostage back into the garage. He forced the rifle barrel into the back of her head and forced her toward the staircase.

"Now you'll behave as though your life depends on it," Peck said, "because it does." He pushed her up the stairs.

He forced her through the door and into the kitchen ahead of him. He steered her toward a living room and thrust her down onto a couch. Shara resisted showing her fear.

Peck was breathing hard. He brushed back his hair as he held the rifle in the other hand. "Drink?" he asked with a sudden smile. He abruptly assumed the tone of a gracious host. It terrified her. "He's mad," she thought.

He pulled off his big down coat and tossed it onto a chair. He walked to the bar, still carrying the loaded weapon.

He poured a dark liquor into a pair of small glasses, glancing at her from time to time. Tossing a sardonic smile in her direction, he reached into a small refrigerator and topped the drinks with whipped cream.

"I call this a Mountain Top. See, the whipped cream even looks like a snowy mountain top," he said playfully.

"You can't imagine how many of these I've had to drink alone," he said as he glared at her. "It will be nice to share it with someone I care for." He walked to the couch and extended his hand. It held her drink.

She accepted the glass. What choice did she have? "Drink," he said as he raised his hand in a toast. A tear rolled down Shara's cheek. She was going to die, she knew it.

She sipped the drink. He just stared at her. She allowed her eyes to roam the room. It was huge. The ceiling was two stories tall, supported by large timbers.

The walls were covered by a faded wood, perhaps pilfered from a ghost town. The chandeliers were made of moose antlers.

A fire was roaring at one end of the room. Over the fireplace, there was a large painting of a buffalo stampede.

"You know what I like about my new home best?" Peck asked his guest. Shara weakly shook her head. "The solitude," he answered. "You're talking to a guy who didn't have much company, growing up. Now, I do it on my terms!"

Peck took an energized stroll to some French doors. He opened them, revealing a small balcony. It offered a view of the setting sun.

He stepped onto the balcony and spread his arms. "Don't you love it?"

Then he turned to face the valley and shouted, "Will someone please help this poor woman?"

He laughed and turned back toward her. "No one is going to come to your rescue, if that's what you're thinking."

Shara began to choke back tears. Peck gave her a disappointed look and said, "Don't be boring."

Through her tears, Shara sensed that Peck was near her. She cringed. He was standing at the edge of the couch. She pulled her feet off the floor and tucked them beneath her.

When she looked up, he was holding out some tissues. She accepted them and wiped her eyes. Peck said, "The point is, Shara, I'm your only hope." She looked up at him. He was trying to smile at her with an assuring look. It wasn't working.

He handed her a second drink. "Don't fall behind," he said in a musical tone. She gulped the remainder of her first drink and took the second glass.

"Take off your fleece, stay awhile," he said playfully. She didn't move.

"Really!" he barked. It startled her and she began to pull her fleece over her head. He stared at her but said nothing. She was only wearing a white tee shirt now, with a Sheep Ranch logo on her left breast.

She shivered, and it wasn't the cold.

Peck was standing in front of her with his arms crossed and saying nothing. He seemed to be lost in thought. The fingers of one hand were tapping the other arm. He was mulling over thoughts known only to himself.

He closed the distance between the two of them and reached out one hand. He grabbed the collar of her tee shirt and savagely pulled it toward the floor. She screamed in horror.

The fabric around the back of her collar cut into the skin of her neck. The front of her tee shirt was torn, exposing her bra and the cleavage of her breasts.

She was crying and tried to cover herself with her arms. She shouted between sobs, "Is this going to make you happy?"

Peck now had a puzzled look on his face. "Shara, life isn't motivated by joy, it's motivated by fear."

His demented face showed her that this was the truth as Peck knew it. Shara was so frightened, she could barely breathe. Peck leered. Then, he picked her up by the arms and led her upstairs to the bedroom.

47

JC parked his 4x4 about a hundred yards away from Bill Peck's driveway. Spotting a moist tennis ball by his front wheel, he picked it up by habit and tossed it onto his dashboard.

JC walked up the road, concealed by the snowbank. He paused at the end of the gravel driveway and studied the impressive new home. He didn't see any movement outside the house. He saw Shara's pickup truck parked in the driveway, and he spotted Jumper curled up and sleeping next to the driver's door.

JC scurried to the left side of the truck. It concealed him from the large windows of the house. He approached the black Labrador to keep him from barking. The dog was in a deep sleep. JC rubbed the dog's head.

It was sunset. The low light gave JC some cover. He dashed through the open garage door. Upstairs, he could vaguely hear voices.

He could see a workbench in the garage. He looked up the stairs to be certain he could move unnoticed. On the workbench, the chemistry lab and tools only cemented JC's belief that Peck was the killer. Fingering the bottles and tools, JC considered how intelligent Peck was. He must have constructed his own deadly weapons.

JC's feet brushed something under the bench. It was a dirty red jacket with a white cross on the back. Of course, he thought, it belonged to Greg Jones. Peck must have handed the cardboard box to Trip Lake. He'd stolen Jones' jacket out of the ski patrol locker and disguised himself. That's why no one recognized the ski patroller.

JC knew that he needed to call Deputy Cochran. He reached for the phone in his pocket. He'd have to return to the road and move away from the house so that he wouldn't be overheard.

But he heard a scream. It came from upstairs. He was certain it was Shara's voice. He could hear Peck talking, too.

JC quietly and quickly advanced up the stairs. The door was open, and he slipped into a kitchen.

To his relief, he could see Shara through a doorway, but only barely. She was sitting on the couch, not saying much. JC's view was blocked by the back of Bill Peck.

Peck was holding a rifle. Then, he appeared to gather Shara and push her up the stairs to another level of the house.

JC had to think. He needed a plan. He'd prefer a gun, but he'd have to settle for a plan.

As soon as they disappeared up the staircase, JC quietly dashed across the living room. Maybe he could find a weapon.

Upstairs, he heard a sound familiar to any skier, duct tape. Then he heard footsteps returning to the top of the stairs. Peck was coming back down.

JC rapidly surveyed the big room. He needed a place to hide. As Peck was descending the stairs, JC pressed himself behind large rocks that formed the fireplace.

"I'll be right back, honey," Peck shouted to Shara in a mocking fashion. "Don't move a muscle."

JC saw Peck's back as he crossed the living room, still carrying the rifle. He walked into the kitchen and out of sight. JC seized the opportunity and, looking over his shoulder, ran up the large wooden staircase.

JC looked from one bedroom door to the next. He found Shara, lying on a bed in a sparsely furnished guest room. Peck had taped her wrists and ankles to the brass bedposts.

She saw JC as he entered the room. Her eyes grew large, with both relief and concern.

He tried to gently pull the duct tape from her ankles. "How did you know I was here?" she whispered.

"Kit figured it out," he told her. He pulled the tape from her wrists.

"Oh great, every party has a pooper." The voice came from behind JC. He knew it was Peck's voice.

JC slowly turned around, saw Peck's weapon pointed at him, and sat down on the bed.

"This is not who was supposed to end up in bed with the girl," Peck said sarcastically.

He was holding a different weapon, a handgun. It was the kind synonymous with the Old West, a pearl-handled, silver-plated six-gun.

"Well, honey, I guess our date is over," Peck said snidely to Shara. "I don't think we should see each other anymore."

JC was pulling some duct tape off of his fingers as he said, "Peck, what the hell is wrong with you?"

In a rage, Peck cocked his pistol and shoved it into JC's eye. Peck's face turned red with anger. His hand trembled. Slowly, he pulled the trigger.

"No!" Shara screamed. They heard the hammer strike but the gun didn't discharge.

Peck laughed a demented laugh. JC closed his eyes and exhaled.

"No, we're not going to make a mess in my new house," Peck said lyrically. "Unless we absolutely have to. But I warn you, that was my only empty chamber. I emptied one, just for fun."

"Ironic, isn't it, JC?" Peck swung his gun in a circle. "I mean," Peck said, "you and I have been partners all the time. I did what a man had to do, and let's face it, I added a little fun to the chore." Peck was bragging. "And you are the one I allowed to broadcast it to the world."

"Don't flatter yourself," JC told the gunman.

"Come on, JC," Peck said. "You news people are vultures. If something doesn't get killed, you don't eat."

Then Peck slammed his open hand on top of a dresser in the room and shouted, "OK, everybody up!"

JC picked up a piece of duct tape and used it to close the tear in Shara's tee shirt.

Peck noted the gesture. "Very touching. They don't make 'em like that anymore, do they Shara? Well, there's a reason they're called a dying breed."

The gunman instructed Shara to tape JC's hands together behind his back. Next, Peck taped Shara's hands behind her.

He told the couple to walk down the stairs in front of him. He marched them across the living room, through the kitchen, and down the stairs to the garage.

He directed the couple to lean against one of the wooden posts, back to back. He told them to sit. Peck secured the pair to the post with more duct tape, wrapping it around them over and over.

"Let's see," Peck was tapping the muzzle of the gun against his forehead. "What to do, what to do."

He began to rummage through materials at his work bench.

"Oh, JC," Shara whispered over her shoulder. "I'm so sorry. Thanks for coming to get me, though."

Peck returned, fabricating something with his hands while he talked.

"JC," Peck asked, "have you appreciated my artistic style? Did you figure out my clues? Marsha Prospect's gambling song?"

"You killed Marsha Prospect?" Shara snapped.

Peck sneered back, "She was a small thinker, nothing like her husband. Small thinkers create big problems." His tone turned more conversational again and he smiled. "I like to think I'm a problem solver."

"You're crazy!" Shara spat.

Peck shouted at her, "That's what got Sally Decker killed, a big mouth! She thought she was better than me!"

JC was just nodding to himself. The last mystery solved, he thought. The gunman noted the look on his face. Peck's tone quieted again. "JC, don't they say, 'The first murder's the hardest?'" Peck snickered as he walked back to the workbench.

"How about that Harrison creep," Peck was ranting again. His hand punched the wooden workbench. "He thought he was so fucking smart. He thought he could rob me blind?" Peck turned back to his captives. "I check the tapes of those machines, you know. When I saw the same thing happening here as had happened in Kalispell, what did he think I was going to do, tell him, 'You beat me fair and square?'"

Peck was panting now. The volume of his voice dropped. "I still don't understand what the hell he was doing, but I know when someone is stealing from me."

"He was so high-tech," Peck began to giggle. "Well, he's so high now, pieces of him are still coming down."

Then Peck looked at JC. "About your forest ranger ..." JC's eyes hardened on the maniac.

"Yeah, sorry about that," Peck apologized. "He stumbled across my secret. What was I to do? But making it look like an outdoorsman died outdoors? That's as good as killing Smokey Bear in a forest fire." Peck laughed, almost uncontrollably.

48

"What's your plan, Peck," JC asked. "You going to bore us to death?"

The gunman was leaning against his workbench, mulling over how he was going to dispose of his guests.

Peck looked their way. "Give me time to think. You didn't have the decency to call ahead." Then Peck walked out the garage door and into the darkness.

JC struggled to loosen the duct tape around his wrists. It wasn't giving way. He could feel Shara's spirits evaporating. He thought that he'd better keep her talking. "You know," JC whispered, "that big head of his is really one for the record books."

Shara looked over her shoulder at JC like he was nuts. "And that mouth," JC continued, "I could freeze water in it and play hockey on his face." Shara began to laugh, surprising even herself. "Don't worry, honey," JC then said, "we'll beat him."

At the moment, JC didn't have a single idea as to how to bring that about. His only weapon, he knew, was his rage.

JC and Shara sat, lit only by the moonlight that poured into the garage. JC stared at a speck of something he saw near the woodpile. He squinted and barely made it out to be a button. A green button, like the ones on the uniform of the U.S. Forest Service. Like Al's.

JC and Shara heard a vehicle start up in the darkness. They heard the tires crawl across the gravel. Could Peck be leaving, they hoped? But those hopes were dashed when they heard Peck's footsteps. The vehicle was still running. Peck had found JC's SUV and backed it into the driveway. They heard Peck open the hood of the vehicle. Then they heard it slam shut.

Peck returned and pointed his handgun at his hostages. He had a hunting knife in his other hand. He approached his captives and crouched near Shara.

His face was only inches from hers. He was brushing her cheek with the blade of the knife. He seemed to get an erotic thrill from the act. He dragged the knife down her neck and shoulder. It caressed her arm. She watched the blade as it moved. She was petrified.

Peck pulled the knife away from her flesh. He cut the duct tape that held his prisoners to the post. He was always careful to remain on Shara's side, out of JC's reach.

Peck ordered JC, still bound with his hands behind his back, to get up. "I can't," JC told him, "with my hands tied up."

Peck leered at Shara, the knife toying with her tee shirt. "Figure it out," he told JC.

The message was clear. JC pressed his back against the post and pushed with his legs. He was able to crawl his way up to his feet.

Peck slipped his arm under Shara's arm and pulled her up. He waved his gun in the direction of the open door, ordering them to walk.

"I'm not going anywhere," JC said. "If you're going to kill me anyway, at least I'll go knowing that I made your garage dirty."

"Oh, I'll kill you," Peck responded. His eyes turned to Shara, "But you don't have to die first, JC." He stroked the knife against Shara's throat.

"Alright," JC acquiesced, "I need to stretch my legs, anyway."

With his hands still bound behind him, JC walked out the garage door, Shara following.

They saw that JC's 4x4 was pointed down the driveway. JC studied the fall line ahead of the car. It traveled across the road and down the steep wooded hillside. He knew that somewhere beyond, there was a cliff and a deadly drop.

Peck pushed the couple toward the vehicle. He grasped Shara's hair violently. She winced. He directed her into the passenger seat.

He fastened the seat belt around her. "I wouldn't want anyone to get hurt," he said. "You're about to have a terrible accident."

He ripped the duct tape off of her wrists, pressing the gun against her temple. "Sit on your hands!" he ordered her.

She didn't move. "Sit on your hands!" he yelled, "or your boyfriend is going to suffer a fatal case of writer's block!" The gun was now pointed at JC's head.

Shara sat on her hands. Peck moved around the front of the car, his gun trained on JC.

Peck kicked at a block of wood to be certain that it was secure. It was under the front tire of the SUV. It was the only thing preventing the 4x4 from rolling forward. JC looked at the gear shift. It was in neutral, probably locked there.

"I could make it look like a murder-suicide," Peck smiled as he lowered the gun at Shara's face through the open door. Peck directed JC to get behind the steering wheel.

After climbing in, JC tested the brakes. They offered no resistance. Peck had done something to the brake lines. Probably cut them, JC thought. Peck slammed the car door shut.

He ordered Shara to pull the seatbelt and shoulder harness around JC and lock it. She did as he ordered. But she saw her fingers covered in a sticky substance. She showed it to JC.

"Glue," he told her in a subdued voice. They could hear Peck snickering. Shara tried her own seatbelt. It was also glued shut.

"We'll just let that sit a bit," Peck mumbled, allowing the glue to dry. He commanded Shara to cut the duct tape off JC's wrists. She complied. JC now had use of his hands, but nothing useful to do with them. He struck the car horn. It didn't respond.

Shara glanced about the truck in a panic. She spied a mauled tennis ball on the dash. Held back by the shoulder strap, her fingers barely reached it. She cradled the memento of her dog in her lap.

JC stared at the path ahead of the truck. He knew that they wouldn't survive the fall. He smelled beer. He looked around the cab of the truck. There were a half-dozen empty beer bottles.

Peck appeared to be making preparations, "We had a beer bottle barbeque," Peck told them. "At least that's what I'm going to tell the authorities. Too bad my good friends overdid it. You know what happens when you drink and drive."

Peck was also holding an odd-looking bottle, skinny. JC didn't know what it was.

Peck pointed his nose away from the container and pulled off the cap. He tossed the cap into the car. He stuffed the end of a small rag into the bottle's opening.

He saw JC studying it. "Oh, I forgot to tell you," Peck informed him. "They're going to be shocked when they find this in your truck. Chloroform!"

Peck was chuckling. "It turns out that you killed your friend the forest ranger. Tsk, Tsk. Didn't they find chloroform in Al's autopsy? I'll bet they did! You really had us fooled, JC. We never suspected that it was you."

Peck was directing his monologue through the open driver's side window of JC's car. "I know, I know," Peck said, careful to remain out of JC's reach. "They'll find the glue in the seatbelts and the cut brake line."

Peck scratched his head, mocking them, as though he was trying to think of a solution. Then a smile appeared on Peck's face. "But not if there is fire!" Peck pulled the odd skinny bottle in front of his face. In his other hand, he held a lighter.

He walked to the front of the car and kicked out the block. The car inched forward, slowly at first. Shara's heart stopped when she felt the SUV lurch. She felt panic, but not paralysis.

She spotted her curious black Labrador standing only a few feet behind Peck. Then, she glanced at the ball in her lap. Shara thrust Jumper's tennis ball into view, yelling, "Come get it, Jumper!"

Peck's arm was cocked, ready to toss the bottle with the flaming rag into the truck. He turned to see the excited dog leap for the ball, Peck in his path.

Peck was jarred off his feet. JC reached out of the rolling truck and grabbed his captor. JC freed one hand to grab the bottle with the rag. The flame had almost reached the highly flammable liquid.

Peck grabbed the car door to regain his balance. JC's grasp, however, dragged Peck along with the rolling vehicle.

They crossed the road and slowly climbed over the elevated berm into the woods. Peck saw the hillside grow steeper. He struggled to free himself. His feet slipped on the snow. His big mouth was open wide.

"Pucker up, Peckerhead," JC snarled. He let go of the man just after thrusting the flaming bottle of chloroform into Peck's huge mouth.

Peck rolled down the hill, away from the car. The flaming bottle protruded from his mouth like a birthday candle.

When his head struck a tree, face first, the bottle exploded in flames. Peck's hair and face and clothing quickly ignited.

JC and Shara heard Peck shriek. Peck tried to get up, but stumbled. He dropped helplessly back to the ground, the flames consuming him.

49

"Ouch!" JC's ribs slammed into the car door when his 4x4 slapped a tree.

JC was relieved by their escape from Peck, as long as ...

As long as he and Shara weren't killed in the plunge over an approaching cliff.

The SUV was bouncing off saplings as it slowly rolled downhill toward the precipice. JC and Shara were trying to uncouple their seat belts, but Peck had glued them shut.

Tree branches and snow crashed into the windshield. The car began to fishtail as it crashed into bigger pines.

The snow was getting deeper, catching the undercarriage. The car slid sideways.

That began to slow the vehicle down. "Hang on!" JC reached out to grab Shara.

The car slammed into two substantial pines, one hit a front fender and one hit a rear fender. The momentum of the SUV rolled it onto two wheels, threatening to flip, but it dropped back to the ground. They weren't moving anymore.

JC and Shara lifted their disbelieving eyes. A few trees were still shaking. Out of Shara's window, there was empty space. The cliff got that close. Out of JC's window, a small fire could be seen up the hill.

Beyond the drop, they saw the lights of Sierra at night. "This is a great view, we've got to come back here," JC said with a smile.

His forehead was bleeding. He'd probably struck it as the 4x4 tumbled down the hillside. Shara was holding her arm. She said that it had hit her door more times than she could count. She wondered if it was broken.

Then Shara looked at JC with a sincere expression. She said, "Did you bring me up here to neck?"

JC nodded his head. "Yep, would you believe that we ran out of gas?" They laughed.

Despite the tilt of the truck, JC reached down and pulled Shara closer to him. He brushed her hair out of her face. She said, "Thank you, JC," and they kissed.

50

The glare of seventy-five helmets reflected in the sun. It was a colorful display for riders on the chairlift overhead.

The seventy-five racers relaxed near the start house with their coats off. The thin layer of their colorful speed suits, reds and greens and yellows and blues, were enough to ward off the mild winter temperatures.

The Dick and Jane Downhill at Grizzly Mountain would be raced down a run called "CAB." Boys against girls. A time handicap would make it even.

JC and Shara arrived at the starter's shack together. JC was wearing his old green and gold speed suit.

Shara wore a blue speed suit with orange stars on it. JC noted how tight it was, "Is that Lycra or paint?" he asked.

"Are you complaining?" she questioned him with a grin.

"My goodness, no," he answered, waving his hand in front of his face as though he was getting very warm. She smiled at him.

The winner of a downhill race had to overcome sometimes frightening speeds, far greater than a giant slalom or slalom. JC and Shara liked their chances. After the episode with Peck, they were not easily frightened.

It had been a few days since the death of Bill Peck, Jr. The race had been postponed in that time. Shara's arm wasn't broken, but it was badly bruised. JC had sore ribs but otherwise was no worse off than before. Both would push cautiously out of the start house.

JC had wrapped up his reporting from Grizzly Mountain. Peck was called the "lone killer" by the sheriff's investigation. The official report found Peck murdered four innocent victims: Sally Decker, Harvard Harrison, Marsha Prospect and Robert "Al" Pine.

Because of his daring brush with the killer, JC was interviewed on national television. He knew that his celebrity wouldn't last the week.

He told Fred Shook what Bill Peck had said: "Paraphrasing a psychopath, 'The attention span of television watchers always needs new meat.' They'll forget about me pretty quick."

Paul Prospect, investigators determined, wasn't involved in the murders. He had never been identified publicly as a suspect, but he wasn't very happy about privately being considered one. He blamed JC for it.

Trip Lake was still unaccounted for, but that was immaterial now. He could happily "ski bum" in Utah or wherever he landed.

The residents of Fort Affordable were informed of their fate. There were about six weeks left of Grizzly Mountain's ski season. Next year, Paul Prospect's subordinate told residents of the ski bum compound, they wouldn't be welcomed back.

The night after Peck's death, there was a bright glow over the outpost of Benedict's Brigade. It was accompanied by the pop of ammunition exploding. The dining hall had caught fire. The snap of ammunition and some small explosions were heard all night.

In the fire, the kitchen and cafeteria of the dining hall caved into the basement. There was nothing left but ash and concrete walls.

JC had asked about Captain Hemingway. A militia member told JC that Hemingway was gone. He'd slipped out of the camp without being noticed.

General Smith suspected that Hemingway had started the fire. JC thought it was a smart way to destroy evidence. Investigators would be looking for the source of Peck's lethal inventory.

It had never occurred to the sheriff's office to charge Hemingway with arson. They'd never heard of Steven Hemingway.

The siege ended within days of the fire. JC paid tribute to TS Eliot as he reported that the standoff died, "With both a bang, and a whimper."

Out of curiosity, JC had looked for Hemingway's Army records. He found nothing. The same held true when JC looked for a record of him in college. A Steven Hemingway never existed.

Before reporting to the top of the race course for the Dick and Jane Downhill, JC had already endured a long morning.

He had spoken to his news director the night of Peck's gruesome end. JC and his boss seemed to be in good standing again. Then another call came for JC this morning. It was the news director again: "JC, do you have a minute?"

JC couldn't think of a reason to have a discussion on the phone requiring "a minute" when he was going to be returning to Denver in a day or two.

"Sure."

"You did great work up there," the news director told his reporter. JC thought this was going to be another "But" conversation.

"JC," the news director said in a tone he probably thought was comforting, "I'm your boss, but I have bosses, too. And I told you, you were pissing them off. We play with their money, and you spent way too much of it."

JC was silent. He knew that the only body parts he needed for this conversation were his ears. "Are you still there, JC?" the news director asked.

"Yep."

"JC, it was called to the ownership's attention that your contract expired a few weeks ago, while you were up in Montana."

JC hadn't given it any thought. He'd let his contract expire before. Management just renewed it when they got around to it, with a customary two-percent raise.

"JC, we're not renewing your contract," the news director told him. JC was still silent. He wasn't certain that he had heard right.

"JC," the news director continued, "you spent a lot of money up there, and it pissed somebody off. Do you know someone named Paul Prospect?"

JC asked, "What's he got to do with it?"

The news director responded, "He's one of the board members of our TV station's ownership. I've met him a few times. He seems like a nice enough guy, but I'm told he has a thing about you. It's all gossip, but sometimes gossip is grounded in truth, JC."

"It's true this time," JC told his former boss.

"Sorry, JC, you'll find another job. Probably better than this one." The news director tried to sound comforting. "We'll get you all the information about severance and health care and all that."

"Sure," JC said. "But right now, I'm on vacation." And he terminated the phone call.

51

The racers were a speeding splash of color. A crowd had gathered at the finish line. Some of the crowd knew who the racers were. They were friends and family.

But the daring of the downhill competitors drew others out of the lodge just for the sheer thrill.

A snowboarder pointed as JC got air over the last headwall. JC held his tuck and scraped to a stop in the finish corral. JC's chest heaved as his lungs tried to swallow air.

"That dude is killer," the snowboarder said to his friends. The boarder next to him nodded in agreement: "He is murder on skis."

Shara was already standing along the plastic netting in the finish area. The women had raced first. With the handicap, they had beaten the men this year.

Shara joined the women doing a little victory dance. JC and the men just smiled and laughed. "Yeah," said one of them. "But we finished second."

JC hadn't told Shara that he was now unemployed. As they stood at the finish line, he told her, "You have a big house."

"Thanks, I guess," she said back to him, thinking that was a bit random.

"You want company?" he asked.

"For how long?" she asked. A smile appeared on her face.

"As long as it takes," he said to her.

She paused before responding, "Sure."

Shara told JC, "There may be chores. You may have to walk the dog."

"Jumper and I have already talked," JC told her. "He negotiated a 'throwing the ball' clause. He drives a hard bargain." Shara had a grin on her face.

The discussion led to the length of stay. That led to "quite a while." Spring arrived, Grizzly Mountain closed for the season, and he was still there.

JC was reading the newspaper in Shara's kitchen one morning. An article told him that his old TV station in Denver had won a big award for "Outstanding Reporting." It was for JC's reporting of the serial killer at Grizzly Mountain.

There hadn't been a phone call to JC, or an invitation extended to attend the awards ceremony. The gold-plated statue was handed to executives at his former TV station. It would sit on a shelf in the lobby of his former employer.

It didn't bother him. He looked at a trophy with a skier on top of it that was sitting in Shara's living room and had JC's name on it. A picture of JC and Al together leaned against it. "I'd rather have this one," JC muttered to himself.

The next morning, JC poked at some ground with a spade. He was on his hands and knees and shoveled the moist soil out of the way.

There was still some snow for cross-country skiing in Yellowstone, but it wouldn't be around for long.

On this particular patch of earth, near Excelsior Geyser, the snow was gone. Patches of plant life were pushing up. There were small pebbles. Not much grass would grow, Al would have told him.

Two ravens were flying overhead. Al had told JC that they mate in the spring. He described how smart they are. The male was doing barrel rolls and generally showing off for the female.

Not far away, park rangers had closed Fountain Freight Road to visitors because too many grizzly were emerging from their dens there. Some would have cubs.

JC scanned the landscape around him. He thought that this was a magical time at Yellowstone. Al thought so, too.

JC's spade hit its target. JC pulled a foil bag out of the warm soil. His surface temperature thermometer had told him that it was just right to warm up some turkey.

JC sat on the ground and pulled two pieces of bread out of his pack. He inserted the warm turkey and some lettuce between them.

He ate his sandwich as he looked at Mount Jackson. He could see two small hills the locals called the "Mae West Mountains."

He glanced in the direction of Grizzly Mountain. He couldn't see it, but he took comfort that it would be alive with new adventure next winter.

Then he hit "play" on his cell phone's collection of music. He thanked God for this life. He thought of Al and listened to bagpipes.

Acknowledgements

Many thanks to my very smart and nurturing editor, Deirdre Stoelzle. She and Carolyn provided support when it was desperately needed. Debbi Wraga of Shires Press overcame adversity to see this project through. Mike Bryers of Yellowstone Alpen Guides disclosed the secrets of Yellowstone National Park to me, over twenty years ago. The late Phil Furie, former Albany County Coroner, advised me on murder scenes. Ed Parham of Rueckert Advertising helped us devise a fun marketing plan. Ronn Bayly, my brother, introduced me to Montana in the 1970s. Ronn and Susan have maintained an open-door policy for us. We can never use it enough. My late great Black Labrador, AJ Kitt, was the inspiration for Jumper. Thanks to the ski racer of the same name for the influence. And thank you to every skier and snowboarder who have never failed to provide interesting tales during rides up the chairlift and gondola.

About the Author

Phil Bayly is a forty-two-year veteran of television and radio journalism. He has lived the life of a ski bum, with a better-than-average job.

He currently lives in Saratoga County, New York with his wife, Carolyn.

Visit Phil at www.murderonskis.com

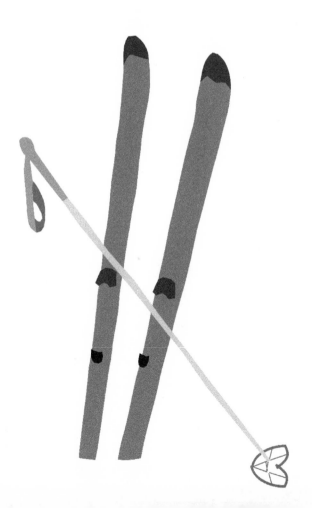

CPSIA information can be obtained
at www.ICGtesting.com
Printed in the USA
FFHW021025041219
56123486-62238FF